The Via Veneto Papers

Ennio Flaiano

The
Via Veneto
Papers

Translated from Italian by John Satriano

The Marlboro Press

First English-language edition.

Originally published in Italian under the title
LA SOLITUDINE DEL SATIRO
© 1973, 1989 RCS Rizzoli Libri S.p.A., Milan

Translation © 1992 by John Satriano

The publication of the present volume is made possible in part
by a grant from the National Endowment for the Arts.

Manufactured in the United States of America

Library of Congress Catalog Card Number 92-80360

Clothbound edition: ISBN 0-910395-66-7
Paperbound edition: ISBN 0-910395-67-5

The Marlboro Press
Marlboro, Vermont 05344

Contents

The Via Veneto Papers

These notes were written at various moments and are not here in chronological order. What I wanted to recollect is a street, a film, an old poet: disparate things that are unclearly mixed up with one another, not only in memory, but also in a diary. The jumps from one time to another have, then, a reason of their own.

June 1958

I am working, with Fellini and Tullio Pinelli, dusting off an old idea of ours for a film, the one about a young provincial who comes to Rome to become a journalist. Fellini wants to adapt the idea to the present day, to paint a picture of this "café society" that frolics between eroticism, alienation, boredom and sudden affluence. It is a society which, the terrors of the cold war now past and perhaps even in reaction to them, flourishes a bit everywhere. But here in Rome, through a mixing together of the sacred and the profane, of the old and the new, through the *en masse* arrival of foreigners, through the cinema, presents more aggressive, subtropical qualities. The film will have *La Dolce Vita* as its title and we have yet to write a single line of it; we are vaguely taking notes and going to the different places around town to refresh our memories. In these last few years Rome has expanded, become disproportioned, got rich. Scandals explode with all the violence of summer storms, the people live outdoors, they sniff about, they study, they invade the restaurants, the movie theaters, the streets, they leave their cars in those very same piazzas which once upon a time enchanted us through their architectural splendor and which now resemble parking lots.

One of our locations will perforce have to be Via Veneto, which is becoming more and more festive all the time; and this evening I took a walk there on purpose, wanting to get a clear picture of it. How changed it is from '50, when I used to go there on foot every morning, crossing Villa Borghese, and stopping at Rossetti's bookstore with Napolitano, Bartoli, Saffi, Brancati, Maccari and the poet Cardarelli. The air was clean, the traffic was light (Brancati rode his bicycle), from the bakery shop came an odor of hot buns, there was a gay, rustic liveliness, journalists and writers would be drinking apéritifs, the painters didn't have dealers yet, people were doing less flying way up to the sky. At the barbershop I used to run into Mario Soldati, and he would say to me: "I'm writing a novel."

How a street can change! Now that summer is coming on it's plain as day that this is no longer a street, but a beach. The cafés, which overflow onto the sidewalks—how many are there? six? seven?—have, each one of them, a different type of umbrella for their tables, like the ones at the seaside establishments at Ostia: and they aren't just street umbrellas but the sort you'd find at a *fête galante*. Some have tassels and straw festoons like those in the Hawaiian islands, others make one think of the Offenbach of *La Vie parisienne*, of the Great Exhibition, of the People's Progress; on every table are little flags of the nations participating in the festival.

Proceeding with little forward thrusts, automobiles glide like gondolas toward the theater, and the public takes in the fresh air and drifts hither and thither with the indolence of seaweed and the false confidence of choir-singers.

Our destiny then remains upon the sea. So fond are we of this idea that we have adapted it in the only way that our laziness will accept it, by transforming streets into seaside resorts, by elaborating a seaside style for houses, for automobiles, for attire and, finally, for citizens themselves, who have the appearance of being—and at heart they are—just so many bathers at the shore.

Even the conversations are seaside resort: baroque and jocular; and they are concerned with an exclusively gastro-sexual reality. All that's missing is splashing water and beach ball games.

December 1961

It is difficult these days to get to Via Veneto at all; and it is also useless, it looks like another city. For a kilometer in every direction there's nowhere to leave the car. I head for it on foot and count four Christmas trees along the way. The season's greetings are written in English. Snow, which paralyzes the city for a week when it falls, is evoked in the shop windows by flakes of cotton on the goods on display. There are stuffed animals three feet high in the bars and pastry shops: it's that American anthropomorphism which is asserting itself in the middle classes, with its animal friends of man, made in man's image: goats, fawns, gun-toting cats, mice with little aprons, dwarfs. Coming out of a tobacco shop I'm struck by a curious sight. A girl is standing in front of the Café de Paris and on her head she is wearing a hat in the shape of a Christmas tree; working a little switch which she has in her pocket she turns the little colored lights in her hat on and off. Poor girl, she's pouting, disillusioned, like a little child who, at a masked ball for little children, suddenly bursts into tears. And the photographers who are bivouacked day and night in front of the café look at her with a mixture of compassion and peevishness. Perhaps if some actor of note should pass by, or maybe Fellini, they could try a forceful solution. "I don't know," a photographer says to me, "maybe if somebody slapped her in the face . . . If it isn't dramatic, we won't take a picture of it."

The girl has crossed the ocean to attempt, in the climate of *la dolce vita,* a career as an actress, and now she is standing in front of the Café de Paris turning her little colored lights on and off. Why don't they go for her gimmick? What does the public want? Nothing?

April 1952

Every morning the poet Cardarelli goes and seats himself in the only armchair in Rossetti's bookstore and is a positive hindrance to trade not only with his witticisms but even more so with his gloomy silences, which make the customers uncomfortable. Rossetti seems not to take any of this amiss but rather to enjoy it. Yesterday a young woman writer came in and began browsing through a pile of books, all the while uttering comments which betrayed a little nervousness on her part and also a desire to attract the poet's attention. Picking up the works of Goethe published by Sansoni, she murmured: "My God, now it's Goethe. What a bore!" Cardarelli, who looked as if he had dozed off, in the sudden silence that ensued, said, as if to himself, "It may be, Signora, that you are confusing him with Golden Gate" (which is a pastry shop on the same street). Today, all bubbling over with joy, another lady came in and asked Rossetti: "Do you have *Le Diable au corps*? I have just seen the movie and now I want to read the book." And Cardarelli, astonished: "My, what an intense intellectual liveliness you manifest, Signora." Then a young poet came in who, after paying him all sorts of compliments, begged him to say something in his favor to a certain magazine where there might be a chance he could get his poems published. He handed him one so he could see for himself that it wasn't cheap stuff. Cardarelli put on his glasses, extracting them from out of the depths of his overcoat, and read the poem, while doing so wrinkling his forehead, as if he were reading a telegram. And finally: "But this is good stuff, the very best, the kind they should put in *La Fiera Letteraria*!" Then, suddenly recalling that it is he himself who edits *La Fiera Letteraria*, he started to chuckle, silently, until his right eye began to fill with tears.

*   *   *

June 1958

One of the first scenes of the film ought to be the one in which the young provincial goes up Via Veneto on foot, without a penny in his pocket but overcome by the glamour of the crowd, repository of his high hopes. For in the rush of gratitude he feels toward the city he has already conquered, the protagonist believes that that crowd is a guarantee of life, of love and also a hypothesis of freedom. Happy faces, laughing mouths, pomp, elegance, nonchalance, a woman who looks at him and smiles. And the cafés, where he will even find a friend, a promise of work, a loan!

The reality is better, in a certain sense: more chilling. The cafés on the street have all been renovated and in such a showy way that one thinks immediately of their winter solitude when—the sunny weather over with—their gaiety will remain in disuse and, like a Luna Park in the rain, will inspire instead a feeling of melancholy. The dreadful interior decorating successfully interprets our thirst for pomp, and the Café—erstwhile bulwark of the bourgeoisie—has become the showroom of the furniture industry. Gone are the leather- and velvet-upholstered seats, the mirrors that multiplied perspectives, the deaf and venerable waiters and the marble-topped tables you could draw on. Now the cafés seem like alcoves, pagodas, nursing homes, family tombs.

April 1952

Things are starting to go to pieces. They are redoing the flower beds along Via Veneto, putting in great rims of cement around them. The ones they had before weren't good enough. Mino Maccari is indignant and tries to pass himself off as a cabinet member, to see if he can talk the laborers into stopping what they are doing. It doesn't succeed. Then he proposes to me that we start a journal together, which we will call either *Obnoxious Tales* or perhaps *The Dotard Illus-*

trated. We sit down. He lapses into a few sudden and disconcerting silences during which it seems he wants to say something important, who knows what, then he abruptly starts to laugh. "Last night I thought for some time about myself, trying to extract some sort of philosophy from my life. Everything I was able to understand about myself I wrote on this little piece of paper. Here, read it."

This is what was written there: "1) I don't know who not to believe in. 2) I have a couple of ideas, but they are confused. 3) I was looking for employment, instead I found work. 4) I have a family I have to support. 5) I try very hard to understand, but I wind up understanding nothing."

June 1958

So we've decided that the film will begin with the young provincial going to a nightclub. He's already in a pretty good job, he is making a living, he is one of those journalists a civilization of sensationalism has produced, that is, he reports scandals, the damned fool behavior of others. He allows himself to be adopted by the same society he despises, he is unbothered at having to renounce his original ideals, which now seem to him not only tiresome but useless to boot.

Towards midnight the movie theater crowd wanders up and at a few tables the talk is about cinema: the only discussions, along with those about different makes of cars, that reveal any difference of tastes and opinions. Towards three it's all over, there's nothing left under the big umbrellas, there are no further meetings with friends (almost always De Feo, sometimes Carlo Levi, with that benevolent country doctor look of his), and it ends in front of the newspaper stand, the only tranquil harbor for our nocturnal lunacy, the immense newsstand full of books and newspapers that never shuts down, like a lighthouse. Some scrutinizing of the sky to see if we're to have fair weather tomorrow or not. When I reached home, found a conch at the edge of the sidewalk

*   *   *

July 1959

At a table of the Caffè Rosati, in one of those rapid introductions in which nothing can be understood but during
which one smiles, I was presented to an American lady—
tanned, dried by the sun, slender, with something coleopter-
ous in her eyes and in her iridescent green dress. Such was the
impression that came into better focus when a friend of mine
explained to me—in that tone of gravity which redeems the
gossipiness of certain stories—that for three months each year
this lady, in full agreement with her husband, takes her sexual
vacation in France and Italy. It seems that it's on her psychoanalyst's orders. The woman accordingly picks out her men,
sustained by her faith that she is getting better.

In her purse she carries a little camera and with this she
takes pictures front and back of her subjects, preferably nude.
One documents as best one can. By now she has an archive,
which perhaps serves to keep her from boredom during the
winter months when the cure is suspended. But personally I
think that this archive of hers represents the tribute she pays
to that modern cult which makes a photographer out of every
tourist, preoccupied with collecting evidence of his own existence (in order to have proof of his having existed).

June 1958

A society as troubled as ours, which expresses its frigid will
to live more by exhibiting itself than by truly enjoying life, deserves its petulant photographers. Via Veneto has been invaded
by these photographers. And our film will have one of its own,
the invisible companion of the protagonist. Fellini has this
character very clearly in his mind, he is acquainted with the
real-life model: a news agency reporter, about whom he tells
me a passably atrocious story. This fellow had been sent to the
funeral of a well-known figure who had been the victim of a
terrible accident—sent there to take pictures of the weeping
widow. But through some carelessness the film was exposed to
light and the photographs didn't turn out. The director of the

news agency said to him: "Figure something out. In two hours either you bring me the widow weeping or I'll fire you and see to it you never find work again." Therewith our reporter hurried off to the home of the widow and found her just then returned from the cemetery, still in her widow's weeds, and wandering from one room to another in a daze of grief and exhaustion. To be brief: he told the widow that if he failed to get a picture of her in tears he would lose his position and with his position the hope he had of getting married, for he had recently become engaged. The poor lady wanted to chase him away: you may imagine that after having wept so earnestly and for such a long time she was in no mood for comedy. But at this point the photographer gets down on his knees, begins to beg her not to ruin him, to be kind, to just cry for a minute, or even to just pretend!—for just long enough for him to take her picture. It works. The noose of compassion once around her neck, the poor widow ends up getting photographed weeping on the matrimonial bed, at her husband's writing desk, in the front room, in the kitchen.

Now we will have to give this photographer an exemplary name, because the right name helps a great deal and indicates that the character will "live on." These semantic affinities between characters and their names drove Flaubert to despair. He spent two years finding Madame Bovary's first name, Emma. For this photographer of ours we don't know what to make up until, stumbling upon that golden little book of George Gissing's titled *By the Ionian Sea*, we discover the prestigious name "Paparazzo." The photographer will be called Paparazzo. He will never know that he bears the honored name of a hotel keeper from somewhere in Calabria, about whom Gissing speaks with gratitude and admiration. But names have a destiny of their own.

May 1952

It may seem strange that Cardarelli chose Via Veneto of all places to live out the last years of his life. If there is one street anywhere which couldn't help but be distasteful to him, it must certainly be this one. At the time we first became friends he never used to leave the Corso district—the shops of Piazza del Popolo, the restaurants of Via del Gambero. Of an evening his most audacious destination was Tito Magri's, a Tuscan wineshop on Via Capo, and now look at him on Via Veneto, in fact, in the best stretch of it, near Porta Pinciana, amidst that crowd of grand hotels, the whistles of doormen hailing taxis, the film extras working in *Quo Vadis?* and letting their beards grow. Today he was out sunning himself and he was looking about at everything with apparent approval, like the old emigrant who has made his fortune and come back to the village. So far as money is concerned he manages to put together enough to pay for a *pensione* and a male nurse. But he has the self-assurance that enables him to feel rich. As for love of his true homeland, he has given vent to all of it in his books, and there can hardly be much more left in him. He knows that this is his last port of call.

July 1958

I ran into an old film extra who for years now, in the midst of our cinematography's historico-biblico-mythological rebirth, has been shuttling from one film to another without even changing his make-up. He is a wise man out of Thebes, an archon of Athens, a counsellor at the court of Pharaoh, a Babylonian priest. In Crete he is watchman at the Labyrinth, upon Olympus he is Saturn, in Galilee an apostle. He asks me for a small loan. I ask him: "Aren't you working?" He extends his arms, desolate. "I may be a Senator—but in September!"

May 1952

Cardarelli, I remember having run into him in Piazza Cavour right after the war—all by himself, reduced to despair by the prolonged solitude he had undergone and happy to have returned, that very day, to Rome. He was counting on the help of a few friends and especially Velso Mucci's, who was preparing an essay for the new edition of *Prologhi*. I remember that we sat on the edge of a fountain outside the Palace of Justice; and that little by little he was starting to resume, together with his calm, his dark mood. "Pretty soon now I'm going to die." "Nonsense. Right away?" "I'd like to die here, at once, but without doing it on purpose," and he was smiling. A few days before, Bruno Barilli had stopped in front of the Caffè Greco. He had lifted up the hem of his duffel-coat and showed me a little roll of twine: "It's the rope I'm going to hang myself with." And that's how these two poets began life again in that marvelous post-war period that so encouraged everyone's hopes, feeling themelves undone now that the outcome they had yearned for had come about.

Now Barilli has died (in princely fashion, requesting a comb); and Cardarelli spends his days on Via Veneto. There is something to meditate upon in this choice of his, a kind of challenge to the rules of the game which require the old elephant to go off and hide himself far away, in order to die. This poet, however, loves to show himself, to impose his presence, with an air about him of spoiling the fun for everyone else.

September 1958

In three months, at the sea, we have finished writing *La Dolce Vita*, and now we're running into the usual problems. The producer refuses to do the film. He has given the script to four or five critics and now they are giving us sorrowful looks and shaking their heads: the story is rambling, false, pessimistic, insolent, whereas the public wants more cheerful stuff. "No," Eliot said somewhere, "the public only wants a little striptease, but what counts is what we get away with doing behind its back, without it noticing."

It's almost midnight and, passing through Via Veneto, I see Cardarelli all by himself, sitting at the last table of the Caffè Strega. "They haven't come to pick me up," he says. He seems like a giant who has lost all his friends and missed the bus. The doorman who has the job of accompanying him home towards eight must have forgotten about him. In fact, he arrives a little later and puts on a little show of surprise: "What's this? No, still here? But I thought..." They go through the gate slowly, weaving this way and that, with a list, like two decadent epicureans after a night's revelry.

At times it seems to me that there is a connection between Cardarelli and the protagonist of our rejected story. A connection which falls apart immediately. Cardarelli, very young and poor at the time, also came to Rome from his native town with the intention of becoming a journalist. When in a confidential mood, he used sometimes to talk about his first steps in Umbertine Rome as a reporter for *Avanti!*. He wrote about everything, furiously. Crimes interested him, ritual bloodlettings, tragedies of passion. He signed himself Simonetto, Calandrino, Calibano! Then sudden illness, a long confinement in the same hospital ward where his father had died. The furor of youth vanishes, he becomes another, he looks within himself, discovers poetry, makes it his creed and begins to write all over again. His first prose works are already perfect. Rereading them today, almost prudently and perhaps with the unconscious hope of finding them old, I become aware that if there is an old man around here, it isn't he. A great deal older and wrinkled are these literary troupers who play clownish games with success... I myself feel very much older.

June 1962

Via Veneto— ever more unrecognizable, swept away now by its own fame, abandoned to tourists, easy encounters and to cinematography. The "intellectuals" have followed the painters to Piazza del Popolo, topographically protected from the assaults of fashion by its ample spaces, by the absence of large hotels in the vicinity, by the few cafés. They no longer come to Via Veneto in the evening, but in the afternoon, to the presentations of new books, and not always even then. Three or four times a week, new books are presented at Golden Gate or at the Einaudi bookstore. Everyone is writing. Whoever isn't writing is collecting material. If the cultural miracle keeps on progressing, we will have a writer for every hundred inhabitants.

Women especially—certain women—are showing themselves implacable. Never mind: you can't have a bacchanal without bacchantes. I have a feminine manuscript here on the table that I should be reading, just to give an opinion, but I'm not doing it. I know what's in store for me: tumid, sentimental, sexual, autobiographical adventures. For this sort of woman writing a novel means telling badly about the very things which she succeeded so well in hiding when she did them.

July 1957

I made a long detour to avoid Cardarelli. I was in a hurry and so I committed this little act of cowardice, but others of his friends do it too. At about eight in the morning, Cardarelli descends from his *pensione*, which is over the Caffè Strega, and sits at the first table of the café itself, in front of the portal of the house. The waiters don't mind; they're happy because they know that he is a great poet and that he won the Strega Prize in 1948. They explain this when the customers show some curiosity about that gentleman sitting over there with his overcoat and hat on at the very height of the heat wave. A strange illness that chills his legs obliges Cardarelli to put on his entire wardrobe each time he leaves his house and has to abandon the stove to which he is practically attached. In short, the waiters respect him, and the owner of the café has given instructions that he be charged prices that would seem ridiculous to anyone else but which don't disturb Cardarelli in the least, because he doesn't know the price of anything and is perhaps convinced that the prices are the same in the other cafés too.

Cardarelli is there for the entire day, observing a precise schedule: from eight till one; then a one-hour break for lunch; and then two till eight. At eight he retires to his room, gets into bed and begins his titanic struggles with insomnia, which abandons him at dawn.

Amerigo Bartoli presented me with a drawing today which shows Cardarelli at the café together with the doorman of his building, the same one who goes to get him in the morning and who brings him back in the evening. Oftentimes the doorman sits modestly beside the poet, and he also gazes out upon that same animated coming and going, upon the swarms of pretty girls. Bartoli's drawing shows Cardarelli and the doorman who, by mistake, have exchanged headgear. The doorman has the poet's fedora and the poet the doorman's *berretto*.

Bartoli's friendship with Cardarelli is of long standing, their fondness for one another is very great but does not exclude reciprocal digs. For example, Bartoli, talking about Cardarelli, says that he is "the greatest of dying poets." A few days later a lady from his own province stops to greet Cardarelli and inquires: "And Bartoli? How's Bartoli doing?" With a sorrowful face the poet responds: "He's not growing, Signora, he's not growing!" And pursuing his allusion to the painter's diminutive stature, he adds: "At night, he's nervous, he can't sleep, so he paces back and forth underneath his bed."

Nevertheless, Cardarelli does nothing but keep on the lookout for Bartoli's arrival, in a frenzy if he's late. But as soon as he sees him appear at the corner of Via Sardegna, he turns his head in the opposite direction, like a lover who has decided to break off a romance, and pretends not to see him.

Today I was witness to this little interview:

"Cardarelli, what do you think about the literary prizes?"

"Don't ask me stupid questions."

"All right, you're against literary prizes?"

"If it's a question of a gift, no. If it's a question of a judgment, yes. I find it indecent that several writers should get together to pass judgment on the work of another writer. However . . . if you do wish to award prizes to the best writers, then every so often you have to give a cudgeling to a few of the worst."

"But what about the great prizes? The Nobel Prize, for example?"

"The great prizes are never given to the writer. They're given to his readers. Poor beggars, they deserve them."

"Have you decided whom to vote for in this year's Premio Strega?"

"Yes, but I haven't read anything of 'his'. It would take—"

"Really? Never anything at all? You're doing it on trust?"

"No. These votes are cast out of a certain contempt."

Evening descends upon Via Veneto with a feverish haste. During certain silences in the traffic you hear the Villa Borghese sparrows flying about in flocks before settling in the tops of the pine trees. I was sitting at the café and I was intent upon divining the arrival of night in the face and in the eyes of Cardarelli, as you can sometimes succeed in divining it in a lake, and in me this brought on a feeling of deep melancholy, almost as if that face reflected my own and my lost day, rendered more distressing by the certainty of another day and then another on this dead-end street. Out of inattentiveness, and in order to utter one of those model sentences that nowadays distinguish a boring conversation, Raffaella Pellizzi, who was sitting next to Cardarelli, said with a sigh, "Ed è subito sera." Cardarelli shook his head, and murmured: "What a profound concept. And what pleasure it must afford."

These are the only moments when one has the opportunity of seeing him smile. He would like to go on but he hasn't the will for it; he hasn't the will for anything, not even to die.

September 1957

The fashionable sort of success is obtained with publicity and is paid for by prostituting oneself to the crowd. Success doesn't change by inverting the order of factors, "suffering" may perhaps render it more lasting. Success obtained through merit and paid for with indifference annoys the public at large and, for some time now, everybody else too.

Today an elegant lady, who in her speech imitates a certain temperamental actress (she always performs in her undergarments), said, talking about a musical she had gone to: "Terrifically funny. I laughed so hard I p——— in my pants." And she doesn't even lower her voice, seeing as we're on Via Veneto. The gentleman who is with her adds politely and with the air of someone who keeps himself up to date: "My dear, you should have your urine psychoanalyzed."

Such a society is no longer in need of anything: it knows as much as will suffice to keep it refined and *à la mode*: and it has a certain faith in vulgarity as a means of defense against anything higher than its own material interests.

May 1955

Raffaella Pellizzi has decided to put a little order into Cardarelli's life; and she has begun by tidying up his room. She was telling me today that while she was clearing off his work table (where he hasn't sat in months), among an absurd heap of books, bottles, notebooks, letters he hasn't sent, letters he has received and never opened, among old mufflers and medicines of every description she found eight fountain pens and six pairs of scissors. The drawer of the night table was open and filled with books that rose like a tottering tower, and among the books were the slippers whose disappearance the poet had, for some time, been lamenting. She found no work of his, neither books nor manuscripts. Cardarelli hasn't been writing anything for years now. He doesn't even like anyone to speak to him about poetry or literature, they have lost their value, like dead things, trash, they leave him gasping for air, and if the conversation happens to turn in that direction it's almost as if he were chewing on some fruit that had a taste of ashes. His body is outliving his spirit, it is with resentment he sees himself live on, in life perhaps seeking extreme degradation, curious to see how far the spirit that sustains him may decay along with his body, maintaining the stoic implacability of someone who remarks: "I told you so."

On these sunny mornings, Via Veneto sparkles with a beauty that is a little offensive, opulent, tenderly crowned with the green of the few trees that carelessly punctuate the flower beds, amidst the continuous flow of automobiles, the indolent pedestrian flow, the somnolent bliss of the people who are sitting at the tables of the cafés. This is the hour when the ladies go in and out of the shops, the hour when the journalists bump into each other and ask: "What are you up to?" The morning mist is dissolving under a glorious sun that pushes the clouds towards the west. It is still the hour when you keep asking yourself whether today isn't the day to go out to the country for lunch, and then to decide that it isn't. Well we know what sort of afternoon will ensue: carefree, empty, then back to the city. Better to stay right here.

Today a photographer who works for a French magazine requested me to pose for him. He had me sit at a table and asked me to speak and act naturally. Someone stopped and observed the scene, which was, for me, one of keenest embarrassment. And all the while the photographer jumping from one spot to another, looking at the sun, adjusting his lens. I begged him to shorten the torture and, taking me under the arm, he pushed me towards Villa Borghese, where we would be able to continue unobserved. Leaning against the trunk of a tree and under the continuous gaze of the photographer, I felt a hand on my shoulder and heard a voice saying to me: "Ah, ha! Caught you by surprise!" I turned around and there was a certain man whose name I am never quite able to remember. And so there we stood: I with a silly smile on my face, he shaking his head from side to side, and the photographer saying: "Wonderful, move just a little, just like that, wonderful."

November 1958

"Oh, how marvelous it is to feel yourself profoundly intelligent, to rave about Sex, to remain indifferent towards women ... To respond to every enquiry, to always have an opinion, to sign petitions, to interpret the situation ... Oh, how wonderful to be in step with fleeting fashion, to be constantly attuned to mass culture ... To swear by commercial art, to repeat that Industry is beautiful, and to conclude the day with a shot from a pistol . . ."

We were crooning in like fashion, Fellini and I, driving down Via Veneto, when a traffic cop blew his whistle and had us pull over to the sidewalk. We had gone straight through a red light—fine: three thousand lire. "I don't have a dime," Fellini said, "but I can write you a check." The officer looked at us severely. "One second," Fellini continued, "you seem to know who this man is. Let's do it like this. You lend us five thousand lire, we pay the fine and we'll come back tomorrow, same time, same place, and give you back the five thousand." Since the officer was looking at us uncomprehendingly, Fellini repeated the proposition: "What can you lose? If we pay the fine, you'll make a good showing with your superiors and we'll be able to get a little gasoline. If you don't lend us the money, what happens instead? We can't pay." "I don't have five thousand lire," said the officer. "Come on, let's not kid each other," Fellini said. "Do you expect us to believe you've never done anything wrong? Come on, be a good guy." The officer looked at us, shaking his head all the time, then, sighing, said: "Go on, go on."

It seems certain that his film will never be made. Even so, Fellini never wearies of thinking about it and spends all his time talking to actors, choosing types, sending out telegrams, acquainting himself with the equivocal underbrush of Via Veneto and its surroundings. He wants to portray an unreal Rome, to reconstruct everything, or to concede that little to reality which is already unreal itself: Trevi Fountain, Saint Peter's, the Roman countryside.

July 1957

These people don't walk to their destinations, they saunter by, brushing past the tables, lingering, as if they were in the main square of a little town during some holiday. Those at the tables sit with their eyes fixed upon the stream of people that flows by on the sidewalks, while the passersby stare at the animated banks of tables. It's as if everybody were tacitly acquainted with one another, a criss-crossing of friendly and befogged glances, which hide—and at this hour, what else could it be?—an erotic assessment. I'm sitting at a table with Ivella, who never gets tired of watching. He has just come back from America, and had forgotten all about this crowd. Finally he bursts out: "What gets me is that Italians are all different from one another. It isn't a race, it's a collection! Just look! Just look!"

March 1961

"Are you working on anything good? Something for the movies?"

"No, I'm writing a comedy, it's for the stage."

"That's interesting. Would it bother you if I asked you to tell me a little about the plot, the problem, the theme?"

"Not at all. This in a nutshell is what it's about this." (He pauses.) "Okay ... everything leads one to believe that in the future, as the population increases, man will be increasingly more alone, especially in the big cities. Increasingly more alone, increasingly restrained by inhibitions, by laws, by reciprocal controls, by the tyranny of machines, by the necessity to succeed, by the enigma of the future, by the terror of a war. And then, one day, even art will end, in the same way that love will end."

"Very interesting."

"But in some provincial backwater, in some sort of depressed zone, the one and the other are still alive, love and art. The people feel awkward about it, especially about love. It's so provincial! 'But other than that,' they say, justifying themselves, 'what can you do here in this little one-horse town?' So they cultivate art and love. They write terrible books, they paint, and, in the wee hours of the night, when they're just getting home, they play electronic music, which by now is utterly outdated, in fact, it's been completely forgotten by the

rest of the world. And then, resigned and in their own backward way, they also make love."

"Yes, it's really interesting. What then?"

"Elsewhere, in the big cities, where poetry, painting and
music have become by this time forms of applied art (art is
something with which one dresses oneself), there are other
problems for these unhappy societies to worry about: the
correct utilization of time, the elimination of waste, total in-
surance coverage, diet . . . Pornography (in literature and the
movies) enjoys a period of technical splendor because everyone reads about and looks at things that he doesn't want or
that he simply can no longer do. The protagonist of my comedy, who lives in one of these cities, is obliged to make a trip
to that little provincial town I was just telling you about.
There, he has a girl cousin, who candidly confesses to him
that she spends all of her time painting and making love. Our
friend feels awfully sorry for her, he tries to find a way to cure
her. To be brief, he too winds up painting and making love. He
discovers that certainty is in uncertainty, repose is struggle,
etc. He discovers this through a 'backward' woman who re-
introduces him first to love and then to art. However, one day
he says to himself that these two activities will finally cause
him nothing but troubles. He leaves his little cousin and goes
back to the city, where, naturally, he kills himself."

"Very interesting. And when will this comedy of yours be
finished?"

"Never."

September 1954

Barilli, Brancati . . . it seems that death is going by alpha-
betical order. It wouldn't surprise me. I've always imagined
death as a hardheaded school-teacher, scouring his attendance
sheet in order to call upon the pupils who are the least prepared. Now, Vitaliano Brancati. A few evenings ago I ran into
him as he was leaving his favorite café—in a hurry. We barely

nod to one another, then he feels the need to come right back and, shaking my hand, he says: "I'll be gone before long and I'm not sure that we'll see each other again. I wanted to say goodbye." I said a few words in reply, joking. He was going to Turin to have an operation . . . Now we're in the freightyard at the station in front of a wagon loaded with a casket. We are almost all there, all of his night-time friends, our faces a little pale thanks to the sirocco. Someone speaks and eulogizes Brancati, the man and writer. Cardarelli is also there, immersed in his overcoat with the fur collar. When it's over, we go away like thieves after a job that has turned out badly, sneaking away, avoiding comments, while two porters throw wreaths and clusters of flowers into the wagon and close it up.

March 1960

Is another reality at all necessary? Is this rosy Roman reality not sufficient? Certainly, it is hard to live and be judged in a city where the one industry is cinema. One ends up believing that life is in function of the cinema, one becomes the photographic eye, one sees reality as a reflection of what lives and palpitates on the screen. A dog bites his tail. He ends up finding it tastes pretty good.

The night is calm. One overhears conversations that go like this:

"In other words, you don't like cinema."

"No, I do like it, I even respect it, I make use of it, I am even something of a slave to it, as I am to all modern comforts. But cinema isn't art or, rather, it is an esculent art, which satisfies a momentary hunger. The trouble is that it pretends to portray reality. So the best film affects me for, say, a year, for three, for ten, then it reveals its limits, its true nature, the emotional necessities that produced it . . . Later on, the passing of time turns the reality which the film presumed to fix forever into something clumsy and absolutely incomprehensible. The best film challenges a generation and then becomes a document, unbeknownst to itself. It looks at this street, these people. Captures them just as they are. Today, the result will satisfy you, in ten years you will find it all old, in twenty ridiculous, in fifty you will exclaim: what a wonderful document! Moral: every dramatic film slowly sets out to be comical."

"And do the directors know these things?"

"Yes, I think so. They know."

A long pause, during which the two friends look at the people who are passing by and are looked at in their turn, for a summary erotic assessment.

"Let's see how far we understand each other. What, according to you, is a director?"

"In the exceptional cases, the director is an artist, a temporary poet, who is never sure that he won't lose his job. The true poet, the true artist, advancing in years, getting older, improves his production, rarifies it, refines it, rids it of dross, enriches its spirit. This is possible because he works by himself and for himself, and his experience with life inevitably brings him to an intuitive understanding of ever new mysteries. A director on the other hand declines after a certain age, because his art has an immediate need of public approval, the basis for which has in the meantime changed. That reality which he believes he is portraying is no longer operative, it's over with, it no longer has customers. And now the problem arises: at what age does it become necessary to kill a good director?"

"Look. There's De Feo, Ercole Patti, Arbasino and Carlo Levi. Let's go over there and join them."

September 1954

Cardarelli spoke to me at length about a cinematographic project of his. He would like to write, or he would like someone to write, a film about 1911. "Of course," he adds, "he would have to do research; but I have that year in front of my eyes, just like a film. It's the fiftieth anniversary of National Unity and in Rome they're preparing grandiose festivities: the

International Exposition of Valle Giulia, the Regional Ethnographic Show . . . The monument to Victor Emmanuel is dedicated, the Ponte Vittorio Emanuele, the Palace of Justice, in short, everywhere, the chintziest architecture imaginable. The Zoological Gardens are also dedicated. Pincio and Villa Borghese are joined together, the Capitoline palaces are joined together with galleries of papier-mâché . . . And again with papier-mâché they built a pavillon in Piazza Colonna, where there's a gallery today. There were cafés, restaurants, a nickelodeon. Here, on Via Veneto, the Excelsior was dedicated. Where we're sitting now there was a shop that sold butter and eggs. In Valle Giulia Zuloaga, Franz von Stuck, Mestrovic, Sartorio, Michetti, Klimt, Sergent and a number of other *pompieroni* were triumphant. It is the apotheosis and the liquidation of the whole of the European *pompierismo*, the triumph of papier-mâché and floral-decorated reinforced concrete. Can't such a film be made out of all these triumphs?"

"Yes, very interesting. But, you see . . ."

"And in addition all the bands are playing to empty seats, because the French newspapers are spreading the word that there is cholera in Rome. All protests are useless. No one is coming to Rome, the deficit is enormous. The beginnings of our patriotic melancholies coincide precisely with the failure of the festivities. We pass the most squalid of summers and in autumn we go to war in Libya. Another series of disasters begins. Can't a film be done about fumbled triumphs and disasters?"

"Cardarelli, that's just what we're doing."

December 1960

Every so often I still find someone who more or less indirectly reproaches me for having had a hand in portraying Rome, in *La Dolce Vita*, as a sink of iniquity. Strange, because I think just the opposite. I would like to answer these people with the words of my friend Frassinetti: "There is a kind of madness which consists in the loss of everything except reason." In other words: is it my fault if Vice in Rome quickly becomes rational and utilitarian? And my fault if, when not fueled by passion, it becomes simply an external feature, a costume, a source of satisfaction, a fashion?

It seems to me that one of the reasons, perhaps the main reason, that keeps Rome from being a city of great vices is its profoundly familiar character, even in the area of corruption. It owes this character to its being an agglomeration of large villages, horrible towards the periphery, all gathered around the nucleus of the ancient city—villages inhabited by first or second generation emigrants who have preserved their provincial habits and customs. So, in Rome, every great "vice" takes on the trappings of a passtime which becomes boring once its novelty wears off. When it comes to vices no one is more difficult than the provincial: none agrees with him very well, and he ends up by finding them all ridiculous or expensive, without counting what they do to one's health.

The Vice capitals of the world base their fame on alcohol, on drugs, on violence, on great passions and, above all, on Remorse, that is, upon the somber reflections of Sin. In Rome today no one drinks except at mealtime. To run into a drunk on the streets in the middle of the night is becoming more and more unlikely. In some bar on the city's outskirts you may run into one, but now look at him: he's not causing a ruckus, he's not threatening anyone, he's not being thrown out like a sack of potatoes: instead, he's talking soccer with a group of ironic young men, and that's how they'll round out their evening. In the bars at the center the city, in Via Veneto bars, we know who the hard-core drinkers are, there are perhaps a hundred of them all told, and after a time they become objects of admiration because they reveal themselves to be seasoned travellers, familiar with the European way of life. Rather than vice-ridden they feel themselves privileged—they enjoy the esteem of the barmen, and every dispute which involves either alcohol or the usages of the *bel mondo* is deferred to their judgment. The other customers drink coffee, orangeade and even milk. With many people, uncertainty over what to order assumes desperate forms until they finally find enough courage to say to the waiter, with a profound sigh that points to an equally profound want of vices: "A coffee ... with a little ... milk." And when the waiter moves off, they call him back to remind him: "Cold! Make sure the milk is cold!" Now these people are not abstemious because they have decided to combat Evil or because they have no money: they are abstemious because they haven't anything to forget and they want to remain lucid, rational—to give themselves up to vice, yes, but all the while keeping one eye open.

Drugs haven't fared very well either. They hark back to the other post-war era and are therefore silly; and the joking the sect's few adepts do about their weakness discourages anybody from imitating it. Finally, the Roman doesn't need to feel that he is different from what he is, to exalt himself; he admires himself enough already, he always wears his best clothes when he goes for a walk, he takes in everything, he considers himself unsurpassable in at least two principal activities of the mind: film criticism and automobile criticism. These two are more than sufficient to support the ambitions of his particular superego. If you see two young men talking at the same time in front of this very café at two o'clock in the morning you can almost bet money on it that they are taking turns explaining why Ingmar Bergman is an already outdated director and which of his too many films is sincerely stupid or theatrical. If, instead, you see a little group of young men loitering like gangsters around an automobile and you fear for the people inside, don't be alarmed: those young men are discussing the speed, the rate of acceleration, the gasoline mileage of this model compared to its predecessor. If another young man happens to come by in an ordinary economy car, a new one, and announces that he just bought it, all his friends will struggle up out of their armchairs to take a look at this utility car with which they are already thoroughly well acquainted, simply to comfort their friend by giving it their approval. And you will see young men, who wouldn't exert energy for anything in the world, wearing themselves out testing the clutch, slamming the doors to listen for rattles, opening the hood to look underneath.

We were talking about drugs. Certainly, there would be a better market for them if Romans could buy them without any risk, just for the novelty. And if their wives and mothers would do their shopping for them, for when it'a a question of price, they're the only ones in the family who know how to buy wisely. Then, in the pharmacies, cocaine would be sold in "family sizes,"and everyone would have a bit of white powder on his necktie; perhaps in the exact spot where now, after dinner, they all have a bit of talcum. Petrolini ever remains the poet of this society: "Rina / lei per me la cocaina / se la prende a colazione / pensando a Gastone."

May 1962

Here's something that will make Mario Soldati happy. I saw his novels and his latest volume of poems, *Le canzonette*, displayed in his barber's shop window on Via Veneto. Though it isn't exactly the barber who is displaying them (you can't have everything in life, Mario). This is what happened: the old barber retired from business and ceded the premises to a Milan publisher, who transformed the "salon" into a bookstore, nay, into an exposition of his products. Where lotions were before, behold Arpino, Butor, Tobino, Soldati. For my part, I was touched. I used to come here too to get my hair cut, and Tennessee Williams must have come here as well, because he mentions it in *The Roman Spring of Mrs. Stone*. The interior design was in the solid style of Ducrot 1920, in mahogany and marble. Now, it being a question of Via Veneto, the architect knew very well how to give the same tone to the decor that all the other stores are taking on. And so I'd say this is the one and only bookstore that is furnished with the mirrors and vestiges of a beauty parlor. The industry of culture is reaching out to a new public that is sensitive to "gifts" and wrapping-paper. But this may be a nice expression of two very flagrant characteristics of our contemporary literature: autobiography and vanity.

Back at home, I spent the evening reading *Le canzonette*, and finally I think I began to understand why Soldati left Rome once and for all: because the city had begun to appear to him like a good-natured demon, accomodating and rational, which was crushing his idea of sin into pulp: that is, like the worst of demons.

December 1960 (continuation and end)

Great passions, great errors? The Roman never commits great errors and doesn't forgive them in others. He who exaggerates is "a fanatic." Rome has no *cours de miracles*, it does not have an undue number of vagrants, the beggars have become parking lot attendants, and theirs is a corporation more closed than the notaries'. Even in the outskirts the subproletariat aspires to "redemption," to stable employment and, lacking anything better, it imparts a seasonal rhythm to its enterprises: in winter, it's automobile theft, in spring, purse-snatching, in summer, hub-caps and spare tires. It takes imagination to find this sort of existence arduous and violent. Perhaps Rome lacks compulsive gamblers, rebels, go-it-aloners, idealists, those who will have nothing to do with money—personages who add salt to a society. It lacks false messiahs, unpublished poets (everybody publishes something), gloomy visionaries, mad speculators, Sunday painters, wandering philosophers: they wouldn't have a public. It lacks, in other words, great sinners. Nay, sin, which is clearly, par excellence, carnal sin, is its only true diversion. How much drama and remorse can it possibly be the source of? Rather, it will be the source of memories and regrets in the old, of new schemes and new hopes in the forever adventurous young.

Certainly, pederasty has its active participants and sympathizers, but also its very numerous mercenaries, a species of manual laborer nowadays being supplied even by the rural areas. It gives rise to no great amount of spiritual trouble, only gossip and an occasional horror story for the newspapers. "Responsible" pederasts have this shortcoming: taken one at a time, they are all likable, witty, intelligent, drawn to the arts, studious; put them together and they make you think of gypsies and mountaineers who immediately form a group, start to sing in harmony or to speak in dialect: unbearable.

What other vices do we have in this *dolcissima Roma* of ours? Literature? But the Roman literati are models of practically every virtue, a healthy exhibitionism not excluded. And in what other town have prizes for literature assumed so modest and familiar a tone as in Rome, where the prizes are awarded right in the house? And where else do there exist the fine organized excursions on the order of "One day in Capri, Blue Grotto included," which bring the Reader together with a Writer of his choice, offering him his book plus a hot lunch, all for around 3,000 lire (wine extra)? And where else can anyone, whoever he is, establish an award and give it time and time again to whichever writer makes himself easiest to read, thereby assuring himself of the understanding of all concerned?

And then there's prostitution. But the appearances which this activity is obliged to assume are so exhaustingly hypocritical that, in the end, it turns into pure and simple work, providing to certain families their sole source of income, a windfall to tourism, to small business, to short-term lenders, security to the elderly and an occupation to pimps: something with a stronger appeal for the economist than for the moralist.

Add it all up and lo! a serene panorama, dominated by reason. The only great attraction remains Sex which, again par excellence, is Woman. But this leaning the Roman has towards Woman never takes on the aspect of a ruinous vice, or of passion. Sex is a comfort, even vaguely para-familial. Last summer Lily Niagara came to Rome to do her strip-show. After four days, in the place where she was performing, members of The National Association for Assistance to Workers were getting in at reduced prices.

March 1962

Today, towards seven, the cafés along Via Veneto were almost deserted and the basement of Einaudi's bookstore was chock-full of critics and writers who had come from every section of the city, and even from other cities, for the public presentation of Giorgio Bassani's new novel. The presenting of new books in this fashion, the way kings used to stand on their balconies and present the newly born crown prince to the crowd, is recent: a few years ago it would have led to an author's being covered with ridicule; today it is accepted as a form of manifest persuasion, a postulate of mass culture. Five writers, who have read the novel in galley proofs, have woven together a eulogy. Most acclaim it. Others, with clenched teeth, admit that it's a fine novel, well written, but it raises no questions, indeed, it's "built out of memories." Proust is cited. Soldati even cites himself. On the way out, pushing through a crowd (which reminds one of those in the catacombs), someone murmurs in my ear the first mindless epigram of the evening: "Isn't it lovely / to live in a place / where Bassani is mistaken for Proust?"

April 1959

Whenever he's invited to some official party or other, Cardarelli borrows his evening attire—a tuxedo—from the waiter at the Caffè Strega. His latest *sortie* was yesterday, April 25, to Villa Madama, where he was invited to a dinner in honor of a writer who had won the *Penna d'Oro*. Cardarelli himself also won a prize recently, the *Torre*, which is given fairly often, and almost to everybody, in a restaurant close to the Campidoglio. At the moment in which they gave him his silver tower he was happy, but the next day he was crestfallen when the doorman, whom he had sent off to see what he could get for that pound or so of silver, returned almost immediately. It wasn't silver.

I accompanied Cardarelli up to his room. The stench was unbearable, I opened the window which looks out onto one of those dark, viscid courtyards, inhabited by cats and sheltering a little cesspool. Here, Via Veneto is only a façade. You no sooner enter these old buildings than the old Rome of narrow portals, of dark stairways, of corridors smelling of cabbage and mustiness grabs you by the throat. Once upon a time, towards the end of the century, the gardens of the Ludovisi and of the Boncompagni were here—the tree-lined avenues, the vineyards, the little woods adorned with statues. Those in charge of city planning didn't go for that stuff though (and they still don't go for it) and decided that Via Veneto (then called Via dei Cappuccini) would be the central street in a district of low-cost housing. The quarter of the rich bourgeoisie, of the high officers of State, of the Piedmontese conquerors, would be instead the Esquiline. "Nunc licet Exquiliis habitare salubribus . . ." Accordingly, they gave Piazza Vittorio Emanuele porticos, like those in Turin, with immense buildings, balconies, caryatids. Along Via dei Cappuccini they put up tenements. Then, with time, as in a quadrille, rich and poor changed places: the poor went into the houses of the rich and Via Veneto became the fashionable street. It filled up with hotels, with cafés . . . But here in this courtyard you get the feeling that everything started out badly. The poet's room is narrow, with a toilet stuck in one corner. His table in a state of precarious order. "I don't have anything anymore," Cardarelli says with a hint of satisfaction. I see only two photographs, groups of friends from his faraway youth. Next to the window, the stove. Cardarelli sits on the bed, with his greatcoat on, like an emigrant who is waiting for the ship's departure, or like an earthquake victim who, sitting on the only piece of furniture that he has left, in this way implies that he is its owner and won't get up from it because he doesn't want to see it carried away.

May 1959

It had to be two o'clock in the morning, but there was a reflected light from the clouds, which were flying low. Via Veneto was deserted, as if asleep since the beginning of time, its buildings shut tight, dark, with those squalid façades which advertising is unable to brighten up. I heard a rattling of drums coming from Porta Pinciana and behold! out from under the vaults emerges a parade. Leading it were a dozen majorettes, with bare legs and white suspenders. They were beating on their drums, and a tall long-legged girl was twirling a baton and catching it in mid-air. Behind them—smiling, responding to the greetings of an invisible crowd—came a group of people whom I seemed to recognize as they passed by: poets and writers, a few painters. An old man, borne upon someone's shoulders and closely surrounded like a saint in a procession, was protesting amiably to his admirers: "You lunatics, what are you doing, just let me down," and he swayed this way and that. I saw Sandro Penna who waved to me, as if apologizing for having to go on. He would be back, later. Sinisgalli was driving a pretty little jalopy in which all his manuscripts and drawings—more than a few of them unpublished—were displayed behind the windshield. I saw Bassani arm in arm with Alberto Moravia, and Goffredo Bellonci between Alberto Arbasino and Italo Calvino: they were singing. Mario Soldati was imitating himself, running from one group to another and reciting a few lines he had written: "About life I am learning the meaning, / how bitter and how hard it can be: / wisdom is got only by suff'ring, / much too late, alas, does one see . . ."

The street, meanwhile, was suddenly filling up with people—as when in Labiche's plays the guests come on stage: from side streets poured forth swarms of tourists, waiters getting off their shifts, cab drivers just beginning theirs, abusive parking lot attendants, married couples emerging from movie houses discussing Antonioni, photographers, tall, gangling Americans, the entire crews of jet-liners, townsfolk, students, girls with ruffled hair, young men with high collars, prostitutes, pimps, street types, playboys. All were applauding, without knowing for what or for whom. At the wheel of his 1937 Fiat 500, the poet Juan Rodolfo Wilcock was declaiming his immortal verses: "Every morning at dawning, this light of violets / sends up a fragrance in the motionless little gardens / turns back from the roof of the first cars it encounters / and enlivens the broken glass scattered among the flowers." I didn't see Pasolini. Where was Pasolini? Could his shyness have kept him at home? No, there he was too, in the middle of a group of young poets and calm, haughty directors. They were following swarms of girls, actors, actresses, directors, the juries of literary prizes, worker-writers, worker-painters, worker-critics, fellow travellers, misanthropes, sons of celebrities, wives of painters, the whole one gay confusion.

Flowers were raining down from above. "Where are you going?" I shouted to De Feo, who was walking along the sidewalk, keeping himself a little out of sight. He answered with a vague gesture. Running, I found myself once more at the head of the parade, which all of a sudden had come to a halt. In the middle of the street was a man and he was waving his hand to indicate that he wanted to speak. It was Cardarelli. In his somewhat hoarse and subdued voice he was saying: "Friends. I have asked you for too much, and you have given me too little. It has been a marriage of convenience and incompatibility. We have not understood each other and we have been unable to communicate. We have suffered so much being together! But now we must go our separate ways."

In the procession's front rank someone asked: "Who is he anyway? What does he want?"

Cardarelli was going on: "But you don't know what it is that's useful to life. Your word doesn't bear witness. What do your silences say? There is no system in your silences or in your words . . ."

"Down in front!" someone shouted.

"You don't know that words, if they have any value at all, have it only by virtue of their implications . . ."

"Enough! Music, let's get going again. Long live culture!"

"Your measure is lacking in freedom and miserly in hope . . ."

"Take off! Cuckold! Police!"

"You cannot imagine all the duplicities and sorceries and abuses of intelligence among men!"

"Silence! Beat the drums! Continue!"

"We have shared a consciousness without horizons. It has forever covered us over and exhausted its continuity. Upon every new occasion, when we have separated, we have been curt and threatening. And now it's time for us to bid each other farewell."

At this point the procession started to move on again, squawking and clamoring. And at this point I woke up.

June 1962

I am reading Sandro De Feo's *Gli inganni*. The story takes place in Rome, in a single day. Perhaps on account of something insistent and breathless in the narrative, it is like a gust of wind that gathers up dust, leaves, waste paper, and even some precious and imponderable material, our own life, our useless illusions, an effort of years, a love for a city which is unique and that leaves one loving it and despising it, depending on the moods and the sights it offers. The true Rome is in shadow, it shows itself with the years and becomes a landscape of the memory, a part of ourselves: the most secret and unique part, from which a certain salvation can come to us. The other Rome can irritate us, but it reveals too much of its complacent game to become really dangerous. One ends up laughing at it. On page 121 and following, De Feo speaks for example of Via Veneto: "So tonight it's Via Veneto. The spectacle of a charnel house under a green marquee is exactly what it is, but undoubtedly my nerves have been chafed by the wind and have made me exaggerate its obscenity and its grotesqueness. If I had the strength to do anything at all, I would start to laugh, the way I laugh when I come to those moments in the stories of the Marquis de Sade where the author goes too far overboard..."

The green marquee... I forgot all about the latest things: the big umbrellas of the café tables have disappeared from Via Veneto, those very umbrellas which made it resemble a beach. They have replaced them with long marquees of iron covered with cloth and also with shingles of transparent material. When evening comes, neon lights go on under the marquees.

June 1959

Yesterday, the 15th of June, Cardarelli died at the Polyclinic, where he had been for a month. A great devotee of Leopardi, he also died (almost) like Leopardi, through an indigestion caused by ice-cream, which then degenerated into bronchial pneumonia. For a month he had been unable to speak: only every so often, when someone came into his room, he would say, softly: "Tedious people."

Fellini is finally shooting *La Dolce Vita* at Cinecittà. In a studio, he has put together a piece of Via Veneto, not the corner where the poet lived but the more recent and crowded corner by the Café de Paris. Standing in front of that implacable reconstruction I almost started laughing, but immediately afterwards a biting melancholy took hold of me. In a projection room, I saw a few clips from the film. Fellini's elated portrait, his amplification of that world of Via Veneto recalls the wax museum, the images of Lenten preachers as they describe the flesh putrifying and corrupting. It reminds me of those big paintings of Valdes Leal that are at the Hospital de la Caridad in Seville, where ornamental scrolls float

over the cadavers of bishops and read: *Finis gloriae mundi.*
Fellini a Lenten preacher? It's a tempting hypothesis. "Perhaps
I could put Cardarelli in a corner, like a sort of premonition
lying in wait." "He died yesterday," I say to him. "Sure, you
see?"

Occasional Notebooks

1956–1960

A soldier asks me for a lift, he tells me he has to go to M., some fifteen kilometers away, to see his fiancée. He's a good-looking, dark-complexioned boy, indolent, with a hint of disgust in his expression, almost as if he were on the point of throwing up. His hair is well combed, he looks at his fingernails, gives his shoes a couple of swipes with his cap. He speaks with an effort, sighing. He informs me that every day when he gets his pass he goes to M., where, in a few days, he's going to be transferred with the rest of his regiment. A month there, then another new base, in C. The soldier also has a fiancée in C. And another in Rome and another in the country. But he's in no hurry to get married, he wants to enjoy life first. He utters these last few words with such disgust as to make me think he's joking. He's not joking at all. I question him a little. He's from "around Palermo." I ask him which he likes better, Sicilian women or "continental" women. He replies: "They all have their defects and they all have their charms." But I insist: "From the looks of you I'd say you're lucky when it comes to women." He makes a wry face and after a moment's silence answers very positively: "My dear sir, I would be lucky, but I'm not much of a talker. Girls like to talk and I don't know how to tell funny stories, jokes and all, all the stuff they like to hear. And besides that I don't know how to sing either. I don't like to talk about my personal life and I don't like to hear about anybody else's. So we don't ever say anything, and since I have to get back to barracks every night at ten and don't have much time to waste, they're always pulling out their hair and saying that I'm rude and insensitive. But I like the truth and I can't stand lies. If I go out with you it's not because I want to make conversation, it's because I want to make love. That's the reason honest girls like me, girls who say yes or no. Hurray for honesty, that's what I say."

A silence. Then he resumes: "Once in C. I was engaged to a girl. She swore to me that she was a virgin and respectable. Okay, good, I said to myself, now we'll just see. One Sunday, we had a cup of coffee together and then took a walk in a little woods. We ate some caramels and in one of the caramels I'd put a sleeping pill that I took from the infirmary. Well, she falls asleep and then I did some inspecting to see if she was honest. My dear sir, she wasn't honest, if I hadn't been careful I'd have fallen inside. When she woke up, I said: "How come you told me you're respectable when you're not? What's the matter, didn't you think I'd love you all the same?" Then she started to cry and I forgave her. We made love for a whole month, every single day. But her parents didn't want me around because they said that soldiers never get married. I'd have liked to have said that soldiers get married just like everybody else, but they marry respectable girls and that's not what your daughter is. But I didn't say anything because they transferred us."

Another silence. The young man passes a hand over his face and when he takes it away I see that he's smiling. It's a chilling smile, inspired by some memory or other. Indeed, he continues: "As far as respectable women are concerned, I once stopped a girl on the street in Palermo. We went for a walk, and I started to date her. Two days later, she says to me, sincerely: 'Listen, let me tell you right away, so there won't be any ugly surprises later on. I had a baby with another man who left me and now it's all over with, because the baby's dead. If you want to keep on seeing me, naturally I'll be happy, I like you. If not, tell me right now so I don't get my hopes up.' So I said: 'You did the right thing by telling me everything up front, you're an honest girl, there's nothing bad about having a baby. I like you because you told me the truth, the past doesn't matter, let's go on seeing each other.' Mister, I made love with her for four whole months, and then I split. Naturally, just as a precaution, I gave her a false name and address, my cousin's name and address. Mister, you can't believe what a riot it was when she went over there steaming. As it happened, my cousin was away but when he got back, my uncle—who would be my father's brother—wanted to beat him to death with his bare hands. And my cousin didn't know the first thing about it. And me, never a word, but inside I was laughing so hard I almost split a gut!"

We continue on in silence. In front of a shack, a girl with blond hair waves to us. The soldier gets excited and, since immediately afterwards we pass a truck stopped alongside the road, he turns around with wild gestures and shouts to the truck driver: "There's a blonde! Over there! Over there!" And to me: "If it wasn't for my fiancée waiting for me, I'd get out right now."

Once in M., the lugubrious Don Juan gets out, once more weary and full of disgust, leaving me to reflect upon his adventures.

He writes down his impressions, hoping that they are poetic. He therefore dwells upon the stupefying, the marvelous, the simple. If he looks at a wall it's because a rose is climbing up its side. He goes out of his house and notices that the sun is shining, or that it is not. If he goes out at night, a star breaks through the clouds, or thick clouds full of rain pass by, driven by the wind. He goes to the countryside: he discovers that the landscape changes color and the death-dealing city advances like a polyp, with its outlying houses. He recounts his feelings during an ordinary stroll outdoors. He stops to watch two little children at play. A woman is singing. Where? He doesn't see her. He wakes up in the middle of the night, believes he is dying and feels the darkness all around him like a quilt. Fortunately, he isn't dead. Et cetera.

*　　*　　*

"One morning," says R., "I couldn't sleep so I went down to the seashore. The sun hadn't come up yet and it was cold. About fifty yards out from the shore, in the calm water, an old man was fishing for clams. He had on a soldier's overcoat, with a shapeless hat on his head, and the water came up to his chest. At that particular moment his drudgery struck me as so damnable that, overcoming a feeling of shame, I called to him, saying I would pay him for his day so that he could go home. At first the old man didn't understand, then he said that he was used to it and went on with what he was doing. He had been making his living like this since he was a child, now he was seventy-five years old, this was the trade he would follow till his dying day. He came out of the water dressed as I said, his legs as sinewy and strong as a young man's. He deposited his catch in a basket and slowly went back into the water, thinking me either a madman or just a tiresome vacationer. He waded forward, like an old man who has his mind set on committing suicide, and when the water came up to his chest, he began to fish again, with a powerful cast of his trap. At one point he raised his hat, dried the sweat from his forehead and looked up at the sky. That same day I made inquiries about the old man. He was from a village in Campania, near Formia. Every year, with the approach of spring, he would make the journey here with the other fishermen, old and young, and with his sons too. They'd sleep in a few straw huts, in the woods. They were able to spend less than fifty lire a day, per head: for their bread and that's all. They wouldn't smoke and would never drink wine. They would all get up before dawn and each would light a fire and put a pot of dried beans (which they'd brought with them, together with onions and oil, from their village) on top of it to boil. They would fish from dawn till ten and then eat their meal, each one in front of his own hut without gathering in a group and for the most part without talking to one another. At nightfall they would dine on a piece of bread. The rest of their time would go into selling their clams, which is just as hard work as fishing for them. With the coming of winter they would take to the road again, back to their village, to go out fishing in boats, as usual. They would carry their earnings back with them, practically intact, and deposit them with the Post Office. This old man never deposited his earnings anywhere except with the Post Office, putting them in an account, not only under his name, but under his wife's too. Now the wife is dead and he has to renew the interest-producing bonds that have matured. The wife's heirs are called in, the three sons, his fellow migrants and fishing companions. The three sons want equal shares, otherwise they won't sign the paper. The old man says: 'It isn't fair. Half for me, half for you.' But the sons retort: 'No, equal shares.' And they won't sign the paper. So no one can collect the savings from twenty years' labor. Every morning, the old man and his three sons, each one on his own, fish for clams. If ever they run into one another, they never exchange a word of greeting. The fisherman who told me this story concludes by saying: 'They're too selfish.' "

Italian actors—all excellent playing the parts of thief, priest, carabiniere. The actresses—all excellent playing the parts of sister-in-law, plebeian, lady of the night. The troubles begin when they want to play lords, ladies, artists, *condottieri,* manufacturers, politicians, professors, scientists. The crisis besetting the élites—you can also feel it on the stage and on the screen.

Nothing entertains me more than to hear Italian actors speaking the lines of an English or American comedy. For example, when an Italian actor plays an Englishman he dresses himself up like the conventional caricature of an Englishman: checkered jacket, foulard around his neck, pipe between his teeth, stiffness in the shoulders when he moves. And the translation of the text aggravates the situation. "*Càspita!*" "You don't say!" says the actor, raising his eyebrows. It's not real at all: in his own house, in a similar circumstance, he wouldn't hesitate to say: "*C...!*" pounding his fist on the table at the same time; and this always supposing that he's in a good humor.

Why does theater "in lingua" provoke neither laughter nor tears? Perhaps because in our opinion the reality of life is always outstripped by the imaginations of playwrights: and reality, whatever it may be, cannot be brought onto the stage otherwise than in familiar speech, in dialect. Show me a scene, if there is one, in which Signora X tells smutty stories in Italian, without it being vulgar. In real life when she tells smutty stories, Signora X doesn't fall in social standing. Show me a seduction scene, in Italian, that isn't comical. In real life they come off very nicely: the protagonists take no notice of the ridiculous pretence. Finally, show me a poet speaking. Impossible. We know that our poets are all blessed souls, systematically benign, and that the only sort of *poète maudit* that we have plays the stock market. On stage, that poet, should he speak in character, would make us doubt his seriousness, we would accuse him of professional fanaticism, of exhibitionism. Don't you see, we cannot have our heroes speak, because they would have us smiling all the time and we would never consider them capable of great actions, of tragical solutions, of "profundity," while in real life they often are. We the public go to the theater convinced we represent a society which acts "in Italian," while in reality it thinks in vernacular. As for the theater of ideas ... does not the average Italian's appeal, his likeableness, have to do with the fact that he has no ideas? Pirandello? We forget that Pirandello, the night his *Six Characters* opened, was pursued by the audience and had to hide himself in a doorway.

I'm at a country restaurant, spending the evening with C. There is a party of campers next to us. They never stop laughing. The young man who is entertaining his companions has the elegance to remain deadpan, or rather gravely frowning.

He glances at us and at the customers at the other tables from beneath heavy eyelids, without moving his head, ready for a fight. He has full, rosy lips, a goatee like the skipper of a raft, and a meaty and powerful chest. His repertory is limited, but this is the reason for his success since the effectiveness of his jokes lies simply in their obstinate repetition. He is a specialist in noises. He doesn't speak a word, he emits sounds, varying them from hisses to meows, from roars to belches. His schtick is to be irresistible. The waiter passes by: he makes him turn around quickly by producing a grunt. A song is coming over the radio: he accompanies it with little hee-haws. An obese gentleman is playing ping-pong and he bends over to pick up the ball: there's a fart. And since he has to bend over fairly often, irresistible the thing does indeed become. The gentleman looks around, his surprise runs up against the frigid dignity of the young man: he tries to smile, after a little while he stops picking up the ball. And he goes away, looked at by everyone as if he were the true author of those sounds. Now it is clear our laughter springs from old memories of school days, and also from this: that the young jokester defines his victims, makes infantile caricatures out of them, but that is exactly why the victims recognize themselves, in some obscure way feeling they have been caught off balance and carried back to an age in which the only funny jokes are those which reveal the animal in us.

He opens his door to the Catholic thieves and discusses with them how to steal necessities from the poor, who have need only of the superfluous, otherwise it's revolution.

Along the road over the Futa, on the walls, at regular intervals: "Viva la Morini," which is not a local girl, as I had imagined for several kilometers, visualizing to myself the felicity of young peasants united at least by this tender erotic collectivism, but the brand name of a motorcycle.

On the door of the church of San Petronio, in Bologna: "The

decorum of the church prohibits the entry of bicycles." This is a warning that would have pleased Stendhal, he who marvelled that in St. Peter's, in Rome, two lovers might exchange notes. In Rome, I think I might be amazed by a sign that prohibited bicycle repairing in church.

Mr Mayor, I think I finally understand how in Rome a street is built in a new district. This way: first of all, poles are installed in the open country with the name of the street which is to be laid down, paying careful attention that the name chosen be without reference to places but, rather, that it belong to some mediocre personality who has been dead and forgotten for at least ten years. Shortly afterwards, houses are built along the proposed street (it's best if they're enormous office-like buildings, at least eight brightly painted stories), preserving, of course, the natural landscape between one house and the next, thereby making sure that they will turn into swamps whenever it happens to rain. The buildings once inhabited (by which time someone has provided for the cutting down of all the trees, which disfigure construction sites and hinder trucks from getting around) stony material is unloaded on that part of the landscape reserved for the future street itself. This material is not, however, to be distributed evenly over the entire area, but rather arranged in little pyramids, which it is best to leave alone for at least a year, to facilitate the games of little children. After this year has gone by, the path receives a summary levelling and summary sidewalks are built, these last having to end up about a meter higher than the aforementioned path to forestall their inconsiderate use by pedestrians. The next year, work begins on the street itself, with its concrete road-bed and the required layers of asphalt. However, it is best to interrupt this work at the halfway mark and to take it up with greater vigor the following year and then bring it to an end. Two days after the street has been inaugurated the useful thing to do is open it up lengthwise for its entire length, in order to install gas conduits. The street, after this necessary undertaking, of great benefit to the inhabitants, now possesses a hump down its middle. This need not concern us inasmuch as within the space of one month (in some cases, within the space of a week) the same street is torn up for the second time, once again for its entire length, and this time with transverse trenches, in order to install the indispensable cables for the transport of electric energy. At this point one might think that we could take advantage of the unusual circumstances to install the streetlights where they are supposed to go along the sidewalks. No, your Honor, it is always best to save this kind of work for winter when the mud renders it more interesting. Anyhow, the arrangement of the said streetlights usually precedes, by scarcely a month, sometimes two weeks, the installation of pipes for the diffusion of drinking water, which requires a third more vast and more challenging excavation of the street and the restoration of the characteristic trenches. On certain streets a fourth digging back down through the substructure (along with a digging up of the sidewalks) may be necessary in order to lay down telephone cables. But, your Honor, we're talking here about "upper class" streets! On streets in the humbler sections of town the installing of telephones will be possible after the reasonable delay of five years at least. Then, once the telephone cables have been taken care of, one may look forward to the starting of the necessary work of rebuilding the road, with all the short-cuts you care to imagine. If someone should then want to adorn our street with trees, in order to render it gay and salubrious, there is but one way to go about it: at convenient distances from one another, with an opportune re-opening of the sidewalks, oleander bushes must be planted, provided of course they're just about dead—avoiding in this way both the shade (not very much to begin with) that these trees cast and an excessive colorfulness that might be to the detriment of the architectural rainbow of the surrounding buildings. Other dying trees that might be planted more conveniently (but only in the alleys) are the dying maritime pine and the dying acacia. The acacia, honorable Mayor, may be the more advisable since its roots, as we know, easily spreading out to the conduits and pipes below ground, can damage them and render necessary a fifth, though not necessarily final, re-opening of the street bed: it being the sixth that is usually reserved for the eventual installation of sewers.

A friend and I are in the country, sitting in front of the gate to his house. We have to talk about a story, for a movie, and neither of us wants to say the first word, lest by our unloosing the modest images suggested, indeed, by the story and its protagonist, this afternoon of ours lose all its meaning and the landscape disapear. Both of us agree that we want to write a true story, with a true character. But what the devil is truth? Ah, just to be able to wash our hands of the whole thing! And so we wait, half closing our eyes, each hoping that the other will continue to keep still; or, if he has to say something, that he will touch lightly on some amiable nonsense about the weather, or about first loves, or about his encounters of the day before, which in the city make for the delight of these working conversations. Now, however, the silence is becoming suspect; going on this way is going to oblige us once and for all to talk about the story and its immobile protagonist. Yes, every passing moment is rendering a serious discussion more and more inevitable. In chorus we say: "It looks like the weather . . ."

But towards the west, the pink sky foretells a calm and starry evening: no need to talk about it. A desperate look at our watches and my friend concludes: "Let's work seriously for maybe one little hour. After that the village will come to life, and we don't want to miss the sight." Fine idea. Let's get to work. And out of the lazy depths of our imaginations there arises, still featureless but already diffident, the face of the actress who is awaiting our decision about her destiny. "She's a kid from hereabouts," my friend says, with an effort I find admirable. "Right," I say. "She's a poor kid from hereabouts who works and wants to go to the city." It's a reasonable enough hypothesis. We dwell upon it for a moment. And now a girl actually passes by. "Don't let her see that you're looking at her," my friend says, "but kindly notice her eyes. Tell me if you've ever seen such a pair of eyes. Eyes like a cat's. She'd eat you up, if she could." The girl, as a matter of fact, has very lovely, oblique eyes, in a face worn out by her mediocre adventures. "Now think about this," my friend goes on. "I recall that she had a fiancé. They didn't have enough money to get married. She had a baby and he skipped out." "To the city, of course." "To the city, that's right. He was never seen again."

Silence. With the speed of light each of us relives the story of this girl who is passing by, each of us thinking that perhaps a character like this, for our story . . . "Right, and then what happens to her?" asks my friend, as if making me responsible for all the many things that can easily happen to her, all of them obvious and hardly exemplary. But the girl is already retreating into the distance, taking with her every fantasy associated with her. "Notice the way she walks," says my friend, who hasn't given up hope. But no, it's already too late. Another girl emerges from her house, mounts a bicycle; she draws near. "And this one? Think about her. She's crazy about dancing, but really crazy! When the orchestra strikes up there's no holding on to her, she becomes somebody else. What do you think of it?" I respond with a moan. "Right, okay," rejoins my friend, one step ahead of me, "and afterwards, what does she do? She marries the orchestra?"

Now four girls pass by, arm in arm, talking up a storm. Upon seeing us they lower their voices, stop talking, one of them covers her face to hide a sudden merriment, surely provoked by us. "Or we could do the story of these four girls," I say. "Village life, dreams, reality. They all work in a tin can factory. One is engaged, the others no . . ." "Or vice versa," my friend says, ironically. A long silence follows. Reciprocal resentment over the futility of our attempts to adapt the life of others to our necessities makes us sulk. Ah, the life of others, made up of days, one after the other, and from which there's nectar to gather only at the end, and then not always! A lady passes by. "Act natural," my friend says, "but take a look at her face. Indomitable!" And he adds, greeting her, "Buona sera, Signora." Then he tells me a few stories about her exploits. And thus, for an hour, the models which reality had to offer filed by in front of us. We were asking from them exactly what they were asking from us: a story. Finally, tired, we decided to talk about it again the next day. One creates nothing out of doors. And to copy it all down, what a headache!

Roberto, who has descended upon Rome to become an actor, wanders through the city elegantly dressed. He encounters someone from back home, a lawyer, who is overjoyed to see him and invites him to the house for dinner. Roberto, who hasn't eaten for two days, is deeply moved. An hour before the appointed time there he is impatiently pacing up and down in front of his friend's house. The dinner passes practically in silence, Roberto is too busy with his food. Afterwards, a laborious digestion awakens his feelings anew. Fighting back tears, he tells his friend about his misfortunes and how in anticipation of better times he is looking for a job, even a humble one, provided the work's honest. The lawyer thinks for a moment, hesitates, finally says: "What about brooms?" And he explains: he has helped a certain person, who paid him his fee in the form of a shipment of brooms . . . It's a question of a thousand brooms, which he has to get rid of somehow, but he dislikes the idea of taking a big loss by selling them wholesale. If Roberto wants to handle them . . . "Why, sure!" Roberto shouts gratefully. He'll sell brooms! And he becomes ecstatic before this humble task that chance has brought his way. Hasn't he read about great men who have started out even worse? They go over to the warehouse to take a look at the brooms: there are three types: extra-deluxe, feather dusters, and regular. It's a question then of making the rounds to all the neighborhood hardware stores and offering this merchandise at a good price. The lawyer adds: "If I had time, I'd do it myself. But I never have time!" Roberto reaffirms his intention to sell the whole lot in a few days. They agree on a commission and Roberto takes three brooms, one of each type, and promises he will make his first round the next day. The only thing he asks for is an advance, which he gets and with which he spends a merry evening.

The next morning Roberto, his head clearer, is assailed by shame. Walk out of the house carrying three brooms? But carry them how? Under one arm? Over his shoulder? Or simply by grasping them by the handle? Finally, his pride suggests the most daring solution: to secure the brooms baldric-wise across his back, like three rifles, and not worry about looking ridiculous. What does it matter if people laugh? Actually, this is probably the only way to keep them from laughing, by startling them. After a few minutes, with his brooms baldric-wise and staring fixedly at everyone rash enough to get in his way, Roberto is on the street and in front of a hardware store window. Here his fine self-confidence deserts him. He hesitates, finally enters. The store is full of young ladies and his entrance brings the gay conversation to a sudden halt. Behind the counter the owner scrutinizes him with implacable eyes and asks him what he wants. Roberto smiles: "I've got plenty of time. Take care of the ladies first," he says gallantly. The druggist insists: no, he wishes to serve *him* first. Pointing to a package of camphor, Roberto says: "Give me a quarter-pound." He feigns to be enchanted by what's on the shelves, hopes that the lady customers will go away and leave him alone; but the owner doesn't let him out of his sight and serves him promptly. He pays, has to leave. Once outside, he's tempted to start slapping himself. And he wants to be an actor, stand on a stage, act in front of a cold audience!

To hell with shame! Isn't his elegant appearance the best guarantee that he doesn't ordinarily sell brooms? He hurries back into the store and, not paying attention, he breaks the pane of glass in the door with his broom handles. He stands there dumbstruck, watching the last pieces of glass fall to the floor, while the owner, more surprised than he, shouts at him with a voice in which, along with anger, there vibrates a desperate curiosity. "Just what are you trying to do? What are you trying to do?" And Roberto, irritated with himself and close to tears, shrugs and in a sullen voice says: "Nothing! I wanted to sell you a consignment of brooms! What's so strange about that?" But even as he utters these words, he has the feeling his whole life has been a mistake, even his choice of an acting career has been a mistake, because an actor who expects to sell brooms (and some are successful at it) ought at least to be smart enough to dress like a broom salesman, in order to pass unobserved.

On an outing with F. to Monte Amiata, to the places where David Lazzaretti once preached. We arrive in a serene, wind-swept little hamlet, ask an old man where we can we find a restaurant. The old man looks at us with a smile and forgets what he was about to answer; he snaps his fingers, in a moment he'll have it. He's a very poor old man, dressed in patched-up clothes and a little cap with the cardboard showing through on the visor. However, he cannot be mistaken for a beggar: the clear look in his eyes attests to a difficult life, but an innocent and straightforward one too. It's only his surprise that impedes him from being of help to us, so seldom does he have the occasion to chat with anybody.

Finally he points towards the next little piazza; he offers to walk ahead and show us the way; we thank him for it. There we are, happy on account of this encounter, in the restaurant. It's a little bar with two tables, but homey, which adds to our good cheer and inclines us to find everything lovely and pleasant. The food is excellent, a girl blushes as she waits on us and, whenever she can, secretly adjusts her skirts or tidies her hair. After a little while we see our old man pass in front of the door, look in through the windows. He enters and sits at the other table, taking the chair in the corner. Without his asking for anything, the girl brings him a plate heaped high with food: a little bit of everything all mixed together. He plainly doesn't have the right to choose, with the little he can afford to pay. He eats slowly, trying to catch a smile from one of us; by looking our way, he risks sticking his spoon into his ear. Since we linger at table, held there by the pleasantness of that warm atmosphere, the old man, who has finished his meal, gets up to leave, wishing everybody good day. He mistakes a gesture of ours for an invitation to shake hands and he reaches forward. A sudden timidity (perhaps he realized his mistake) makes him back up; he overturns a chair, laughs and apologizes.

There we are ourselves now in the little piazza looking at the panorama, filled with a more and more unreasonable happiness. The old man crosses the piazza and it is obvious that he is waiting for us over there. He pretends confusion, pretends not to see us when he finds himself in our path. The way we take ensures that we'll meet him, and finally there we are face to face. He gives a start, laughs, and the question which has been cooking up inside him for some time suddenly comes clearly to his lips, as if he were afraid of forgetting it: "Are you happy you came?" And since we assure him that everything has been wonderful, he breathes a sigh of relief. "It's a good place," he says seriously. Then: "Should you come through again, ask for me." And he adds: "Actually, I'm not from here, I live on top of that mountain." He points it out to us. "Not on the very top," he laughs, "there, where those beech trees are." "Alone?" The old man nods his head: of course, who else would be up there? Who else can live way up there, if not an innocent old man, who comes down in the evening for someone to look at and to walk around the automobiles, to read the license plates, and to take comfort at least in this?

Our car is already moving when he remembers he hasn't given us his name. He runs after us: "Ask for Arittimetica! That's me!" And the old Lazzaretian apostle stands still and looks after us, waving his hand until he sees us vanish around the first curve; without supposing that his appearing, his surveillance, that unconcealed need of his for love and friendship has given us this quiet joy, this sudden faith in the evening that is about to descend, something he certainly cannot imagine; or, were he able to, it would seem like a joke to him.

After tranquil and by now predictable dreams during the night, wakening, as I lie abed, brings its menacing symbology in more abject dreams, prompted by the mail and newspapers. Here's the painter who is sending me an invitation to his show and on the catalog he has had one of his paintings printed: in what incubus have I ever seen anything to compare with it for chilling uselessness? My eye, still weak and hurting from the light, drinks up this vision and a shiver takes possession of me under the covers, a shiver all the more absurd when I think that I am awake, well protected by these four walls, by the floor, by the ceiling, and not wandering in the limbo of the night. Other letters follow the first, all dreamlike: an invitation to a wedding, another exhibit, the menacing prospect of having to see a bad film, a department store catalog, a childhood friend who still remembers me, three exhibits, a convention, a calendar-gift that proclaims the coming new year with the cruelty of an impatient creditor! And then the newspapers. In what torpid, sirocco-provoked dream have I ever lived moments more thick with fear and pity, for myself and for my fellow creatures, than those in which I live wide awake reading about domestic massacres, ferocious homicides, about inevitable insanities, collective disasters? And every particular, just as in the dreams of once upon a time, is described with a precision that approaches art! Names, sex, age, last words, final convulsions! Often the pain is such that I refuse to bear it and with a shout I go back to sleep, seeking comfort in my innocuous dreams, which never go beyond an hypothesis or a desire; dreams which unfortunately glide like shadows, modestly, into the loudest noises from the street that is waking up, eager to live.

*   *   *

"And now, after you've succeeded so well in this, your first murder, what else are you planning that's nice?"

"Well, actually..."

"You mean you don't have anything planned, nothing at all?"

"Well, yes, I'd like to carry out an old idea of mine, a mass-murder, but it's premature to talk about it."

"Thank you. We're all certain you'll be able to pass this hurdle and arrive at the peak of your fame. And now, to finish up, is there anyone you'd like to say hello to?"

"Yes, first of all I'd like to say hello to the Department of Justice, then to my dear mamma. Ciao, mamma!"

I'm just old enough to remember the first resignation of En-rico De Nicola and just young enough to be able to stroll along Via Giovanni Giolitti.

In his first year as a stud, the celebrated race-horse will attempt no more than twenty-four mounts. In the two following years he will accomplish forty mounts each year. Every mount will cost about two million lire. An American breeder has telegraphed, booking all the horse's mounts for the first year. The sire of the famous horse mounted regularly until he was twenty years old, for a grand total of nine hundred or so mounts. There's no assurance, however, that every mount will result in a colt as sure-footed as the sire. That depends as much on the dam, on her reproductive organs and on how the mount itself turns out. Et cetera. In short, the interest that this horse's future gives rise to is enough to warrant that the above-mentioned mounts be conducted in public, possibly on holidays and in a stadium. There should be no problem arranging it if part of the draw goes to the benefit of ... of whom? Oh, here I foresee conflict. It would likewise be opportune if the celebrated horse were elected senator, so as to go back to a period of Roman history that we have been doing a very good job of imitating.

"And tell us, Signorina, were you always so beautiful, even as a child?"

"Oh no, as a child I was a rather ugly little thing, so ugly that my family decided to have me study. I went through three years of high school, repeating one year to gain time, until at sixteen I improved, physically speaking."

"And this permitted you to abandon your studies and to devote yourself to prostitution."

"Yes, that's correct."

"Then we can say in all truth that even you have had to struggle to win a name for yourself!"

A race-car driver writes an article giving hints on how to drive an automobile. For instance, he recommends that on curves one should always keep on one's own side of the road and that one should always maintain the proper posture while driving, "above all because it is more elegant." Elegant! Here's the word, here's the topic I've been looking for for so long! Yes, because elegance is our only concern. We allow any reservation to be voiced about our conduct, but any doubt cast on our elegance upsets and offends us deeply. Oh, to be able to apply this method of criticism to thieves, to murderers, to swindlers, to establish once and for all that robbing is not elegant, that murdering is not elegant, that swindling is the height of inelegance. The day reprobates are smitten, not by the contempt of moralists, which actually excites them, but by the veiled disdain of elegant people, the maximum shall have been done, and we shall be able to dissolve the police corps, which, moreover, has shown it understands the true exigencies of the times, having adopted in these last few weeks a new and exceedingly elegant uniform.

*　　*　　*

If the proprietor of a movie house, finding he needed (we propose a desperate hypothesis, one that borders on the extreme) to buy a book, should enter a bookstore and, after having asked for the title he wanted, should hear by way of reply: "Signore, it's all yours, in fact, kindly hand over your money and pay for it; but before you settle down to read it, please lend an attentive ear to the following recitations"; and should he be constrained, on pain of forfeiting the money he has paid, to listen on the spot to (a) an extract from the forthcoming novel of a writer he detests; (b) a poem on the manufacture of chocolate; (c) a sonnet on the excellence of certain detergents derived from the processing of petroleum; (d) a stirring and joyous account of the least interesting events of the past week, namely: the dedication of an ugly church, a livestock fair, a speech by a political figure connected with the government, a game of football and a party for incoming college freshmen; and then, after a brief interval, (e) a colorful lyric on the Amalfi Coast; (f) the addresses of a certain number of retail stores; (g) a demonstration of the advantages he would derive from using a certain model of vacuum cleaner; and finally (h) a record with three Neapolitan songs: if that movie house proprietor should, then, have to listen for a half-hour to these and similar spiels before coming into possession of his book (which he has already paid for and for which he has dragged himself into the bookstore) merely because the bookseller earns a certain personal profit from his capricious impositions, would he not perhaps have the right to shout death to all bookstore proprietors and to cut himself off from the pleasures of reading? Of course, and who would dare to criticize him? Nor, on the other side, could the inconsiderate bookseller have anyone to blame but himself if his customers deserted his bookstore for good, preferring, instead, to spend their money in the movie houses, where these outrages are not permitted.

*   *   *

In the same way Lady Chatterley found the most striking thing in a woods to be its gamekeeper, so our newspapers see in life only its most sensational aspects. The piety of reporters is on the side of sentiment and sex. The names they have been dwelling upon for so many years have by now become a zodiac-like heaven of fixed constellations, with each month pushing forward a heaven of its own that we would like to forget, but it isn't possible. Oh, the periodic and inevitable return of these names! I won't write them down, they provoke in me a suspicion that is even orthographic, but I know them by heart, like everyone else. We will forget the names of our teachers, the name of the person whom we loved for a day, but not the name of this vile gang, not their smiles, their vulgar self-assurance, which derives from the simple fact that they have survived unpunished, and which then defies all criticism. And moreover how could we forget them? The newspapers are on the alert and every time we show signs of weariness they redouble their piety. The same newspaper that published one hundred photographs of the lady murderess, today deplores the publicity she is after; and publishes, if need be, photograph one hundred and one. The distaste which overly photographed faces inspire in us comes from this: in any one of them may lie hidden our own incubus of tomorrow.

To whom it may be of interest.

"And now we come to our last question: for thirty pieces of silver can you tell us the exact place where, at this very moment, Jesus of Nazareth is to be found?" "In the garden of Gethsemane." "Your answer is absolutely correct!" (Applause.) "Guards, let's go!" (Exeunt).

Let's splash around in the slush. The snow statues of Stalin, with pipe in mouth and broom under arm, are melting in the first rays of the sun. The sculptors, who used to oblige the citizens to kneel worshipfully before these statues, are now throwing dirty snowballs at one another, weighting them with a stone inside. One of them hails a passer-by: he wants to start a dialogue. And with this dialogue to demonstrate that they have indeed been wrong, even if for internal reasons they had to maintain that they were right; but that everything is going to change and that from now on they will always be right.

A friend of mine is an enthusiast of vaudeville shows. He tells me about a company that performs in a little movie-house in Trastevere. We walk in and a skit is already in progress and, naturally, what's unfolding is the Two Superpowers number. It's a number that never fails to be on the program. Russia and America are on stage with Pulcinella, the cunning servant of two masters. The sketch itself, more than the entertaining material it contains, offers the usual material for reflection, and at the end we leave the movie-house quite saddened. Sadder than I is my friend, forced to take note of the fact that while we were away they've stolen his spare tire. This theft is altogether a continuation of the sketch, or at least it adheres to its spirit. I try to make my friend understand this. But I think that he is too irritated by the theft to be consoled by a philosophical digression on "our" character.

One of the points upon which the unknown author of the sketch dwelled is in fact the capacity we have for "sticking it to" our neighbor; a capacity which the author defines: intelligence. Pulcinella, for example, boasts of having despoiled the American down to his shoe-laces, of even having stolen an ocean liner right out from under his nose. At this allusion to a Neapolitan tale that circulated in the days of the black market, the audience burst into applause. On the stage the Russian, while congratulating Pulcinella for his craft, admonishes him severely, allowing him to visualize the eventuality of a forthcoming trip to Italy of his own. "Nobody," the Russian says, "jokes around with me, caro Pulcinelloff!" Pulcinella looks at him with an air of smiling pity, winks at the audience, and replies: "But have you ever been here before?" and this

several times, miming: "But have you ever been here before?"
He means: in Italy. And when the Cossack responds that no,
he's never been here before, Pulcinella lets fly the witticism
he has been keeping in reserve: "In that case *come* and then
you'll see!" A hurricane of applause drowns out the Russian's
rejoinder, which in any case can't have been very important.

The applause of the audience moved us for a moment to
feel a certain sinister pride in this capacity of ours to laugh at
national defects. Except that the audience and, before the
audience, the author and the actors of the sketch do not think
it can be spoken of as a defect, but rather as a virtue, an
ancient, solid, eternal virtue. One of those virtues that even
suffice to level out the political differences between two rivals, who find themselves possessing it together. A virtue, just
to be clear, which at that moment gave the spectator the
subtle and invincible assurance of being safely above every
criticism and suspicion, of being safely beyond the fray.

Four or five of us are together, we are on Via Croce, we know
an American professor of Italian origin, very quiet and *simpatico*. Introductions, the usual jokes. The professor asks V.
where he was born. V. responds: in Ravenna . . . Jotted down
here is the dialogue that ensued:

"Magnificent city, Ravenna. I wrote the finest pages of my
Byron there."

"You wrote a book on Byron? But whatever for?"

"Because Byron interests me. Ravenna inspired my best
pages. I used to go into the pine grove . . ."

"Alone?"

"Alone. I was in 'their' company, however, Byron's and the
Contessa Guiccioli's. In Ravenna, as you know, Byron was the
guest of Contessa Guiccioli."

"More than just a guest! He *thrust* himself into Casa Guiccioli, he ate, drank and made love to the contessa there. In
Ravenna, everybody knows about it. Nice way for a poet to
behave."

"But Byron was in love. It was a dreamy period for him. He used to go into the pine grove with the contessa . . .

"And you call that acting like a gentleman?"

"Byron and the contessa went for long rides on horseback."

"Right. And then?"

"And then nothing. Byron declamed verses and the contessa . . ."

"Spread her . . ."

"Come on! What are you saying! It was the purest sort of love. Byron drew his highest inspiration from it."

"Riding horseback."

"And he immortalized those moments in the sixteenth canto of *Don Juan*. Remember the beautiful invocation of the Madonna?"

"I don't believe so."

"Read it!"

"If you think I have time to read Byron."

"Do you trust Carducci?"

"No, not at all."

"Well, even Carducci . . ."

"What? Even Carducci . . . in the pine grove with the contessa? She must have been a little old lady!"

"No, Carducci wrote the famous ode in which he says, remember? *'Una di flauti lenta melodia . . .'* "

"Wonderful, now it's a flute too. Great stuff you're trying to defend, professor. And now let's shed a tear over the critical state culture is in."

And the dialogue continues in this tone. The professor can take a joke, but he is a bit worried all the same. That behind the joke there may truly be no respect for Byron?"

My young communist friend greets me, looks steadily into my eyes, talks about the weather, about a film he would like to see. His calculated indifference finally saddens me. I search in vain for a shadow of doubt or of shame in his eyes; there isn't a thing, not even a trace of disappointment over this friendship that is coming to an end. We know that from now on we will avoid greeting each other, shaking each other's hand, because I neither greet nor shake hands with institutions, with associations, with mafias, with dogmas, with raisons d'état. A comparison comes to mind which is perhaps odious, but nevertheless spontaneous. In France, to talk about a country that has a communist party in the same condition as ours, amongst the rank and file of the party many voices were raised to condemn the aggression in Hungary. There were declarations, resignations, protests: a sign that Men are not yet dead and don't intend to die. From us, a few letters that were not sent, a little deploring, promptly watered down. The agitation of the young was limited to a rather cynical calculation: was or wasn't the party too weak to allow an outcry? The Russian tanks eliminated every doubt in their minds. They would speak, finally, only out of vanity, or in order "not to be among the last." Now they want to have us believe that they gave precedence to jointly held opinion over personal opinion. We know that it isn't true, that it had been fear alone counseling them, a fear rendered all the more mean-spirited by the fearless dreams of brotherhood that they nourished and which now, quietly, they are disowning; a fear that they hope can be swapped for security. Instead it's a question of rigidity, probably the rigidity of cadavers.

I follow Togliatti not for his political program, which doesn't interest me, but for his philological coquetries. In the days of the blue double-breasted Togliatti, the communist chief used to indulge a certain fondness for grammar. Oh, those little professorial delights that led others to say of him: "He's a good man, if he loves the Italian language so much." Today I read in *Unità*: "counter-revolutionary hoodlums," in reference to the insurgents in Budapest. An inexactitude, professor! We've already heard suchlike talk, in '44, when the SS used to speak of *"delinquenti badoglianti"* (Badoglio's criminals) with reference to those assassinated in the Fosse Ardeatine. How quickly the brothers of peace, the breeders of pigeons, the planters of olive trees, the open dialoguists have taken as their own that language which only properly belongs to jailers and slave-drivers!

Unità: on page one, insults to the dead of Budapest; on the other pages, the sports headlines, this is your house, ladies, how to cook a nice little lunch, the serene life of the Chinese, et cetera. Chilling, like an executioner telling funny stories.

Whatever else they may suffer from, Fascist students are persecuted by the curse of having to graduate. They don't know how to do anything except make noise. Look at them, with their little thirteenth century berets, covered with comic and pornographic insignia, running through the streets in the center of town (it's safer there), blowing whistles, looking at the girls, glad to be out strolling, having fun, convinced that they're being admired and that they're exhibiting their disdain, while actually they are succeeding only in provoking the disdain of whoever is looking on. During the final years of fascism I recall them "demonstrating" only once: to demand an *A* on their exams. Whenever Pulcinella protests he steals a plate of macaroni.

J.P. Sartre: an existence spent in joining and leaving the communist party. He's the little man with the umbrella on certain barometers that indicate thereby if we're in for good or bad weather. Today he doesn't approve of the Kruschev rapport, because it has undermined Stalinism and "rather than contributing to the reduction of the party's dictatorship, has reconfirmed it." Hence, they should have dismantled Stalin only when the dictatorship of the party had entirely disappeared, that is, when there would be no further for need for it at all. In the meantime, Sartre would have obeyed the "fetishes" of the party, volunteering to yank the ears of all those who, after Hervé, had called it into question. It is the reasoning of the gardener's dog, who detests cabbages but who will have no one touching them.

At the first news of the revolt an enormous painting was begun; its title was "The People of Budapest Are Fighting against Tyranny." Work on the painting continues, but the title has been changed to "The Glorious Soviet Army Crushes the Reactionaries". With a view to an award it has, however, a third title in reserve: "Tanks and Figures."

Fascism: a stopped watch that tells the exact time twice a day. It is a question of a moment. But in that moment it shouts: "Right on the dot!"—and everything ends there; Time doesn't stop moving.

One may reproach Herod for the slaughter of the innocents. But a court historian successfully demonstrated that those little babies, who were too little to understand anything anyway, weren't sincere democrats in the first place. And besides, their mothers got all the pride and satisfaction that comes from making a sacrifice, the more praiseworthy for having been dedicated to the Throne. Without mentioning that during the ensuing melee unleashed by the reaction, a good dozen or so executioners, all democrats, suffered severe bruises.

"Ladies and gentlemen, technical difficulties have caused us to suspend our broadcast. Once the trouble has been cleared up we shall, within a few days, resume those society game-shows of ours, which give the life of the nation that feeling of vivacity that so becomes it. We will be looking forward to introducing you to more fools and half-wits, to exhibitionists of every tendency, we will hold a few spicy courtroom trials, we will publish your memoirs, we will purchase Hungarian soccer-players. The essential thing is to get through to the coming summer with faith intact; for our beauty contests, our literary prizes, our festivals and dances once back in operation, we will be able to affirm with heads held high that the outside world is envious of our happiness.

He is so vain that he can't resist his own charm. He's ruining his health doing his self-portrait.

A hero of our times. In 1943 he took off his badge at two o'clock in the afternoon. In '45, running into me, he said: "We will put everyone like you up against the wall." In '46 I saw him again in a restaurant: he was singing a Russian song. His teeth were black, he had stopped brushing them. In '48 I found him at night writing on a wall. In '49 he sang me the praises of a horrible film and recommended it as an expression of progressive popular art. In '50 he said to me: "Your haggard group of intellectuals . . ." I saw him again in '54 and he warned me: "Our duty as intellectuals is to engage in an open dialogue." In '55 he embraced me: "I've just got back from Russia. We'd never be able to live there, but you ought to go. It's an experience." Two months later he smiled at me: "Did you see the Russians at the Biennale? Sickening." Finally, the other day he said to me: "I know what you're going to say: that Suez signals the sunset of liberty."

For the littler ones. A mouse falls into a trap and starts to struggle furiously: "I don't want there to be any misunderstanding," says the mouse to those who gather around to watch him, "I'm not protesting against the trap, which works very well, but on account of the poor quality of the cheese." This is the thesis which the communists have offered us in order to explain the Hungarian revolution, informing us that they have already taken steps to improve the quality of the cheese and to reinforce the trap.

*   *   *

Someone calls me on the phone and tells me he's conducting a little survey. He would like me to respond to this question: of what nationality would I like to be if I weren't Italian.

We live in the century of questions. I close my eyes, take a deep breath and answer: "First of all it might be a good idea to determine whether I really am Italian. Let's see if I can do it by means of reverse logic; but I'm not too hopeful. Well then: I'm not a fascist, I'm not a communist, I'm not a Christian-Democrat: so there's perhaps a twenty per cent chance left that I am an Italian. I don't write or speak my dialect, I don't adore the city where I was born, I prefer the uncertain to the certain, I'm resigned by nature, I detest paternalism, dictatorships and orators. I'm not crazy about soccer, I would be able to put up with it if there were twenty-two thousand players on the field and twenty-two people in the stands. I don't listen to the radio and I don't watch television: I am unacquainted therefore with the heroes of these two pastimes, about whose miracles and life stories everyone can tell you. I pay my fines, I don't have friends in high offices and it would be painful for me to participate in any sort of contest. I don't know how to sing and I don't like to hear others singing, except at the theater. I don't write poetry. Am I Italian? I have always kept the same friends, I like to travel in Italy and almost every place in it enchants me and makes me want to stay here. Seen in this light I could very well be an Englishman. The great problems of the world leave me perplexed and I don't have a precise and definite judgement to make about any of them. Am I perhaps an Indian? In addition, I consider myself reasonably cautious when it comes to judging my neighbor and I find that the majority of the persons I'm acquainted with are excellent people and I wish them nothing but well. Eskimo? I read books by Italian authors, both classic and modern, and I admire our artists; and here you could say I was an American. I adore the sun, the warm sea, Etruria and Campania; and in this you could take me to be German. I don't talk loudly when I visit museums and if I go to the library I'm not tempted to make away with a book or any of its illustrations. Am I perhaps a Swede? Trials, scandal sheets, worldly life don't interest me. A hermit? I don't scribble my name on ruins or on the walls of monuments. An illiterate? I pay my debts, I even try not to incur any. I don't admire the great qualities of peoples I'm unacquainted with. Death doesn't frighten me, I willingly go out for a walk at night, and I become frankly bored in the company of more than four or five people at a time. Spanish? On the train I don't recount episodes from my life, nor do I express opinions on Southern Italy, men interest me for their character, in women I also greatly admire intelligence, which doesn't arouse in me feelings of envy or contempt. Nevertheless, that I am Italian appears impossible to deny: in fact, I like to sleep, to avoid boring things, to work little, to make jokes, and I am very bad-tempered, at least around the house. Very well, if I weren't Italian, at this point I wouldn't know what I'd like to be. Probably I wouldn't be anything and this demonstrates, after all, that I really am Italian. What now? Your question doesn't have an answer. But console yourself by considering that for many 'Italian' isn't a nationality, but a profession."

The story goes that when a German official who was looking at his painting *Guernica* asked Pablo Picasso: "Did you do this?" he answered: "No, you did."

The story goes that when a Russian official who was looking at certain ceramic plates of his in Hungary asked Pablo Picasso: "This your work?" he answered absent-mindedly: "No, yours."

The little boy who plays with a soccer-ball all day long outside my window and whom I have often been tempted to murder, meets me on the street and says hello to me. Since it's the first time I've ever seen him, not with his soccer-ball, but with a bundle of school books, I enquire about his studies. He's in the fifth grade and today he was given a theme in class. The theme was *If I Were a Magician*. Here's the idea that guided him in developing it: If I were a Magician, I would rule the world. Almost all of his classmates manifested the same inclination to world domination, today altogether possible with those works of magic that science fiction has acquainted children with and that scientists are wearing themselves out trying to bring about. We are preparing ourselves, I think, for a lovely old age.

Nevertheless, what struck me more was the theme itself, which recognizes magic as not just a human activity, but even as a professional one. Obviously, the magician of the lady teacher is not the wise old man of the fairy tales with conical cap and real magic wand, but rather the modern magician, of the city, with a consultation office and with testimonials from ministers and actresses on the walls of his study. He is the magician-haruspex and healer, who goes to the premieres of the opera and who keeps a doctor on a salary in order not to be accused of illegal practice. He is the magician who writes in newspapers, the big brother of all the fortune-tellers and astrologers, that vast underworld of charlatans (*"ciarmatori"*—from *charme*—they were once called, and the meaning is pejorative through no one's fault but their own), who prosper today thanks to collective fear, to advertising, to our disorientation. Perhaps the lady teacher would have been satisfied if my soccer player had answered that, should he ever become a magician, he would manage the lives of big-name celebrities and write a horoscope column for the newspapers.

Evening at a performance of the Peking Circus. A precise order, painted on silk, that would have taken the pen of Bruno Barilli to describe. For the two hours of the performance I did nothing but think of him, of his prestigious and elegant way of taking in Life and Art. I was thinking that perhaps Barilli would have known how to explain to us, in the same style of these minute, finely scrubbed and combed acrobats, the subtle uneasiness (truly Chinese) we occasionally felt watching their feats, feats full of lightness, of grace and of abnegation, too precise to be true, enervating owing to the anticipation of a catastrophe which never took place and which, in my heart of hearts, I reproached them for.

The next day, F. tells me that he happened to be there, at that communist celebration, on the opening night and, turning around to look at the audience while on stage a tranquil Chinese was imitating the sounds of domestic animals (and even the chugging of a train), he saw the same faces he had seen at the Party Congress, equally serious, approving, restrained and hypocritical. Were they already adhering to the Chinese line on equestrian circuses, were they already ready to follow it? At the end of the performance, somebody with a microphone in his hand had asked him what he thought of the Peoples Republic of China. "Extremely graceful," he answered, "but somewhat monotonous."

Another image which suddenly came to mind: a photograph preserved at the Museo Criminale di Roma. Perhaps it's still there, yellowed with time. Two Chinese—each shut up in his own box, each with his head emerging that he may breathe, and the one placed facing the other a meter away—photographed a little before the closing up of the cell in which they would remain alone with each other. The two condemned men know that they will have to look at each other until the last moment, they know that in the eyes of the other each will seek his own oncoming end or that he will hear in the other's screams the echo of the madness that will stupefy him. Clearly, an exercise of skill which, in its very simplicity, is worth a nice round of applause.

Padre A., a Capuchin friar, an excellent and candid old man. I don't remember why but the discussion comes round to the Devil, and the padre tells me that, when a young man, he once saw him. It happened like this. He had recently taken his vows and one summer morning, in the extreme heat, he was returning wearily to the monastery. On the white and dusty road a woman was waiting for him at the entrance to a path. She was standing motionless and smiling. When Padre A. was a few paces away from her, the woman raised her dress and showed him her naked belly, while at the same time her eyes became torpid and enormous. Padre A. stops abruptly, makes the sign of the cross and shouts: "Get thee gone, Satan!" Laughing, the woman slipped off along the path and very quickly disappeared. "And you never saw her again after that?" "Yes, but only once or twice. I was transferred." "And what makes you think she was the Devil and not just some unfortunate exhibitionist?" Padre A. doesn't know what the word means, he shakes his head: it was the Devil. Moreover, she had on a red dress... But that it was indeed the Devil I am myself beginning to believe when I think how Padre A., after so many years, still remembers the episode and relates it with such emotion, as perhaps his one and only great sin.

Naples. Piazza del Municipio, dolled up like a main thoroughfare at the annual Milan Fair, with illuminated fountains spewing vertical jets in parallel rows. There's another new fountain in Piazza San Ferdinando. It serves as a traffic divider and almost seems temporary, a superfluous decoration in this unique piazza—of an old-time elegance, narrow and with wide entrances, but not at all suited to municipal water displays. The inadequacy of these fountains, even the surprise that they inspire, comes from the fact that Naples has no need whatever of fountains: she wants nothing to do with them—one might say—because they compare so feebly with the Gulf, which is Naples' one and only true fountain. It is perhaps because of this that even the memorial to Santa Lucia, the Immacolatella, rather assumes the air of a triumphal arch than of a proper fountain. One could conclude that the only fountains that become this city are the old shops of the water-vendors, cool grottoes where lemons, zinc and bottles combine to make inspiring decorations, and in front of which it is so pleasurable to linger.

*   *   *

The youngster who looks after the cars near City Hall is ar-
rayed like a municipal guard in gala attire. He even has a
helmet of black cloth, with the city's coat of arms. I stood for
a few minutes admiring him going about his duties. Slender,
skilful, he guided the cars out of the parking lot with ample,
assured gestures and a seriousness that commanded respect.
He made one realize the potential usefulness of suchlike personages, fallen, especially in Rome, to the rank of inept beggars. Here the boy was rendering himself useful with an
enthusiasm that elevated his intervention to the level of work.
I'm thinking about how this idea of dressing himself up as a
guard came to him, about the mother who gave her approval
to the project, about the tailor who cut and sewed the diminutive uniform; but, more than anything else, about the psychological finesse of this dressing-up, which today gives him
decorum and which one day will give him a place in society.
I see him later, in the evening, in front of a delicatessen, his
helmet pushed back a little above his forehead, busy eating a
fried *pasticcio*. He speaks vivaciously with two men, who
listen to him and answer with that seriousness with which, in
the South, men treat boys, and children generally, who work.

Admission to the Nativity in the sacristy costs fifty lire. Two
young men seated behind a table stack the tickets and keep
each other company. I raise a curtain and immediately I have
the crèche in front of me, arranged on a large platform perhaps five meters wide and as many deep. The idea that seduced the scene-painters is this: the Sacred Event occurring in
the monumental port city of Naples. The anatopism would be
presumptuous were there not an approximating geniality and
a laudable sense of economy about the whole thing. The cradle of the Baby Jesus is in the Palazzo San Giacomo and all
around, in painted pasteboard, are the Maschio Angioino, the
Palazzo Reale, the old houses, the new highrises, all framing
shepherds, ladies, saints and bagpipers from the eighteenth

century, remnants of an older, richer Nativity, their height equal to that of the buildings. The Castel Sant'Elmo dominates the scene, surrounded by latecoming shepherds. To give the setting more life, a little electric train circles around the manger, disappears into a tunnel, stops in front of its station, departs again, passes in front of the Baby Jesus. One can hear, in the silence of the sacristy, its minute and tireless clattering over the tracks. It's not a bad idea, this little train: I almost feel as if I'm the author defending it, saying that in this way even the Baby Jesus can amuse himself.

Visit to Pompeii. We take along Maiuri's little guidebook and the *Guide to Naples and the Surrounding Area*, by Gino Doria, not because it is likely to be of much use to us in Pompeii but because it's an excellent little book, which I've carried in my pocket since I've been here in Naples and to which I owe my best moments. I've never read anything written with such affection for this city, which this gentleman presents to us as an extremely likeable person, of whom we will become very fond and whose very shortcomings we will recognize as familiar to us, perhaps as part of ourselves. So we take these two books along and get onto the autostrada, which Doria defines as "the most beautiful in the world," and no doubt it is, but at the same time it is also the best suited for reading: the whole stretch of highway is lined with advertising billboards, inviting and peremptory, at times big enough to hide Vesuvius from sight. The countryside can no longer be protected from such things.

While we're in the Villa of the Mysteries, a monotonous rain comes down and it gets cold. We draw our visit out, we could leave but we stay to look at the rain, and then in front of these paintings we even experience the sensation of not being there for a mere visit, but of having to remain there and that the rain is a determining element. I recall the line from a French poet: "Puisque ces mystères nous dépassent, feignons d'en être les organisateurs." Organizers of mysteries! This is how it ends up, with the wish to understand something about them. I envy these guards and custodians, who can hang about here all their life undisturbed by mysteries, sometimes drifting within close range of them without being struck by their lightning, only soliciting the boorish visitors' complicity to the point of letting them take a look at "the dirty picture," hidden from the sight of the ladies by a divider or by a bit of cloth.

At the turn of the path, the seaside restaurant is heralded by a black chimney sending smoke high up above the old building. At the grade crossing the guard wished me a "buon appetito," a sign indicating that the only reason anyone comes this way is to get to the restaurant, which is indeed famous. Rain is falling on a landscape fragmented by houses and gardens. Old Mediterranean-style buildings, with vaulted construction, are mixed in among new inexpensively built little houses, made with humid blocks of tufa, the balconies unfinished, terrace roofs. Alone in a truck garden stands a cube of a house, nay, a storage place, upon which the word SALONE is written; and from the other side of the glass door the barber watches me pass by, despondent in the chilly weather. The dining room of the restaurant is enormous, bare, whitewashed. Not a single decoration, only tables and chairs, so that one's gaze is at once drawn towards the sea and remains there, spellbound by the play of the rain that is coming down in sheets, with shifts of light accompanied by distant thunder. Clouds cover and uncover Capri and the Sorrento headlands, rapidly and over and over again. Two parties sit at their respective tables, more or less immune to the power of the landscape, immersed in the seriousness Neapolitans display at mealtime. I walk outside, the sea is directly beneath me, foamy, ugly, juxtaposed with the black rock deposited by Vesuvius. But on top of the not very high cliff, at its highest and holiest point below which the froth heaves in abrupt slaps against the rock, and just where the Greeks would have built a shrine to Aphrodite, there is the booth-like structure housing the toilets.

At the Teatro San Ferdinando, where the actors of the Compagnia Scarpettiana perform. They are putting on a three-act play by Eduardo Scarpetta, elaborated out of an old French sketch, confirming that the only language French can be translated into is Neapolitan, because Neapolitan preserves its brio while shunning that exactness, that finish, that intransigence which renders French as arrogant as an only daughter. The curtain rises and we are in the country, in an olden days setting: at right the hostelry, at left a hotel, in the background the blinding landscape surrounding Naples. In comedies like this one, whose title is 'E nepute d'o Sinneco, two characters begin explaining the situation, after which we pass to good honest entertainment. The actors of the Scarpettiana are all excellent, possessing a natural comic gift; and the comedy itself, based on equivocations of person and of men disguised as women and vice-versa, lends itself to their play, seems even to be one continuous invention and thus redeems itself from its own mechanisms. The presence of a French actress, Hélène Remy, doesn't appear altogether arbitrary, but rather alludes to the Naples of the café-chantant, to its ties to the Paris of the same spirit. De Vico, Sportelli, Pupella Magio seem to me exceedingly accomplished actors. But among them all there is one whose polished elegance and whose adherence to a precisely defined reality makes me think of a Naples inserted live into the sketch. His name: Pietro Carloni. His character, still more so his style, call to mind a Pulcinella of distinguished but now much declined family who is obliged to find some undemanding job and to perform it graciously. There is a point in the comedy which is the key to the whole thing. Constrained to silence by a friend, when he perceives that by keeping still he's bound to lose his job, he bursts out disdainfully: "I have to speak, my dignity is at stake!" But shortly after he adds: "Worse yet, my bread is at stake." And he comments to himself, having recognized the plebeian strength of his line of reasoning: "La zuppa!" The audience is, as they say in Naples, *"aux anges."*

Driving my car, I turn into a street that suddenly dwindles into an alley, clogged with pushcarts, with children, with chairs, even with a trunk. Four or five people who have been discussing their affairs stop and with severe expressions on their faces wait to see how I'm going to extricate myself; I don't know whether they merely want to witness the catastrophe or have decided to provoke it. Becoming nervous, I try backing up, without good results. I'll have to try it again. A little crowd has gathered, the passers-by are waiting, the children are shouting, I'm in danger of entering a gateway from which I'll get out only with the help of the fire department. And at this point, seeing I'm beaten, everyone comes to my aid: the pushcarts disappear, the chairs and the children are removed, the trunk is hoisted up. It's a quick, happy contest of courtesies, which enables me to get through. I leave, bidden a friend's farewell.

That evening in the hotel I open the journal Melville kept of his European travels, in the French translation of Ledoux, just recently released. There is the journal of a trip through Italy, with a stop in Naples, and the date is exactly one century ago: 1857. On page 214 I read: "Acrobats in a narrow lane. Obstructed street. Balconies full of women. A cloth spread out on the ground. [The acrobats] parted to let us through, after having begun their performance, thereby giving proof of a very natural calm. Gaiety. I turned around to offer them a simple and grateful thanks. Handkerchiefs waving from the balconies, exclamations of good humor. I was prouder than an emperor."

It is probable, I think, that the narrowness of certain streets renders these incidents inevitable, and has for centuries. But that the people should still continue to put up with them with the same cheerfulness, as if these incidents were part of a comedy they are conscious of and that even warrants their presence out of doors, this is a mystery which cannot be explained except by accepting the simple verdict of R., who comments on the episode this way: "They are a spirituel people."

I stop in front of a bookstore window, a small boy asks me to give him something. I don't have any small change but I don't like sending him away disappointed. I give him a bill, asking him to change it for me; he takes it, assures me he'll go change it "over there where they sell gasoline," and he runs off. I go into the bookstore, already regretting my impulsiveness, and when I come back out there's no small boy. Considering my fine display of foolishness, he has found no cause to come back. I can't really blame him, but I am annoyed; and as I walk away I think about the severe little lecture I would give him if, by chance, I should ever run into him again: a useless little lecture which very soon fades away before the sights of the street and a sudden downpour that has the passers-by gathering in doorways and sends others dashing off holding newspapers over their heads.

A few days later the same small boy is there in front of me, on the same street, and once again he asks me for something. I look at him sharply, relishing my puerile revenge. "You recognize me?" I demand. He shakes his head, pushing back his hat; however, he scrutinizes me and his little body is already tensing, imperceptibly, in case he has to make a run for it. But no, he doesn't remember. Plainly though his curiosity is at least as great as my ironic satisfaction. I remind him of the incident, certain he will be crushed. He is silent for a moment, then suddenly lighting up with the magnificent excuse that occurs to him, limpid as a line of verse, he exclaims: "Signore, that must have been my brother! But never mind, tonight, when I see him . . ." And he goes away, indicating with a gesture that I need not worry, he'll see to it that I get my revenge.

*   *   *

Impossibility of feeling oneself a stranger, seeing that the people won't permit it. Drop into a café for a brief moment and the bartender is already offering you a pretext for conversation, not only a plausible pretext but an intriguing one. He has studied you in a flash, he knows that he may never see you again, but that's not important, he has to show in whatever way he can that he is a living being and full of likeable qualities. Twisting his neck, he eyes the book on the counter, comments: "You're a professor?" ready with respect should I admit to being a professor. Since I deny being one, he makes a gesture of comprehension, as if to say that it's okay all the same, not everyone can be a professor and anyhow, if I wanted, I could be an excellent one, you can see that I don't lack intelligence, that I've been to school. All that with a simple gesture, which he follows with a look that implies this reservation: "Probably you really are a professor, even though you deny it. I don't care. That's your business. Anyway I believe what you tell me."

And the man who sells fake fountain pens who, when I refuse to buy one, suddenly discards his insinuating tone, becomes serious, gives way to confidences. "Signore, ever since Christmas through the whole of February, there hasn't been much doing. Sixty more days of this, just have to hold out that long, then we'll have the tourists back, the weather will be nice again, and then . . ."

On Vesuvius, we stop at a bend in the road to look at the gulf. A breath of wind wafts the cloud on the summit from sight, and the silence is complete, enlivened by a few faraway, startlingly distinct blasts of a claxon. The landscape and the colors are still those of certain genre paintings, with sea and sky blending into one another, the red of the factories, the burnished blue of the islands. All around, the lava has coagulated in violent and decorative forms, something like Henry Moore's sculptures, but with a more dramatic touch and in overabundant quantity. Heading in our direction, jumping upon these rocks, are two young men, covered with blue from their heads to their shoes. Indeed, they have a big canister full of this very color and two brushes, and they're going around giving a touch of paint to the high-tension towers. They too are alive to the landscape, they comment on it, they name for us localities on the plain below, joke around. Then they talk about Vesuvius as though it were a surly lord who will come to life again someday, it's just a matter of time, he has a temperament all his own and you have to be patient. It's as though they were asking us to excuse the delay in his performance. Then they talk about their work, which is neither easy nor happy, but they prefer it to any other, because they can go about freely anywhere on the mountain and furthermore "it's painting, after all." They would willingly stay awhile, but they have to get back down otherwise everyone will remain without light. They go away humming a tune, drunk with a carnival-like happiness which renders them, splashed with color as they are, altogether fantastic.

G. tells me that one morning in his hotel, which they're renovating, a certain man came into the room, crawled underneath the bed and began to hammer on the wall. Wakened this way, G. jumps up, thinks he is being murdered, but the smiling face of an electrician pops out from under the bed and reassures him: "Go back to sleep, signò', I'm just putting in an outlet."

Evening in a little vaudeville theater. A singer enters—a fat little woman with coal-black eyes that wink slyly while she waits for the orchestra to strike up the first notes. She's dressed in overalls, the trousers adorned with gilt foil, she has on very high-heeled shoes and a wristwatch. She starts to sing in a voice loud enough to frighten the audience, and goes on like this for several minutes. She's followed by a young man who is the darling of the balcony, where a little group of throbbing hearts has gathered in a corner. The singer gets with it right away; casting provocative glances at the young people he bears down upon the more incendiary phrases of his song, the whole while winking at the audience so that no one will have any doubts about him. His fans applaud, send him kisses, the public protests, laughs, whistles, while the orchestra, distracted, lists like a sinking ship, worsening the disaster, at last taking hold of itself with a roll of drums meant to recall everyone to order and which causes the other singers to poke their heads out from the wings to see what's going on.

Taking the Via Domiziana, detour through Cumae. We enter the countryside, quite mild despite the winter season, a densely cultivated countryside with peasants' houses built upon the ruins, with the shore vanishing in the direction of Lake Patria and with the summit of Mondragone covered by stunted growth and the whole scene hardly changed at all since the day Aeneas landed there. The sea is the same, a sea for peasants, without boats, the shore wild and windswept. The Acropolis is in front of us but the gate is shut and a guard informs us that it's impossible to get in: "The *Belle Arti* are on strike," he says. And so, upon this wise and certainly sibylline call back to reality, we get back on the road to Rome.

Sadness and mortification of the flesh, sense of ultimate punishment, of corruption and vermination that one has walking through the streets and looking at advertisements for movies, at the covers of magazines and detective stories. Sadness, here the petty act of sadism performed in the home, there the act of exhibitionism performed the most cheaply, using the modest models that we have and who bring to mind nurses, girls seduced, prostitutes. Oh, why is sin always so sad, cheap, ugly?

Chance brings us to the entrance of the Chiesa del Gesù, which we haven't visited in so many years. The vast ceiling is overflowing with free, healthy nude figures, flying towards either a supreme pleasure or towards a supreme damnation. They are rosy and fleshy nudes but it's understood that it couldn't be otherwise. Even this hastens one's thoughts to pleasure, to that pleasure in particular which the Jesuits of the Counter Reformation invented to renovate their churches and adapt them to the times. It was the period of Saint Sebastian, of the Saint Theresas in sweet ecstasy, of naked penitents, the period in which the body was not only becoming idealized in its forms but also in its agitations. Baciccia performed miracles here. In comparison, Rubens becomes an excursion into fancy dress, and pretty wearisome. Fragonard becomes a modest court counselor. In this ceiling the limbs are full of life, the breasts powerful, the flanks soft, the eyes gaze steadily at you and beckon; and in all the bodies there is a sweetness, a happy irresponsibility. It is a Saturnalia in flight, among clouds that seem like screens. Coming away from it you come away disturbed and, I have to add, converted.

Rome, a corrupted city? I don't believe so: too many employees. Here it would be a corruption based on early payment of monies due, on an unflinching demand for raises and on the prompt payment of settlements. And will this ever be possible?

As time goes by the Montesi trial little by little reveals itself for what I feared it would be: a political and literary trial. It will not signal the end of a certain kind of politics, let's hope it signals the end of a literature. He who is able to will understand me. One need not, I trust, insist upon describing and somehow versifying into heroes such cheap, scheming characters as these, compromised on the left and on the right, incapable of a single truthful impulse, solely preoccupied with exhibiting themselves and therefore at a goodly remove from tragedy. Ours is in fact a tragic epoch, but it hasn't found its poet. This it thinks it can remedy by describing minor characters, those very same who, in the great works of tragedy, are wet nurses, confidants, messengers and assassins. But their veracity is not sufficient. What is needed is the larger, the great truth, and it is undiscoverable: the protagonists hide themselves, they do not assume responsibility: and what their personal histories teach is missing. Must we then be content with this little Balzacian world of nickles and dimes? An ex-chief of police that weeps; a gentleman who says: Impossible for me to have been in bed with this girl, during that period I had a problem with my prostate; a penniless conjurer who does a parody of the event doesn't understand how it came about; a small crowd of witnesses from whom we wouldn't ask, I won't say for testimony, but for directions on the street, so much reticence do they have in their blood, like a secret defense. With all that, the Montesi trial remains seductive. It reminds me of that scene in one of Charlot's films where the tramp helps the blind girl by holding her skein of wool and, inadvertently at first, then deliberately, lets her unwind his vest to nothing. Except that here the scene takes place the opposite way: and from a fat ball of wool we will end up with a lovely little *farsetto* (waistcoat).

Never was there a period so favorable to narcissists and ex-hibitionists. Where are the saints? We will have to content ourselves with dying in the odor of publicity.

Visit with a nouveau riche. Since Brueghels have been in style for a few years now, it doesn't matter whether it's father, son or grandsons, he too has a Brueghel above the fireplace. He angles for some admirative remarks from me but, after I have easily ruled out its being either a Pieter the Elder or a Pieter the Younger, or even a Jan or an Ambrosius, he's surprised to learn that Jan had seven sons, all painters. Seven's too many, they diminish the value of the magical name. Do you think he's ruffled? With that swift adaptability which enabled him to get rich, he lets out a laugh of his own and says: "The fact is,

I'm in court with the person who sold it to me." All his strength lies in this: he knows he has something that's false but, as long as he can, he pretends to have something that's true, thereby gaining, if nothing else, at least a little time.

Nicola Chiaromonte kindly cites me apropos of a comedy of manners. When he asserts that "behind certain modes of being" of our society there is not even such a thing as manners, but only "nothingness," he is right in a way. And from that it follows that today a "theater of manners" is impossible. Theater is based on the strength of a society which rejects the accusations of the comedy writer or at least ends up being scandalized by them. Shaw's success was founded on the hypocrisy of his audience. Nowadays, our good society isn't hypocritical, on the contrary, where it comes to itself it pushes sincerity to the most bare-bones naturalism, its professed instincts are reproduction and self-preservation. The most ferocious satire leaves it cold because on the stage it always turns out to be inferior to reality, and is consequently flattering. On the screen it simply turns out to be more unpolished, because it allies itself with an irritating realism. To stir this society one must shift into sentimental symbolism and, to disturb it, into sexual tragedy for which however it has little feeling, since it is also profoundly healthy, natural, or animal. And then too, in these two fields, theater wouldn't have a chance against cinema. Religious problems have never touched this society either, absolved in advance as it is; it resolves political problems with its age-old sagacity; it entrusts all social problems to the Christian-Democratic Party, moral problems are the concern of the Ministry of the Interior. After the first world war French comedy used to go over well with it, but now it performs its own much better and every day, in its own homes, which resemble theaters, bars, nightclubs. Is the theater of manners only possible in this one, absolutely comical sense? Perhaps. He who would like to write for the theater today has but one problem to come to terms with, that of poetical order, bearing in mind that it is society that authorizes theater and that our society has no apparent poetical problems to resolve. But that does not exclude our society's having them and being able to appreciate them. One never knows. After all, nothingness is the best sign. A comedy writer isn't born out of nothingness, but a poet yes.

Little Italian town. Remains of ancient walls, laundry hung out to dry on them. From a van parked in the middle of the piazza a loudspeaker, speaking with a Northern accent, is saying: "This old scrooge wants to control your very digestive processes, take a look at *our* propoganda folder." Faded but still intact election festoons, with unknown names printed on them. Other manifestoes, among which one shows a woman sitting at a sewing machine inside a large "S". At the movies they're showing *Dondi*. The church is brightened with a recent coat of whitewash, gray at the edges. The Buzzoni family thanks all those who shared in their struggle. A gas station, where they're selling a hitherto unknown brand of gas. Four girls strolling this way and that way; one of them has on gloves, not on account of the cold, but for elegance. The people have a civil and calm way of looking at a stranger. From the tobacco shop, a little girl buying a one-lira caramel.

The little town was founded in the eighth century before Christ. Destroyed by the Gauls. Rebuilt, and destroyed immediately after by Sulla. All the inhabitants put to the sword. Rebuilt during the Empire and destroyed by the Goths. Settled then by the Visigoths and razed to the ground by the Vandals. Everyone dead. Rebuilt, and destroyed by Countess Matilda. Exile for the inhabitants. Rebuilt, and destroyed by the Saracens. Half the population taken off into captivity. Rebuilt, and put to the torch by Duke Valentino. All dead. Two centuries of calm, then the eighteenth century earthquake . . . All dead. Another two centuries of peace and then the bombardment of 1944. Many dead. Be that as it may, nary a trace of weariness. The people stroll this way and that way, today there was even a bicycle race. Births are on the rise. Worthy of note: the tablet to those who fell in World War I, with the additions of those who fell in World War II, with the additions of massacred partisans. In the piazza there's the usual dog who is everybody's friend, who comes by to give us a sniff.

Little letter. "Dear Benedetti, in the brief biographical note concerning me that appeared in your *Espresso*, issue number 12, there's an inaccuracy: that beyond being a script-writer and a scenario writer I am also a movie director. I am not. It also seems prudent to add that I am not an actor, cameraman, musician or producer. Usually I am a spectator, many years ago I was a critic and I stopped being one because it seemed strange to me to be writing for the cinema and to be judging the films of others at the same time (but it's done, constantly). As for my pastimes, they are tourism, astronomy, calligraphy, etruscology, vulcanology and literature; in short, the same as everybody else's. Yours truly, E.F."

"Towards the beginning of the second half of the twentieth century the sect of laymen, strengthened by repression and discontent, began its missionary activities and achieved its first successes despite the vigilance of the dominating powers, which took to concerning themselves with ideas that were somewhat diffuse, this having considerable impact upon the cultivated part of the bourgeoisie and above all upon the young. In substance, the laymen (that is, those not belonging to the clergy; therefore, the minority at that time) supported ideas which nowadays might seem obvious because all peoples the world over have acquired them: the non-meddling of the various Churches in the affairs of the State, the extension of civil liberties to all, freedom of religion and of lay teaching. With the number of the initiates growing as it was and then with the persecutions instigated by the clergy, public meetings were no longer possible and the surviving laymen began to assemble periodically and in great secrecy in an abandoned cave, from which came the name that was given to their movement as a sign of contempt: catacombism. But by 1970, though only in Rome, the catacombs were already ten in number. Almost every quarter of the city had its own and, during the following years, in which repression grew more fierce (one memorable incident was that in which the laymen were accused of having made a mistake in the urban plan and of having destroyed the ancient center of the city), the catacombs were the focus of lay thinking and also of art and poetry. The splendid vestiges that have come down to us testify to the fervor of that subterranean life, where the initiates ("friends") flocked in ever increasing number. Conventions were held in the catacombs, meetings, and even schools were established there. Thanks to the assistance of officials of the State who had converted to the new faith, the simple lay rites came to be celebrated there too. Divorce was discussed, as was birth control, school reform was studied, the struggle against monopolies was initiated and finally the Constitution was revised. Such was the strength this movement acquired that very quickly one no longer *became* a layman, one was born a layman. By the end of the twentieth century, having become uncontainable by this time, laicism was able to return to the light of day and embark upon a course of action that, by means of incoercible concessions and recognitions, finally carried it to power and caused the collapse of the clerical castes' temporal supremacy. The total victory of the laymen, however, came about only when popular assemblies restored the old law which imposed vows of chastity and poverty, or at least nominal adherence to them, on the clerics and on their anonymous societies. Nevertheless, the outmoded religion of Catholic temporal power survived for some time in the countryside, in the pagus, and from that got its name of pagan." (From the *Brief History of the World* published in Rome in 2957.)

*   *   *

Spent the evening reading *The Essential Tourist.* Curious and agreeable reading. It is a little work that will be very useful to all those who travel for pleasure, even in our country. The most interesting part, it seems to me, is the conversational manual, rich in "useful phrases" that we will search in vain for in similar Italian and foreign publications. The author is certainly a person who has travelled a great deal. In the preface he explains that the melancholy which invades the Tourist—and which everyone is familiar with to some extent—comes mainly from the fact that, not knowing certain "useful phrases", he winds up feeling that he's a stranger to the real life of the country he's visiting. I am copying in my diary the phrases which, to me, seem the most useful.

On the train. "Signore, will you please remove your feet, your hands, your head, your suitcase from my feet, from my ribs, from my stomach, from my esophagus?"

"Signor conductor, this passenger has taken off his shoes, his boots, his socks, his stockings and is showing me his feet, his big toes, his heels, the soles of his feet."

"Signora, your baby, your new-born, your little infant has wet my new purse, my new hat, my new gloves."

In the hotel. "This room, this chamber is small, narrow, dark, expensive and looks out on, faces, opens up into a courtyard, an alley, a noisy playground, and has a bath that's filthy, broken, out of order, unusable."

At the museum. "I do not desire a guide, a companion, a monograph, nor any reproductions, postcards, copies of famous paintings. I only want to see, visit, admire the museum, the gallery, the picture gallery, the statue gallery."

Out for a walk. "I'm sorry, Signor Beggar, I don't have any small change, loose change, spare change, quarters, dimes, nickels, pennies; but only banknotes, paper money, bills of State, one-dollar bills, five-dollar bills, ten-dollar bills."

At the restaurant. "Waiter, there's a mistake, an error, a difference to my disadvantage of ten cents, twenty cents, thirty cents, a dollar."

"Waiter, can you tell, advise, instruct the violinist, the guitarist, the mandolinist, the harmonica player not to stick his fiddle-bow, his arm, his elbow, his hands, his instrument into my plate?"

"Waiter, in the soup, in the roast, in the parsley, there is a blond, a brown, a chestnut, an auburn hair, a lock of hair, a periwig."

"No, waiter, this is not my new overcoat, my new trenchcoat, my new raincoat, but the old overcoat, the old trenchcoat, the old raincoat of some other guest, customer, patron."

At the theater. "Signore, what you are saying, relating, hooting about, crooning about is keeping me from enjoying, from listening to, from hearing the music, the comedy, the farce, the ballet, the review, the duet, the drama."

"Signora, this is the second time, the third time, the fourth time that you have burnt, ignited, set fire to my overcoat, my jacket, my vest, my trousers, with your cigarette, your pipe, your cigar."

On the phone. "It's been one, two, three days that I've been waiting for a simple message, a simple call, a simple reservation. Will you have the kindness, the courtesy, the amiability to ask for it, demand it, beg for it again?"

At the post office. "No, Signor Postal Official, I do not want to collect, to acquire, to purchase lottery tickets, calendars, commemorative stamps, but only to send, to dispatch, to forward a telegram, a registered letter, a money order."

At the police station. "They have stolen, taken, made off with my automobile, my motorcycle, my motorscooter, my bicycle, my suitcases, my knapsack, my bag, my camera, my binoculars, my purse, my clothes, my cash."

"I did not know, I was unaware, I was ignorant of the fact that this money was counterfeit, adulterated, forged, withdrawn from circulation."

"This cabman, chauffeur, truck driver wants, is asking for, is claiming ten, twenty, thirty dollars more than what was agreed upon, contracted, stipulated."

"No, Signor Police Lieutenant, there's been a mistake, a quid pro quo, a misunderstanding. I am not the thief, the counterfeiter, the swindler, the driver, but the robbed, the swindled, the passenger, in a word: the tourist."

We believe we have a name, we repeat it to ourselves and we write it down all over the place, but society admonishes us. It's not our name that is of interest to it, but our function and, in a bureaucratic sense, our position. So that time and time again we are bystanders, members, underwriters, onlookers, passersby, contributors, users, beneficiaries of, claimants, subscribers, associates, those who have recourse to, the faithful, the believers. We are addressees, senders, depositors, drivers, entrants, spouses, parents, purchasers. We are in charge, in an auxiliary capacity, on leave of absence, on vacation, nonresidents. Thus do we sparkle all the time under different aspects, but for precise motives, never for what we believe we are in essence. And whenever we do believe it, then there we are again: those who impute to.

Three in the afternoon. Stretched out on the bed, I feel the room shaking slightly and I see the lamp vibrating. The next day I read in the paper that the brief and harmless earthquake had its epicenter in the Apennines; which, "given their young age, are still in process of settling down." The thing I admire in these reporters is the grace, the simplicity with which they adopt a scientist's manner of expressing themselves. And they have an air of adding: "So you didn't know about the Apennines being young, eh, and that they're still in process of settling down?"

The next day at three in the afternoon there I am on the bed again, my eye fixed on the lamp, waiting for a tremor, perhaps because we attribute to natural phenomena that punctuality which we are incapable of observing in our own daily behavior. The lamp doesn't move. I'm disappointed by it.

I wouldn't want the Apennines to have already entered into a riper and more reflective age. I am thinking of writing an essay on the Appenines and the problems of the young; but at four o'clock, seeing that nothing is happening, I give the idea up.

The novelist had somehow managed to let his characters slip a little out of sight. If he remembered correctly, in the last chapter he had left them in bed together; now he couldn't figure out what to do with them. Continue, describe them waking up? Was he being too indulgent as far as erotic scenes were concerned? He said to himself that, after all, that's how his characters were made, they loved each other and they hated each other, he couldn't do anything about it. It's the characters who choose their novelist, and it's the characters who make up the story. He was a witness and had to tell the truth, to relate. Take courage then. He went to the table, put a blank sheet of paper in the typewriter, reread the last lines of Chapter X, and began:

"Chapter XI—Upon awakening Roberto felt the nausea mounting in his throat like a sour wine, which added a discomfort to his intoxication. He was tired and for a moment he found it hard to understand where he was; then the room, the naked form stretched out next to him brought back memories of the night he had spent. And now the sharp, sing-songing voices that were coming from the street gave him . . . gave him . . . (*what did they give him?*) gave him the certain knowledge that nothing had changed (*good, the sense of tedium, boredom*). A ray of sun (*no, better: a blade of sun*) a blade of sun entering from the half-closed window (*check to see if they left it open the night before*) went, as in certain mannerist altarpieces, to strike (*isn't that a little like D'Annunzio?*) went to strike the large and delicate breast of Camilla who, crinkled and disheveled as she was, seemed (*what did she seem? here, an image*) seemed a castaway from a shipwreck lying on a deserted beach. But when she stretched out on the bed and said in that hoarse baby voice of hers,

'What do you think you're doing, come here,' he experienced a sudden hatred for that flesh which the sun, as a kind of game, was charging with a hint of desire. (*What do you want from me anyhow?*) Roberto approached the woman, crushed her nipples, and when she let out a cry he came back with a 'Shut up' so brutal that Camilla, frightened, fell silent, knitting her eyebrows (*Or is it eyelashes? I never can remember which is which*).

At this point the author paused and fell to drumming on the table with his fingertips. And now? Another day was beginning for his characters. He could send them out for a walk, have them argue and then make up. He could describe the street, or the slow *toilette* of the woman, who enters the bathroom naked, or digress upon the feelings of the man, who is watching her. He counted the pages he had already written and experienced a sense of comfort: about two hundred pages. Roberto . . . Camilla . . . what idiotic names. What if he were to change them, right now? No, this was just an excuse to waste time, to distract himself with trifles. He had to forge on to keep from losing his momentum. A little idea popped into his head. Here's what he could do: he could put Roberto and Camilla (tentative names) back in bed, have them argue, and then have them tumble, still grappling, out of bed and onto the rug. The advantages? An obsessive variation of the theme. The disadvantages? A sense of boredom. But—doesn't that perhaps turn into an advantage, if it reflects on Roberto? So he wrote: "Roberto lay down beside her, keeping a steady eye on her . . ." but he stopped once again. Didn't he already have a scene like this in another one of his novels? He had to check. Now it is just on account of this mania for checking that inspiration is deadened, deviates, stumbles, dries up.

The journalist Mario Tavolino di Riccardo, thirty-five years of age, born and raised in Rome, woke up at nine-thirty and immediately asked for and received a breakfast of coffee, milk, toast and butter. When he had taken a look at the blue sky, he said to himself: "Today being Sunday, there will be an exodus of the population en masse to the beaches and neighboring hills." He was content. He put on a suit of grey flannel, a white shirt, a sky-blue tie, and black shoes he had acquired at a well-known shop in the center of town, and left the house. The doorkeeper, a certain Mariangela Dadini, née Antonio, forty-nine years of age, born in Terni, greeted him and about him noticed nothing out of the ordinary. He pulled out in his creamy, grey-colored car, license plates Rome, and drove off in the direction of Via Veneto, which at that hour was alive, as far as he could tell, with the usual Sunday crowd. In that throng of people, thought the journalist, a grain of rice dropped from above would not have reached the ground. "Very well," he said, "I'll mix in with the springtime crowd that is in the process of invading the sidewalks and go for a brief but salutary stroll, looking at the shop windows and admiring the merchandise on display there as I pass." Instead, he met a friend whom he hadn't seen in many years. He was a certain Francesco Trono, né Arigo, thirty-six years of age, born in Rome and residing in Venezuela. So they eventually started to talk about Italy, marvelling together at her economic revival and the initiatives she was so fervidly taking in every field, both social and artistic. Of Rome, they said she is a city unique in all the world, both for her millenary history and for her beauty. As for the Italian woman, they admired her elegance. Passing on then to discuss the city's traffic problems they were in agreement that the competent authorities must be enjoined to take drastic measures. "The whole conversation," the journalist was thinking, "is taking place in an atmosphere of lively cordiality and is lasting approximately twenty minutes."

Having returned home at one o'clock, the journalist consumed, with evident satisfaction, a lunch all'italiana composed of noodles, braised veal, dessert, fruit, and coffee. And, having settled down to read the newspapers, every once in a while he looked up at his wife, a certain Diomiri Luisa, née Michele, thirty-three years of age, born in Treviso but residing in Rome, and at his two children as well, Ada and Giulio, aged six and five respectively. Thus he saw that his Diomiri's face still retained its youthfulness and that she was wearing a simple tailleur of brown tweed, with matching shoes and perhaps also with matching gloves and matching purse. He looked at her chestnut hair (tending towards blonde), and at her grey eyes (tending towards green), and put his reading aside. A strange feeling of malaise had come over him. "Perhaps," the journalist thought, "the rapid ingestion of food is causing a hepatogastric condition which might, if not taken care of in time, prove fatal to me." And he further thought: "I ought to be promptly accompanied to the hospital by my loved ones and there subjected to an energetic gastral lavage by the doctors on duty." But it wasn't a question of a physical malaise. It was something different, perhaps a feeling of disappointment, even of bitterness.

"What's the matter?" Diomiri Luisa said to her husband, watching him with a worried look upon her face.

"Nothing," the journalist answered. But now he knew. From the sunny days of his youth, a memory had come to disturb him. "My God," he thought. "And yet I used to be so clever in Italian!"

The film director, stretched out on the couch in his studio, was peering at his mother through half-closed eyes. He was saying to himself: "Her face will do, but I'm afraid she may not know how to talk and act. Okay, it's only a question of two scenes, and I could dub in her voice, but will she be natural?"

His mother, sensing she was being observed, was smiling. "You want something to eat?" she asked.

Keeping his gaze fixed upon his mother, the director got up and said: "Mammetta, would you mind lying down on the couch for a moment?"

The good lady put aside the knitting she was working on and sat composedly on the couch, trying to understand.

"Mamma," the director then said, "I told you to lie down. When I say 'lie down' I mean 'lie down,' be good and don't make me repeat myself."

His mother lay down on the couch and waited, while her son went on looking at her, thinking to himself: "She's reasonably lifelike." Then he said: "Now, mammetta, close your eyes halfway and look at me, as if you felt you were on the verge of... being sick."

"But why, *figliolo*, what are you up to?" his mother asked apprehensively, starting to sit up.

"Down," the director ordered. And he added: "Nothing. Just look at me as if you were sick. Leave everything else to me. Say whatever comes into your head, but speak in a subdued way, with difficulty—understand?"

"What should I say, I can't think of anything," his mother said.

"That look!" the director exclaimed, already irritated. "Is that what you call a mother's look? More soul." He lit a cigarette and continued: "You have to look at me with despair, but at the same time you're holding yourself back, you know that you won't be seeing me again. Come on, let's try it once more. You want a little music? Rachmaninov? Puccini? Okay, okay. I'll put *Butterfly* on for you."

The director put on a recording of this opera and the notes of a romantic aria filled the studio. His mother felt ill at ease.

"And now what should I do?" she asked without taking her eyes off her son.

"Speak, close your eyes, whisper, and let your hand fall along your side, to the floor," the director said. But when his mother had executed this movement and re-opened her eyes, she saw that her son was gazing at her unhappily.

After a life of hard work from which he made a fortune, the self-made man amuses himself playing the role of a connoisseur of art and fits his house up like a shop, with furniture and rare objects. One day he invites to lunch a young dealer in antiques who has a solid reputation as a counterfeiter and, in the euphoria of a suppositious communion of ideas and interests, jokes about his methods, calls him "our expert." During the course of the lunch the joke becomes insistent and the diffidence of the antique dealer, who limits himself every time to smiling, renders the host more audacious. He arrives in this fashion to "our dear old junk-man," and the antique dealer, who had accepted the invitation in the hope of future business dealings, loses his patience. He doesn't understand how much love his host is putting into his joke, and how much he wants him to forget his wealth for his newly-acquired culture and how much he wants to vindicate himself. "Now," he says, rising, "let's take a look at the situation." He examines furniture, paintings, antiques. And he starts in. The table they have been sitting at, which would be worth three million if it were authentic, and for which he probably paid one million (the host nods), is worth a hundred thousand lire. The two vases would be practically priceless. The only trouble is that the antique dealer can furnish him with two others, almost identical, which have just come off the boat fresh from China—can furnish them for a much more modest price, and still make a profit. That Arcimboldi there was painted in Naples two years ago and isn't one of the best jobs he's ever seen. If you were to scratch the canvas you'd probably find a fruit trophy instead or a fake Salvator Rosa or a portrait of Garibaldi. The Venetian chandelier is the work of a chandler friend of his who lives in the Rione Ponte. If his host had taken the antique dealer's card with him, he would have paid a fair price. Et cetera. The only other things now are the chairs. The antique dealer examines them one by one and concludes: "Of these eight the only original is the one I was sitting on. The others are from Via Vittoria." And he concludes: "Sell it to me. In a few days its presence here is going to become unbearable. As, I imagine, mine already has."

That said, the dealer in antiques realizes the damage he has done and bursts out laughing.

His host brightens up: "You were joking," he says.

"Yes, I was joking, or I was trying to. I beg your pardon, I won't do it anymore."

Together they step into the parlor for coffee. "And what can you find in here," the host asks, "that's fake?"

"Nothing."

"You're mistaken," says the host, "look at this little Degas. It's a copy. I know it's a copy but I hold on to it because I like it."

"Copy?" exclaims the dealer in antiques, having by now repented completely. "It looks authentic to me. They must have been kidding, selling it as a copy." And a little later, in the silence, he adds: "Unless, if you scratch the canvas, there's a Watteau underneath."

Sunday, it's early in the afternoon, the center of the city is empty, the streets have got back their freedom, their calm, the scheme of the architecture reappears. I see corners again, the style of houses, caryatids, gateways which the flood of traffic in all its fury had submerged during the week. As after a rowdy banquet, what remains are the street signs, the tangled disorder of electric wires cutting the sky, the traces of white paint on the cobblestones, a gray soot which dirties the base-work, throwing the moulding into relief and saddening it. It is the disorder of a house after the passage of thieves. Our city was made for taking walks in and today it exudes the sadness of its forced adaptation to the times, a distressing camouflage which exposes its oldness, not of years but of abandonment. But at least it's still breathing.

The stage-mother is by now a definitive category. She is even a rhetorical figure, a big woman usually, fat and authoritarian, outspoken defender of her daughter's rights, guardian angel of her virtue, et cetera. It's tempting to think that the truth is quite different, while instead it's exactly so. And it would make no sense to talk about her if actresses weren't being spawned like mushrooms in this country and didn't each and every one of them have a mother. L. tells me how one of these mothers, bragging about the innocence and purity of her daughter, whom she never misses a chance to have photographed top and bottom, confided in him: "When my daughter gets married she'll be a virgin, just like I was. When I got married, believe me, I didn't even know what a man looked like without his clothes on . . ." And then: "My daughter is very attractive. Nice tone, can you tell how firm she is? Nothing's fake, it's all real. Well, the Marquis So-and-so, a very wealthy man, started to give her the eye. But I'm of noble family myself and I'm not impressed by anybody's pedigree. Ho, ho, if he thinks I'd ever let him lay a finger on her."

With the aim of taking convenient advantage of the natural and artistic beauties of our country, he and she met each other for the first time in Venice. Leaving each other with the lagoon as a backdrop, they swore to see each other again, and in fact we came across them once more in Portofino, in Assisi, and in Rome, on the Old Appian Way. A misunderstanding, as is generally known, separated them. In Pisa, on the Campo dei Miracoli, each reproached the other for his wrong-doings. In Cortina d'Ampezzo they didn't make peace. Not in Taormina either. A year went by. And while he was on his way to Capri, she preferred the Amalfi Coast. In Naples they avoided each other. Reunited by chance in Florence and still in love, they betook themselves to Sienna, there to attend the Palio Festival. The final scenes, for lack of funds, were shot back home.

The sums of money allocated for literary and artistic prizes, slightly greater than the sums of money budgeted to fight illiteracy. Here's a point that should make illiterates pause to reflect.

The problems of the South. A mother at a window, who sees her son having a conversation with a poor devil on the street:

"Antonio, don't compromise yourself, remember you're a college graduate!"

I'm returning home after having seen a film about the Wild West, the finale of which was a fight with bare fists. Precisely aimed blows that would have smashed down a wall. The boxing technique won the audience's admiration, as did the correct behavior of the disputants for whom the encounter became a duel, governed by rules of honor and without hard feelings at the end, in fact it was resolved with a handshake. It's sport, the pleasure of beating each other up fair and square, an everyday pastime in American films, where a fist-fight between heroes has the refreshing effect of a shower at the end of a sultry day.

On a deserted Via Nomentana we have to stop because two cars are blocking the street. One of them has bumped into the other, and a fender has been dented. Heated discussion of the two drivers. Fingers pointed and shaken underneath noses, coarse language, a fight is becoming inevitable. So the two drivers begin to shove each other. Clumsy shoves, which they accompany with an "*Aoh!*" in which the surprise of receiving the blow is mixed up with a stubborn determination to give one back. Neither of the two wants to be the first to stop and so they have to pass the time each thrusting his body against the other. Suddenly the weaker of the two grabs hold of his opponent's hair, as if it were a rope thrown off a cliff to save his life. He pulls with all his might. "Let go of my hair!" howls the offended party; but the other, frightened by his own audacity and by the advantage which he's taken possession of and which he despairs of being able to maintain, clings even harder to the hated head, not caring about the blow or two he receives as a consequence. "Let go of my hair, you rotten bastard!"—but they're words thrown to the wind. The wife of the imprisoned man starts hammering with clenched fists upon the shoulders of the tenaciously unfair fighter. "Let go of his hair, you son of a bitch," she howls, nonetheless addressing him in the polite form, *lei*. After a minute the contestants let go of one another, both of them breathless and pallid with fright, each straightening up his tie, arranging his jacket, pants, and hair. Suddenly, the offended party, in a fresh access of rage, launches himself upon the other and tries to deliver a kick to his stomach. He does not succeed. The foot is grabbed in mid-flight, a short dance ensues. "Let go of my foot or I'll kill you." Hopping about all over the sidewalk, they finally tumble into a flower-bed, one of them knocks his head against a tree, the other takes a picket in the back. They insult each other and come back to blows as best they can, while still stretched out on the ground. "Oh my God, someone get them apart," the woman shouts dramatically, tearfully. Someone makes the first move, and the legal part of the dispute begins: who was at fault? The discussion flows back and forth. An expert is called in, witnesses, policemen. Every so often, a coarse epithet, and it seems as if the fight is ready to blaze up again. But the pleasure of arguing and recriminating, of establishing how things took place is certainly winning the day. Now the whole street is blocked with automobiles and with people who arrive in a hurry "to see the corpse."

We return home very happy; the duel was entertaining and, more than that, it appeared that fantasy had triumphed over technique. And happy that, in short, even for us there is still hope.

Confidences of B.: "If there's one thing that keeps me from dying it's the spectacle of a funeral cortege trotting along amidst traffic, causing back-ups, ignoring red lights and finally going into a gallop down the last open stretch, neck and neck with a trolley car in which the passengers don't know whether to stand up, remain seated, make the sign of the cross, or continue reading the newspaper."

Giorgio spends half an hour at a dealership that sells American automobiles. Something is disturbing him. "Is it possible," he wonders, "that the need for vulgar display alone accounts for the baroqueness of these ornamentations? No. There has to be a deeper reason. Could it be a religious motive, a totemic residue? Or perhaps it makes more sense to suppose that the American automobile is an unconscious attempt to glorify the female body with that technique of decomposition which the cubists simplified. Of course! It's clear as day! There's a breast—look, there's another one, this is a belly, these over here are legs. You need simply ask a driver whether he prefers to be aboard a Venus Callipygous or the Three Graces. And this would explain why Praxiteles' contemporaries all knew a good statue when they saw one and today everyone knows a good car when he sees one. Neglected by the Arts, the human body inspires Industry. The more Art becomes extra-human, the more objects of everyday use become anthropomorphic." Satisfied by these thoughts, Giorgio decides to purchase a red and white model that reminds him of Leda with the Swan, and also of the Laocoön.

As a small boy, Montaigne was wakened, every morning, upon his father's instructions, by several musicians who would play him a concerto. The intention was to spare him an abrupt passage from his dreams to reality. We ourselves are wakened by silence, which doesn't bode anything good, because it is a silence which seems as if it were a part of what we were dreaming, while it is really a brief cessation of reality. To avoid our having an abrupt passage our musicians would have to cudgel us into consciousness.

One of the reasons we are impeded from having a great theater is that public life, illustrated by the press, is already an adequate stage where dramas unfold and get tangled into plots, each one carrying its characters along with it. An intolerable general weariness follows from this, because that certain perversity in the news, its shamelessness, its jargon and facile resolutions are exactly the opposite of the standards all theatrical art sets for itself. One may add that the news, through its impartiality, exalts rascals and humiliates the righteous—necessarily, indeed. Whores, adventurers and half-wits ascend Olympus, they serve as models for the discontented, who are the majority. One ends up having to imitate them. He who really is unable to keeps quiet, satisfied with himself; but he is left with the suspicion that he is in some way unsuited for this world and—with the times as they are—for the next world as well.

A large villa by the sea, built like a confection, entirely made out of glass. The interior shows forth at night when the lights are on, a great dollhouse, with the owners and guests placed inside to demonstrate its perfect and gracious functioning. It isn't a house, but a project, perhaps a reckless one. There are people in the living room. They are conversing. About what? About the fashionable vices they don't dare partake of themselves even though everything, their boredom and their wealth, fully enables them? No, they're imitating the game-shows on television. They continuously burst out with applause and protests, and every time they do the dogs in the garden start barking. Then the notes of a song rise as loud as can be, one of those usual songs heard on the jukeboxes. The singer cries and laments his fate in American. "Assholes!" someone finally shouts in the night. A shadow appears on the terrace. "Asshole yourself," it howls in the dark. The answer is a quick raspberry. You can see for yourself the atmosphere is already spoiled. There's no way in the world we will ever be brave, authentic, normal Americans.

Fregene. A little boy not more than six years old who goes to play the pinball machines every single day; from the house he carries with him a stool, without which he will not play. Another boy who buys a water pistol and tests it at length, sober-faced, finally appearing to be unsatisfied with it. A well-heeled youngster of about twelve, on vacation, who travels around by himself, his expression serious and absorbed. He already has his own motorcycle and doesn't make a move unless it's by motorcycle. It has rendered him indifferent to all other things, he acts like a man in his thirties. At certain times he's at the seaside, looking spellbound at the sea, but he doesn't like it. He has no companions, not even girl companions. Yesterday he got off his motorcycle at the newspaper stand. He was smoking, inhaling deeply and letting smoke dribble out elegantly from his nose. He asked: "Has *Mickey Mouse* come in yet?" "No," the news vendor answered. "Then give me *Dennis the Menace.*" He looked around with heavy eyelids and added: "*Dennis the Menace* number thirty-five, I've already got thirty-four."

Faust is in his study, he's re-reading the proofs of the first volume of his *Complete Works*. Disgusted though he is with all his vain knowledge, see him now as he looks nostalgically at his early writings: love, his youth. He invokes the Prince of Darkness, who appears; and he proposes the bargain we're already acquainted with. Mephistopheles, who has thoroughly the air of having rushed hither to confirm his suspicions, smiles kindly and excuses himself. In exchange for his soul he would gladly give Faust back his lost years, to which memory is providing such a rosy tint. But today everybody is willing to be damned for a great deal less, without asking anything in return, there's the man who damns himself out of curiosity, for instance, or out of boredom; he, Mephistopheles, is therefore turning down a great many offers pursuant to that law whereby things are cheapened when they are in over-abundant supply. As if he should accept every soul there happened to be! Faust, ironic and irritated: "Will I have to save myself at all costs then?" Mephistopheles responds, with the implacability of a banker: "No, Excellency, you will be damned for nothing, that's all there is to it." Faust starts to protest, he implores: "And what about my years, what about love, about life?" Mephistopheles, in a fairly chilly tone: "Fleet-

ing moments, Excellency." Then, bending down and re-
entering his hole in the floor, he adds severely: "Better to go
back to your proofs and make sure they're correct; there's
nothing worse than a book full of misprints."

On the beach, today, a lovely lady, passing by with her friend,
says: "Last night I had the most atrocious dream. Just imagine,
I dreamt about the Aztecs." Her friend, greatly surprised (but
then their whole conversation has been based on continuous
surprise, since people nowadays imitate the talk-show come-
dians without even intending to and every cue has to be
underscored by the astonishment of the listener), her friend
then asks: "But, darling, how could you have?" The lovely
lady, shrugging her shoulders and declining to explain the
mystery: "I don't know what to say. I dreamt about them,
that's all." Her friend insists: "But are you sure they were
Aztecs? Maybe you just made a mistake." The lovely lady, a bit
offended: "Are you trying to say I don't know Aztecs when I
see them?"

The influenza epidemic has become the most entertaining
theme of the year. Whenever the topic is mentioned, as in a
game show, everyone has to have a quick response.
    I find the most freakish one so far in today's newspaper,
attributed to a Socialist Party deputy (Bettoli): "As far as pre-
ventive measures are concerned," Bettoli said in Parliament,
where they were discussing nothing but the epidemic, "I think
that the population ought to consume large quantities of fruit
and citrus instead of just peperoni."
    In another paper, the response of a doctor, which is the
wisest of all: "The best way to fight the epidemic is to stay
perfectly healthy."

The young American tourist who asks me to take him a few
kilometers up the road is a student at Harvard. He knows
French and Italian, and in other words can't be at the foot of

his class. He's also interested in literature. He has read, in translation, the *Decameron* and the *Life of Benvenuto Cellini*, which, along with Dante's *Inferno*, are the only Italian texts included in the Anglo-Saxon universal series. He has also read some French writings, in the original language, but now he's given it up. For this he gives me the following justification: "With my I.Q. I manage to read about seventy pages an hour in English. So I can't waste my time with a language like French, where I can only read thirty pages an hour at best." I look at him full of admiration: "My God, but why do you even bother to read?" Reply: "For relaxation." After a long silence, he asks me: "You're not really afraid I'm going to attack you, are you?" I answer that at this point, from someone like him, I can expect anything at all except an act of aggression. He seems disappointed: "Why?" "Because," I say, "you have a high I.Q. and nobody commits acts of violence carrying around a backpack, a camera, and a cooking pot." The student laughs and congratulates me on my policeman's eye for observation: "You're right," he says, "when a person strikes for real the first thing he has to remember is to keep both hands free, and then not leave clues." He becomes thoughtful for a while and then finally bursts out, triumphantly: "But I could have a gun in the cooking pot!" Inasmuch as I take a better look at him, he laughs immoderately. "No, I'm joking, I don't have a gun, only some nice Italian souvenirs for my family." And he opens the cooking pot: it's full of coin-purses, wallets, powder compacts in tooled leather, stamped with curlicues, enormous florentine lilies, the stuff sold around monuments, in a word, junk.

Longanesi. This morning's newspapers [September 28, 1957] bring the news of Leo Longanesi's death. The newspapers bring nothing but bad news nowadays, one of these days we will even end up by reading about our own death in the news. But this morning's was more than just bad news: it seemed insidious to me and disheartening. Longanesi dead is more than a friend lost, it is the end of an encounter and the end of a performance. I thought about him during the day and realized that I loved him and that he loved me because of it: but it was the love of "once upon a time," which doesn't proclaim itself and leads to continual reciprocal acts of forgiveness. I remembered how I made his acquaintance, twenty years ago, in an alehouse where, after chatting awhile, he said to me: "Start writing and don't waste any time." He ordered me to do it out of the blue, without explaining his reasons to me, which at the time I didn't see clearly. It was his way of convincing lazy and disappointed types like me, in that youth of ours that fascism had, if not seared outright, at least covered with soot. Six years later we worked together on a film and on the 8th of September the fascists broke in on him while he was directing it. It was his first film, never finished, the story of an old anarchist who places a bomb under a building and then goes to warn all the tenants that they have only ten minutes to live. (The old anarchist was certainly Longanesi himself, but the bomb at the end turns out to be a dud. Longanesi wouldn't have hurt a fly.)

Then we lost touch with one another. I was to see him next in Milan, in the severe winter of '46. One December evening we were walking along peacefully when he stopped and said: "Write me a novel by the first week of March." I burst out laughing, but he was in earnest. His lively and lucid eyes, always full of empathy and indignation, were looking at me steadily, with surprise. When I had said (just to say something) what kind of novel I had been turning over in my mind, a story so fantastic that I didn't imagine it taking place in Italy but in Africa, in the Africa of Herodotus and Solinus, Longanesi said: "If you begin right away I'll give you an advance." And so the effect of these words, of Longanesi's off-handed way of doing things, which enabled him to put art on the plane of business and vice versa, had now bound me to the hard work of illustrating my ideas, which I probably didn't know how to do. But the thought of disappointing Longanesi

was practically unbearable, because his faith served to uncover our qualities and set them in motion, a faith which did
not elicit disappointment. So I began to write and, during the
first days of March, I sent him a manuscript, which he published. Later we once more fell out of touch. A year or two ago
we saw each other again in Rome, but our friendship, and it
had been such ever since the outset, was reserved and respectful, we avoided speaking what was in our hearts, perhaps
in the hope that someday we might do so. The memory of him
that remains with me now is of a man who had the best
possible qualities and the best possible shortcomings and who
always spoke plainly, without ever wanting to please me or
surprise me, quick to argue and to be the first to extend his
hand. And also the memory of a man who had the genius of
getting us to take ourselves seriously, which is everything. I
don't know how much irony he put into his polemical poses.
He did it at his own expense and they were also the smoke
that hid his dedication as an artist and as a writer. There are
chapters in his books and pages in his *Notebook* which I will
always remember for their perfect sense of melancholy,
slightly disguised, out of modesty—that journey of his through
Italy for instance, his days in Naples, his return to Rome. He
had what he used to call "the eye" for taking in his surroundings; nothing ever escaped him. About Longanesi I also admired his faith in work, in labor, in manual application. He
believed in the strengths that we find in ourselves and none of
the rest counted. One day I told him that he kept what he was
working on in a state of continuous repair, like certain never
completed monuments. He smiled. Had he been more prudent—prudent people think—he would have been able to
focus himself and "dig in," an expression he detested. But
prudence wasn't his forte, he had, rather, the prodigality of a
genius, giving everyone his attention. I remember him in short
as an artist and as a sincere man, never "personal" in his odes,
which were so happy and impetuous, an enamored and implacable critic, an admirer of the intelligence of others, not

one of those many who seek to attaint us with their protection and consent. I can pity the person who has neither seen him this way nor known him this way, because he has missed knowing a man with a great heart.

Fregene, October '57. How lovely these lonely days are at the seashore, how you regain touch with time and lose yourself in the sweet abandon of limpid autumn! This morning's paper announces that the Russians have launched a satellite into space. It weighs 83 kilograms, it's flying at an altitude of 900 kilometers and at a speed of 30,000 kilometers an hour. It's even going to pass over Rome, perhaps it already has passed over Rome. Let us consider this prodigious feat a victory for Man. "We're already in the future," I say at table. "Just think how happy Galileo must be." My wife observes: "Why do you always have to splash on the tablecloth?" After dinner we decide to have a neon lamp installed in the garden, for now it's starting to get dark early and the night is saddening, though on the other hand it's this selfsame solitude that fortifies one's character.

At five two electricians arrive in a white van, accompanied by a boy whom we already know. His name is Mauro, and he began working yesterday. Before this, he used to keep an eye on people's cars for them while they were in swimming. He's carrying a long ladder. The two electricians have toured the garden and now they're saying they didn't know they had to put in a lamp, they've brought everything with them except a lamp. They send Mauro back to the shop and then sit down for a smoke. "I say it'll fall down," one of them says. The other responds: "Your grandmother'll fall down." When the boy returns, it's already starting to get dark. Nevertheless the two electricians pull out the wire, staple it down, fasten the transformer under the gutter. In the dark one of them bangs his knee with a hammer, he climbs down and starts to curse, softly but inconsolably. It's impossible to see anymore, they'll be back tomorrow to finish up.

The evening papers talk about the satellite, some with that confidential tone that the press usually reserves for Philip (the Duke of Edinburgh), for Ike (the President of the United States), and for our Italian actresses. By the year 1980 man will be going into the cosmos, as soon as we've constructed space stations for him. Later, over the dark woodlands appears the Moon, with something genuinely stupefying about its broad face, which is perhaps only a figment of our imagination. We look at the sky, perhaps we will be able to see the other Moon speeding by. In bed, I pick up D'Annunzio's *Alcyone* by chance and reread the "Madrigali per l'estate": "Come scorrea la calda sabbia lieve / per entro il cavo della mano in ozio / il cor sentì che il giorno era piu breve..." ("How smoothly the hot sand fell, lightly, through the hollow of the idle hand. The heart felt the day was shorter now...") How true it is! I myself experienced this sensation of languid nostalgia for the departing summer. And now autumn...

The two electricians fail to show up the next day. At the bar I run into Mauro who is playing the pinball machine. There is nothing he can tell me. At the shop the young lady says that the two electricians have gone to Rome, they'll be back, sooner or later. The evening newspapers publish imaginary drawings of the satellite and an interview with an astronomer. "In order to launch a satellite," says the astronomer, "a velocity of 8000 kilometers an hour for the first two or three seconds is all is that is required to get the rocket off the ground, then the velocity must be increased. It's probable," he adds, "that other planets besides ours are inhabited."

The next morning, a single electrician arrives. But he hasn't brought the ladder. "I'll go get it at Mauro's house," I offer. "No, no, you might get the wrong one. I'll go." He leaves and I never see him again. And I have an article to write, how can I if I have to hang around waiting for him and his ladder? What distractions! Later I find Mauro at the newspaper stand: he doesn't know anything, because the shop is closed from one to four. The newspapers are talking about the likelihood that

Mars may now be visited to determine whether it is inhabited. The distance could be covered in about forty days. The return trip presents no serious difficulties, it ought to be planned for that period when Mars and Earth are in closest proximity: this would then require a stay of six months on Mars itself. At home the maid hasn't returned because the buses are on strike. She'll come in tomorrow morning on the train, unless I go pick her up.

The next morning, at the shop again. The young lady isn't there, she has the flu. It's Mauro who's there, playing songs on the record-player. I decide to buy a flashlight, just in case I have to go out at night. Mauro gets up on a chair, takes a number of different flashlights from a cupboard, but he doesn't know how much they cost and can't find the right-sized batteries for the one I want. While getting down, he breaks a record; he's angry with himself, he goes and hides in the back-room. He'll be saying goodbye to his whole week's salary unless he can conceal the broken record. I go back home. The satellite continues to go round and round, irritating and impudent. According to the government newspapers it seems that it ought very shortly to disintegrate. According to the newspapers of the opposition it can continue its course in the service of science and of peace for another hundred years. I read an article that censures the satellite, which has violated divine law. I read a poem that approves of the satellite, *à la* Vincenzo Monti. There is also a favorable verdict from somewhere in the Vatican: "Every new scientific truth further bears out the highest theological truth." I'm surprised, though, not to have come across the news that an Italian engineer is building a satellite. Perhaps it will be there tomorrow. The telephone to Rome isn't working. In fact, it has rained. Sometimes at night, and always because it has rained, the lights go out. It's been happening like this for years now, in Fregene. Fortunately we have a reserve of candles and a kerosene lamp. On the other hand, if it doesn't rain, the lights go off all the same because the hydroelectric reservoirs are dry.

The next morning I return to the store, having decided this time to complain. Mauro isn't there. Instead it's an old man who's there, repairing an electric range. He's the proprietor. He doesn't know anything about a lamp, he's been out himself, he assures me he'll see to it that the work is completed in a day. He's a smiling old man, docile, simpatico. While speaking, I absent-mindedly touch the electric range and receive a shock that hurls me against the wall. I thought for sure I was going to die from it.

After dinner I go to Rome. Meeting of the technical commission of review for documentaries. The projector grinds on for three hours; we see thirteen documentaries. The stupidity of these documentaries is equalled only by the indifference of the public that puts up with them. Their makers no longer know how to use their imagination, they are made in order to win prizes, and they win them all, too. When you arrive at this point where slovenly workmanship and lack of ideas prevail, it's useless to complain. We are a country of artists, we work elbow to elbow, everyone copying his neighbor's theme and asking the State for aid. Or, rather, the State ought to aid us, but it also ought to leave us free to do the infantile nonsense we feel like doing. However, Italian cinema is not a phenomenon to be judged differently from Italian journalism, or from Italian politics, or from the Italian economy, or from the Italian building industry, not to speak of Italian schools, sports, life and customs. The principle of communicating vessels applies even to to the activity of a nation and each of them expresses and reflects the others, or at least the general conditions that determiine them.

At the Caffè Rosati, where I go afterward, a heated discussion about the satellite. All of my friends are there, and some politicians. D. maintains that the satellite is merely an application of scientific thinking, inferior, actually, to the splitting of the atom. "True revolutions are those of ideas and of sentiments." I agree. B. rejoins that thanks to the satellite Russia is now in a position to impose *its* revolution of ideas and *its* sentiments. "The satellite isn't a joke," he concludes as he's leaving. "It's an application," retorts D.

He goes on to tell a story, about the adventure of a writer who is something of a go-getter. He has unhooked himself from the communists after the Hungarian business and now he's taken his ladder round to the newspapers and to various government ministries. The satellite gives him his cue, he goes to see the Honorable F. In anguish, he tells him that a new crisis is brewing, he is even willing to disown marxism, because only in the Christian faith and in its political concretization in the Christian-Democratic Party does he see salvation for Italy and calm for her distressed soul. F. is purported to have replied: "But then you'd better hurry and go talk about it with your confessor!" We all laugh at this apt witticism. To myself I'm thinking that perhaps today, during my absence, the electrician will have finished his work.

The satellite is called Sputnik. One newspaper has calculated that, given its size, it should only weigh sixty kilos. A mysterious question arises concerning those extra twenty kilos. The Italians, in any case, have had a satellite project on the drawing board ready to go since 1951. Saturday morning I see an electrician arrive. "How are we doing here?" he asks me cheerfully. Before my remonstrances he starts to pout: he had a sister come in from out of town, to take care of a sick cousin, and he had to collect the arrears on a pension for his father. He sets to work, and at noontime he calls me: "Go ahead, switch it on." The lamp doesn't go on. "It needs a little time to warm up, that's all." After five minutes he says: "The trouble is when everything's new it's hard to figure out what doesn't work. As far as I can tell it ought to work." "But it's clear as the sun up above that it doesn't work," I answer. I'm not angry, only curious to understand. The electrician studies, observes, tears off a wire, decides it's the fault of the transformer. The satellite continues going round and around. The Americans will launch a dozen of them within the next month. The night is quiet now, the dogs no longer bark at the Moon, which doesn't rise till late, and which continues to linger high above the sea, when day is done, ravelled out towards the west.

Monday morning, the sports results. The satellite is also spoken of. The vector rocket, which detached itself from the satellite and was following it, overtook it on the 130th orbit and is now five minutes in front of it. The electricians come back. Somewhat chilly greetings. I ask Mauro, who's carrying the new transformer, what he thinks about the satellite. He doesn't think anything about it. I say to him: "When you grow up, will you go to the moon?" "Mah!" he answers. The transformer is put in, now the lamp works. A painful discussion on the agreed upon price ensues: the electricians' original calculations didn't include the cost of a transformer. As soon as night falls I turn on the lamp. It gives off an extremely lively light, perhaps the usual sort of lamp would have been sufficient; but to leave one outside, here, through the winter—they'll take it for sure. Seen from far away my house looks like a pizzeria. Sadness being alone now that the Moon will be rising later and later in the sky. The lamp draws butterflies, crickets, and bumble-bees. In the evening's paper, a professor writes that the time is near when man, already ruler of the universe, will be able to divert satellites from other planets, should such a thing make our life easier, and put them in orbit around the Earth. A few little satellites of Jupiter, which has eleven of them after all, one of them only ten kilometers in diameter, could be drawn into our gravitational field; we just have to go there and give them a nudge with some big rockets.

Someone rings at my door and, when I open it, a sweet and very gracious girl hands me a package of kitchen cleanser and begins to explain its use to me. Gratis. She does this work to earn her living and therefore she inspires a sense of appreciation in me for her honesty and for the respect she has for herself. When she's finished, before going away, she concludes: "And now allow me to tell you, Signore, that washed white used to be all right but today it's no longer good enough." She goes away blushing on account of my happy surprise, like a little girl who has recited a poem and who now curtsies to the audience's applause. It's going to end up, I think, that even the most innocent, unexpected and finally pleasing encounters will take place under the aegis of advertising. I remember Charlot and his exceedingly fine film, a testament to defeat and to melancholy, which the public rejected because of the disillusionment that inhabits that film, the same disillusionment that prompted it to reject *Monsieur Verdoux* in '47: a disillusionment vis-à-vis certain conventions. The dialogue that has been initiated between author and public is not to be broken off by the sudden voicing of disagreeable truths, untimely truths. The truth can be discussed with those who are our familiars, with the scurrilous, with the bold, with the mawkish, those who move us, who make us feel we're poets, sensitive, generous, "open" to problems. From Charlot moreover we want entertaining and sentimental truths. When Charlot suggests that today it is necessary to re-make one's face, because nobody likes the one we have, he is saying a truth which is at present disagreeable but which Advertising will before long make popular. "Signore, and now allow me to tell you that your face used to be all right but today it's no longer good enough," our sweet and gracious girl will say one day, when we shall uncautiously have opened the door to her.

A. is a perfect intellectual. He believes firmly in statistics and in pornography, indignation cloaking his belief in the latter; believing in the former in order to keep himself up to date. He simulates the interests of the young, he worships the public. His contemporary idol is an idiot from yesterday with the prejudices of tomorrow.

Confessions of C.: "My life isn't exactly a novel, it isn't even a good story. It's a gazette. Things that have happened to me every day for years now, and which will repeat themselves again and again for years, until they become boring. If I were at least hard to please I could transform some desire into vice, some caprice into passion, my modest genius into talent. Many people do it, but I'm happy the way I am. My daily life then is only a newspaper, which, as soon as it's been read and paged through, is already old and a bit loathsome.

Or else: having worked all our life, detesting every form of oppression and violence, honoring our mother and our father, loving our neighbor, respecting the property of others and fornicating only out of pure, absolute necessity, and then finally having it dawn on us that the description of the alleged murderer is the same that a friend might in good faith make of us.

Poet and peasant, yesterday. Today, prose-writer and landowner, essayist and direct cultivator of the soil, philosopher and employer.

Today, in the stationery store, there was a boy of about ten, with a worried look on his face, who asked for a book of worked out themes. They gave him seven of them to choose from. The boy is one of the ones who all day long play in the little piazza on Via M. under my window. He has the opaque look about him of a little bully, a hard face, raise your hand howsoever slightly and, instinctively, he ducks, used to expecting a slap on the head. But here he is without all his fine boldness, he's just a victim of compulsory education and he ends up becoming, for me, *simpatico*. He pages through the volumes, wetting his fingers, he scours the table of contents of each, he doesn't know which to choose. The theme he's looking for ("How I Spent My Summer Vacation") isn't there. Dismayed, he explains: "That's what they always give." He can already feel the blow between his head and his neck that will be coming one of these mornings soon and he would like to protect himself, but his theme isn't there. "So just tell what you did then," the shopgirl suggests. The boy looks at me with an expression of disgust on his face, as if to say: "You make everything sound easy, you two." He goes away disappointed. So it's a book of worked out themes that I then buy, in order to get a grasp of the problems of this childhood I'm unacquainted with. At home I browse through it. It's worth the trouble. There are themes of gentle inspiration, for good little children: "Dreaming about a Little House in the Mountains." Or: "To Candlelight: Surprise and Emotion When the Electric Lights Go Out." There are themes for extremely good little children: "It's Raining . . . A Little Boy Knocks at Your Door." (It's a question of a little boy who is poor, who is "sad and sickly," to whom their mommy will give "some food and a pair of shorts.") Another theme for sensitive little children: "Music, Manifestation of the Human Spirit, Which Is Becoming Refined by It." (At its sound, our feelings are uplifted; in music we experience, depending upon what our mood chances to be at the moment, happiness, sadness, serenity, emotion. Music transports us into the world of dreams.) For the little delinquents from the neighborhood there isn't anything. How is my friend going to dig something out tomorrow when they tell him to relate how he spent his summer vacation? If he tells the truth he goes right to the reformatory, and as for lies, he hasn't the knack for making them up. I leaf through the book again. There are some lovely moral themes. For example: "True Riches Are Not What They Are Commonly Believed To Be." ("Then what are they?" asks the boy in the stationery shop, looking puzzled and mistrustful. Answer: "True riches are health and a good conscience.") Or another theme: "The Sacred Mission of Woman." (The boy at the stationery store lowers his head and smiles to himself, darkly.) Or: "My Thoughts on the Twilight: Whether Happy People Always Feel a Little Twinge of Sweet Melancholy." ("What is that there twilight, exactly?" wonders the boy at the stationery store.)

While I am reading, the usual gang, led by Filettoni Luigi, has assembled in the little piazza, and the scholar without ideas is also there. Sitting on the ground, under the protective cover of a little wall, they begin to play trumps and seven-and-a-half. Placing their bets, they gamble with the money they've stolen from their dear papa ("who, when he comes home tired out from his day's work, strokes our head caressingly") and they trade insults with short and constant outbursts of rage. They throw down their cards with a violence and a pleasure that inspire envy, for they're sincere. When the lights go on their voices arrive more limpid from the deserted little piazza. After a long silence a sudden quarrel breaks out; I go to the window to see what's up; two of the players are giving each other fierce shoves, thumps on the head, kicks. And then Filettoni Luigi gathers up the cards, shuffles them calmly (why should the twilight trouble him?) and says, as severely as a schoolteacher: "Okay, sons of bitches, you gonna cut it out?"

A street fair of paintings on Via Margutta. The "artists" need to feel that they are in the thick of things, that they are included. They have solicited the recognition of the Municipality, which has accorded it to them. It also had lights installed and at the street corners it put up enormous purple-colored standards in the Capitoline style, with the inscription: 7TH EXHIBITION OF VIA MARGUTTA. Roman imperial characters. Inside, the usual fair of the last few years, aggravated by the impression you get that it is no longer a joke, but a chore. A few important painters, who put in a coquettish appearance; the rest is laughable stuff. A golliard-like pretext for putting onself on display, in order to feel that one is in the wake of great movements, in order to say: We are artists. Bartoli once wrote: "Nature is for painters, Art is for crackpots." They all begin at the point where the others, the great ones, after long toil, ended up; and they believe they have to disperse this inheritance, which hasn't even cost them a little patience. The exhibitors have the mental age of a seven-year-old. They maculate their canvases as if they were in kindergarten, without shame, but also without innocence, so true is it that today everything goes, their role has taken on all the trappings of legitimacy. They don't even have to fear the public's ridicule, at this point. The public doesn't say anything, it knows that the Bohemian enjoys State recognition, it looks, keeps quiet, walks along the street, buys hazelnuts and nougats. In the air there's the same odor of vanilla as at the festivals in the Trionfale district. But no cheerfulness. When a people gives more "artists" to the world than land surveyors or public accountants or capable clerks, the equilibrium is broken, and no one laughs anymore.

I never used to believe in the crisis of the Cinema, but in the course of the last few days I've begun to believe in it: ever since they "called" a conference on the relationship between Cinema and Literature. By and large, as far as we in the Cinema are concerned—I'm not disclosing any secret—, when the literati take part in a conference, that's the sign that the end has come. I have no idea why: maybe it has to do with their laziness, which is driving the literati to concern themselves with literary questions. A number of different writers, and some excellent ones, a single producer, a few official personages participated in the conference on the Cinema. There was a great deal of discussion about the sex of angels. Someone even spoke on the relationship between Literature and Internal Revenue. The producers were generally accused of being greedy and simple-minded: and this is so very well known that there was no need to meet just to discover that. The producer—strange as it may seem—is the type of man who is always looking for a way to make money. Incredible. Some time ago he found out at his own expense that noble ideas don't go over, the public prefers ignoble ideas, it feels more at home with them. The producer is almost always the mirror of the public.

The writers have proclaimed that in the article of quality

they are ready to help the Cinema. A certain man asked whether a professional scribe with at least a college education shouldn't have a part in writing every screenplay. But in the Cinema everyone has a college degree! Moravia, always the most sincere in these cases, said that if he has to think about something for the Cinema, he prefers to write a short story or a novel. Although this confession could explain his extraordinary fertility as a writer, a first conclusion is already urging itself upon us: the writer, morally, is contemptuous of the Cinema. But even this isn't news. "To do cinema," for many, or for everybody, is a subsidiary and secondary activity; and reversibly it is so only to the degree to which the writer believes it is. And then why this conference? Perhaps because Cinema is remunerative?

In 1923, Giuseppe Prezzolini wrote (in *La cultura italiana*, page 327): "It took the big earnings bestowed by Cinema to induce artists to involve themselves in it; but they did so disdainfully. For a while it was like journalism, to which a writer gave only the energies left over from his real work, as if to a disagreeable job put up with only for the sake of making a living. Even today a writer who wants to move the critics or a patron to pity can declare—almost threaten—that he is being forced to give himself up to Cinematography."

Many years have gone by and a shadow of that disdain yet weighs upon Cinema. Look at Mario Soldati: he has two desks, one for writing screenplays, the other for writing his wonderful stories and novels.

There is a tendency then for the average Italian writer to consider himself as inviolable as a priest. He wants to say Mass for the cannibals,but he cannot stand the thought of martyrdom: he wants to convert his readers, but he is worried about his rent and his percentages; he wants Freedom but admires, even wholeheartedly, the enormous State press-runs in the Soviet Republics.

The relationship between Cinema and Literature could, all things considered, be the same as that between Literature and the Building Industry. Why should they be greatly dissimilar? Cinema is an industry, or at least everyone would like it to be an industry, forgetting that the few fine works of Italian cinema, those which made it possible to talk about the existence of an Italian cinema, were made in opposition to Industry, in opposition to producers, and above all in opposition to the public. The day that Cinema, in this country, truly becomes an industry, writers will be able to go back to telling us about their first loves. They will no longer serve any purpose, not even for making films of protest.

It's obvious that everything derives from the equivocal idea that Cinema is Art. Cinema at this stage is a public service, a comfort. It can enter the sphere of Art, but—obviously—only through the work of an artist. There aren't very many of them. And often even they are half asleep. But let's leave the art film aside and let's move ahead to the normal state of affairs: to make these films Cinema asks the writers for their collaboration, nothing else. And Cinema takes it entirely upon itself to address an audience that writers very often claim to know nothing about, and to have the right to know nothing about. The writer who "enters into" Cinema—unless, unlike ourselves, he's an innocent—always knows what's in store for him: another kind of disdain, this time of Cinema for Literature. However, the decision to collaborate is his own, no one's forcing him. To want Cinema to be completely literary is the least literary idea imaginable. And it is equally useless to complain that producers are incompetent and that they are averse to the art film. If it weren't that way, they would be writers themselves. What a happy world! Perhaps even Cinema would wind up being useless. Everyone at home, writing.

One more thing: the writer who complains about the producers' lack of understanding vividly brings to mind the story about the man riding a tiger who complains that he can't get off whenever he wants. To lay the blame on the tiger, who, obviously, is running to catch his prey, is silly. It isn't necessary to mount tigers like horses. You may rejoin that riding them is a somewhat scary business, but it pays well. But this is another discussion, we are talking now about a conference on Literature and Finance.

We are acquainted with writers who have collaborated on excellent films. They have always been reproached by their friends and by the critics for having made mediocre literature. Probably the remedy consists in making good literature in order to make bad films: which amounts to writing excellent stories and excellent novels. And in fact when a writer (getting astride a tiger) adapts one of his good pieces of writing for the Cinema he always makes a bad film. There are no examples to the contrary.

This conference would have turned out to be completely useless were it not for the fact that it concluded with a visit of the writers to Cinecittà and with a banquet at Cinecittà's restaurant. The day before, the participants had been received by the Undersecretary of the Performing Arts, who, a paternal man, concluded his toast (I'm quoting from memory) like this: "Whenever you want me, here I am, ready to listen to you. Let's see each other often."

Let's put it to the test, friends and fellow writers. Let's give him a call, one of these days.

Nobody talks about anything but escapism. As far as the Earth is concerned, everyone is already beginning to hate it. It's finished, it no longer has a future. If we at least had Time . . . The trouble is that we only have Space.

That the strongest inspire a natural sympathy in us (Bruno Barilli once wrote: "The Italian flies to the aid of the victor") was roundly confirmed this year—I am told—at the reception which the Russian Embassy held to celebrate the October Revolution. Everybody was there, while the year before, for the same occasion, nobody was there. It's only natural to ask oneself why and then to find the simplest answer possible, which is always the best: this year, two satellites, Sputnik I and

Sputnik II, have flown around the Earth, the year before, two other satellites, Hungary and Poland, rose up in rebellion. We will be preserved from all global catastrophe then for the single purpose, perhaps foreseen by biology, of designating the winner by acclamation.

The distress and suspicion normal persons give rise to in a world where only the Exceptional arouses interest, in all its varieties. Thus it comes about that in the upright man one is obliged to see the scoundrel of tomorrow, or a scoundrel who's concealing himself, while in the scoundrel of today one discovers inspiring qualities. Abel's brain is subjected to an autopsy, Cain is invited to write his memoirs.

Snapshot. One of those types who, in order to find his own peace of mind, has to make others lose theirs.

A lovely day spent at the Aid to Literature Conference. It is a conference made up of people from the Cinema, an attempt to resolve the crisis of the Book. Everybody is there. Festive ambiance, beautiful actresses who, off the screen, among men assembled for the purposes of discussion, assume that timid and domestic air which touches me and endears them to me. I see quite a number of directors, quite a number of producers, not a single writer. How come? Pride? Actually, yes, there is one literary man, they point him out to me: he's standing off to the side of the stage and smiling politely into the void whenever someone comes up to pat him on the shoulders and say: "Have courage, we're here, the Book cannot die."
The President extends his greetings, reads a few telegrams, mentions the conference on the relationship between Literature and Cinema, held by the writers in order to resolve the crisis of film. Applause in gratitude. Then a producer gets up to speak, a certain Massaciuccoli. An enormous man, cordial and vivacious. He begins by saying that the crisis of the Book is undeniably serious, but not desperate, and that he is going

to leave its technical aspects for others to deal with, he will limit himself to the bookselling industry, which is in crisis "because it doesn't know how to delve into its own successes."

They ask him what he means by that and he goes on to give an example: a month ago, confined to bed on account of a sprained ankle, he read a book. "It's true, gentlemen," he immediately stresses before the murmur of dismay from the pit, "I read a book and I can even tell you what the title was: *I promessi sposi.*" The audience claps and Massaciuccoli adds: "See, I'm not making it up." Then he enlarges upon a criticism of the book, with eulogies for the author who, in his judgment, shows himself to possess a great deal of talent. He would be happy to make the acquaintance of this Manzoni and to be able to shake his hand. In the back of the audience someone shouts: "He's dead!" But the speaker is just joking, he smiles and continues: "Yes, I would like to shake his hand, but also I would like to ask him why he didn't take advantage of this book's success, which, they tell me, was enormous. This is the only thing I would like to ask him. And do you know why?"

The audience keeps silent and waits. Massaciuccoli resumes: "Because, gentlemen, after having read this book, I myself entered a bookstore [murmurs] and I said to the owner: 'Give me the sequel.' Well, what do you think the bookstore owner did? Did he perhaps give me the sequel? No, he told me that the novel doesn't have a sequel. I asked him why. And he replied: 'Go ask Manzoni why.' "

Massaciuccoli stops talking, gazes at the ceiling and goes on slyly: "Then you tell me this, someone writes a book, he has it published, he is aware that it's finding an audience, that it pleases, that it's successful, and that's all there is to it? But that's suicide ... I no longer wonder that there's a crisis of the Book, rather, I wonder what else you could expect. As a matter of fact I'm sure I would ask in vain for the sequel to many, many books, should I ever read any. I am sure that thousands and thousands of books are sleeping at this very moment on their laurels, unproductive, inactive, closed, and without a sequel."

Massaciuccoli appears calm; suddenly, he pounds a fist on the table, and shouts: "But what did we do when the crisis of film was tearing us to pieces? Didn't we make sequels, didn't we make sequels to our successful films, maybe ten, twenty, a hundred times?"

Here the audience burst into applause. Massaciuccoli allowed it to run its course and added: "In a few cases we probably even went overboard." (Voices: "No! No!") "Yes, we went overboard, but it was necessary to save the principles of repetition and of delving into things."

Further applause, Massaciuccoli is calm, he means to win hands down. He says: "Let's go back to our *Promessi sposi*. I said to the bookstore man: 'No sequel, eh?' And the bookstore man looked at me and said: 'No, no sequel.' He even seemed surprised that I should insist. 'In other words,' I said, 'we have all these magnificent characters, one more beautiful than the other, and no sequel? We have the unforgettable figure of the padrone, of ... Don Rodriguez, we have the priest, the friar, the cardinal, the Unnameable, and the nun; and no sequel? Why, if only for the nun, if I had time, I would write a book myself, and you're telling me: no sequel?'"

More applause. Massaciuccoli reaches out his arms and concludes emotionally: "I'm not insisting. But let's remind our friends the writers that a single success, the magical flower in the desert, is not enough. It is always necessary to expand one's ideas and out of the desert to make a garden, a garden of hope."

A deluge of applause bursts forth. When calm is restored, the director Crestini speaks. His manner of speaking is easy and impetuous. He begins by saying that to his way of thinking, today's public is detaching itself from the Book precisely because the Book lacks ideas. After the initial applause, he continues: "Many of *us* instead have ideas for books in our desk drawers at home, because for us Literature is a perennially alive and interesting matter. But what can we do with these ideas?"

His question remained without an answer, and then he continued: "We let them keep on sleeping. I, personally, have offered my ideas to some of the top writers in the country." (Voices: "Their names!") "No, I won't tell you their names . . . Anyhow I humbly offered them *these* ideas of mine; an idea for a novel whose setting is at the mouth of the Po, an idea for a novel that takes place in an electric power plant, an idea for a novel that takes place in a women's reformatory; and every time I did I was met with a courteous refusal. Courteous but clear."

As soon as the murmuring in the room subsided, Crestini began again: "And I'm sparing you the excuses: 'The publisher doesn't want it. The topic requires a lot of research. I *would* like it but I'm not free to do what I want. The reader isn't sufficiently mature.' One writer even answered me with: 'But isn't the mouth of the Po all flooded?' Now, what does this sort of cynicism demonstrate? That the writers are in this crisis of theirs from fear of what's new, from fear of reality, from fear of our ideas and even from fear of the Quantitative Method."

A voice cries out: "They're all rich!" Crestini smiles and picks up from where he left off. "Okay, I'm telling the writers in good faith: out of a hundred books why don't you write at least twenty using purely quantitative principles? Why not accept our ideas about islands, about beaches, about salt-ponds, rice fields, tourism, floods, good children, fun-loving priests, girls in the flower of youth, the return to the earth and the blossoming of first love in the slums? Wouldn't twenty such ideas every year be enough to waken the reader, to restore weight and fame and dignity to the Book?"

Applause. Crestini bows his head and concludes: "We are here, friends and writers, we are here. Ask us what our ideas are, we will not refuse them to you."

After Crestini, in the already heated atmosphere, the only writer present, a certain Forletti, got up to speak. He's timid but likeable. He's an unpublished author. With a fixed smile, almost as if he wished to apologize for the absence of his greater colleagues, he said: "Friends, I mean brothers." (Applause.) "I hope that Literature will welcome your words with open arms. As for myself, I've been lacking in ideas for a long time now, I am ready to accept all the ideas you are willing to suggest to me." (Voices: "Bravo!") "I ought only to warn you that... that ... that I don't know how to write."

The disappointment of the assembly was very keen. It was followed by a banquet.

Today, Sunday, being at loose ends, I headed, out of indolent curiosity, towards the *borgata* on the outskirts of town, beyond my neighborhood. A long walk. Then I entered the playing field adjoining a big factory to watch two teams of young men playing soccer. From what I saw I got the impression that the young players weren't nearly as interested in kicking the ball, which often remained at a dead standstill in a corner of the field, as they were in punching one another. At the end of the first period two young men wound up being taken away by car, in search of first aid. At the end of the second period the crowd that was watching the game poured onto the field, which wasn't fenced in, and manhandled the remaining nine young men of the defeated team who were still uninjured. I then listened in on the remarks that were being made in various groups. The spectators, all of them from the *borgata*, were satisfied by the way the match had been played and by its result. The opposing team had been eliminated for a couple of weeks at least, perhaps forever, and those young hearts were not a little aroused by this outcome, with its promise of more heated and meritorious victories ahead for "their" team.

I wanted to question one of the more loquacious young men. He told me that he loves the sport, he dedicates all his free time to it as well as those rare moments he can steal while at work. And here's how: he goes to the games and roots as hard as he can for his team, he then follows the write-ups in the sports pages, discussing them with his friends, he gambles every week on the odds and sometimes wins, modest sums but heaven-sent nonetheless. His hates are defined with precision, and he wouldn't know how to live without them. For example, the mere color of an opponent's jersey is enough to put him in a dark mood and to spur him to sarcasm. One day, he and some of his other friends showed the extent of their devotion by following a lady for half an hour, harassing her as she deserved, because she was wearing a dress with the colors of a rival team's jersey. Finally, to teach her a lesson, they snatched her purse. I asked the young man if he takes part in any other sport. And he answered: "And where am I going to get the time? From you?"

I'm going back home and along the way I run into the philosopher and sociologist Frassetti, to whom I pose other questions about Sports. He maintains that Sports are a source of income, they mitigate delinquency, and they are a substitute for civil war. He maintains finally that, thanks to Sports, thanks even to the single game of soccer, the Nation is happily returning to its socio-historical origins, reconstituting the communal republics, the Polis and, in certain cases, the Tribe. In every large city today there now exist two tribes, each one of which desires nothing less than the extermination of the other. For this reason they conclude both secret and open alliances with more distant tribes and this favors better understanding and exchanges between the various linguistic groups within the Country.

Later, I push on towards the center of town. There has been a big game between the teams of the two municipal tribes and the streets are being invaded by young men of the tribe that has won. Heated and dishevelled by the furor of victory, some carry great banners and flags, others symbolical biers and gallows; shouts and ferocious songs erupt from everybody's chest. Traffic is at a halt, the traffic cops smile wanly, an automobile gets overturned, the driver chased. I enter one group and see one young man of the losing tribe who, surrounded by his implacable foes, is eating a lizard.

The streets of the new district that is going up on the fields of the Nomentana are named for those writers who, in histories of literature, get lumped together in the last chapter and treated with an affection that tends to the summary. Having lived on horseback around the turn of the century, one or two have had their books republished, the others, no; and now they have their own streets, as it befits writers who lived unassuming lives: narrow, for the most part, and full of curves. Better than nothing. I gladly go there for walks because the streets are fairly deserted. Already asphalted, with the new houses sinking in the landscapes constituted of fill, their yards still admitting sunlight, they run between the hills of the old grazing lands. The street signs are wooden, the sidewalks are grass, on the edge of the ditch sits an Abruzzese shepherd watching his flock. Far away, a hunter shoots at starlings and sparrows: feeble shots, as if from a toy gun. Every so often a truck arrives with words written on the cab: "Rome Power" or "Hauling for Carolina": it unloads earth and garbage, filling up the meadows with clumpish mounds where the dogs from the construction sites go rummaging, with the air of excursionists.

Via Ugo Ojetti is the most important street, in fact it's a grand boulevard. They've asphalted only half of it so far, down its entire length, the rest is left to the imagination. One day young pine trees will divide it. For now it ends in a ditch, beyond which extends a soccer field. It's a sunny street, where the stone-crushing machines and the asphalt-spreaders go sluggishly up and down. Via Grazia Deledda ascends towards a meadow (a tortuous route) and ends abruptly in another ditch. Four bricklayers are sitting on the curb eating their lunch. Via Ettore Romagnoli, which intersects Via Ugo Ojetti, has a large number of hundred-year-old pines arranged in parallel rows. Via Antonio Fogazzaro, which twists back and forth its whole length, is already weighed down with houses that seem as if they were bought already made and set there to dry. On Via Emilio De Marchi they're putting up tiny little villas that, once painted, will look just like toys. Seen as they are now the houses resemble automobiles and bathrooms; and the sight of them always manages to make me sad, even though I'm used to it. The poet Mario Rapisardi's street runs between landscapes that are still pretty and fenced in; but they will be developed. It crosses Via Luigi Siciliani, of whom I have never read anything. Between Via Francesco D'Ovidio and Via Achille Torelli (*I mariti!*) rises the local church: built, that's all you can say for it, with an undulating roof. How come this church? It's simple: as far as the building codes are concerned we are still in the Agro Romano and if one wants to build a "nucleus" it is first necessary to build a church. Therefore, here's the church: little and ugly, economical, with a belfry on top, one meter high.

Via Carlo Lorenzini leads to the Nomentana: it's still a little topsy turvy here. Via Emilio Praga branches off from Ugo Ojetti Boulevard (finally two friends) and goes off into the distance between a group of large buildings. The stores, all new and cheerful, stand in single file: Pork Butcher, Bakery, Oils and Wines, Radio and Electricity, Florist, Dry Cleaner's. In the evening, when the lights go on, the words *Dry Cleaner's* appear written in red, blue, yellow, pink, green and violet. You take Via Isidoro del Lungo and after about two hundred meters of co-operatives you merge into Piazza Guido Gozzano: an open area, not very large, surrounded by new houses in the worst possible taste. All of these houses are for sale or rent. My favorite street is Via Giacomo Zanella. He is a poet of whom I read only a very little in my green years as a schoolboy, but his street is a ribbon of dark asphalt that traverses an endearing meadow. It has yet to be taken over by construction sites. From here the prospect extends freely, and one is alone. The women come here to collect chicory, automobiles from the driving schools come here too, with their students clinging to the steering wheel while they practice going into reverse and backing up.

This morning, Sunday, a large family drove up in an automobile that was practically new: everybody got out, they threw open the doors, removed the seats, began to clean it. The women were shaking out the floor mats and carpets, the men were polishing the chrome. Other drivers by themselves, in the little cross streets, had opened up their hoods and were looking inside at the motor. The communions of Man, when he's alone, are not with Nature these days, but with his car. Nature and the landscape, so lovely here where the country dwellings have the Tivoli mountains and the valley between the Sabine Hills for a backdrop, suggest no other thoughts to Man than those connected with the mysteriousness of the machines he possesses.

Rome is far away, on the other hand, and sends forth a bellow that echoes only softly here. A curious society is being born in this district. The greater part of the inhabitants are peasants whom the sharecropper reforms have suddenly transformed into city dwellers. They have sold their two and a half acres of land and come to the city to work as porters and gas station attendants. They are contented. They will make their sons study by dint of head-slappings, they will arrange marriages for their daughters, and on Sunday they will continue to collect chicory in the meadows. They will never "seize" Rome, contenting themselves with the heat of her presence.

The houses under construction seem on Sunday as though they have been abandoned. The assistant manager waits for buyers, the watchman's dog barks. A cooperative building is called Virgo Fidelis, the builder is the engineer Rebecchini, son of Rome's former mayor. How everything ossifies in this city! The stucco on many of the houses, scarcely finished, is already starting to flake, to swell up like a biscuit. They have skewed balconies, painted in lively colors.

In these disturbed meadows, then, lives a class of people in the making, which looks at the markers with the names of all these poor writers on them, and asks itself who in the world they could be. They are names that go well with these new streets, without sewage, without anything. But just to be here is already something. For many, the essential thing is to be in the city, to have broken the fetters to life in the country. They find everything lovely and convenient. A brief conversation with a certain man, who confides to me: "Maybe next year I'll put in a telephone."

From Via Ettore Romagnoli you finally wash up in Piazza Pier Luigi Talenti. Perhaps he's also a writer? Whatever the case, he was a relative of the developer who subdivided the lands he owned in this zone into lots. Piazza Pier Luigi Talenti is sunny, high on the hill, the best spot. The air here is fragrant, the sun heats up the homey asphalt, the evaporation gives a trembling look to the fields and shrubs roundabout. Young couples pass by, dressed for a fiesta, holding hands, just as they do in the country. Upon the veranda of a vacant house a woman and her husband appear: the assistant explains where they are on the map and points out the panorama. Plenty of sun. Five-year mortgage.

Peace and quiet, for now. A little airplane renders the silence more agonizing, makes me think of certain mornings on the lakes, of the buzzing of a motorboat. The airplane banks in wide circles, always on the point of stopping in mid-air and of falling without cracking up. A few years ago this was all country here, the only road used to run through the pine groves towards Mentana.

Today the sports reporter of a daily newspaper, writing on the soccer match between Italy and Northern Ireland: "The referee Mitchell, a man as dried out as parchment and with legs like a spastic..." Of course, the reporter was thinking he would give his readers a good laugh, he had a good laugh himself before anyone else. In Rome, in order to offend somebody, or even just to define him, the words currently being used are: *morto di fame* (starveling), *sinistrato* (accident victim), *sfollato* (evacuee), *alluvione* (flood victim). And one can even understand this; the trading upon their misfortunes that is done by so many in this country is such as to arouse the cynicism latent in the hearts of the Romans to fever pitch. It's now become a disease that strikes in early childhood. Vulgarity dulls the heart. In our reporter it is rather a case of moral baseness, which neither compulsory education nor a humane profession have succeeded in curing. We are up against a stolid low-browed cynicism against which there is no means of defense, it is purely gratuitous and in its expressions pretty ignoble. It is the style of the day.

December 8. In Piazza di Spagna, at the foot of the column that commemorates the dogma of the Immaculate Conception, this year, once again, a great tribute of flowers. With a variation: a few of the tributes weren't anonymous, popular or communal. We had floral arrangements sent, with cards, from the following corporations: Sogene, Fiat, Peroni Beer, Molini Pantanella, Snia Viscosa, Autolinee Zeppieri, Palmolive Soaps. A little conversation: the lawyer T. maintains that it offends religious sentiment because the offerings were plainly made for purposes of publicity. The writer A. relates that in his home town the procession on Good Friday is accompanied nowadays with enormous church candles that bear the name of the concern which donated them. Professor N. wonders what the crucial point of advertising will be in the offering of flowers to the Madonna in the next few years. The poet M. recalls D'Annunzio: *"Di sull' agile colonna / la Madonna / benedice / lo spettacolo felice"* ("From upon the slender column / the Madonna / gives her blessing / to the merry show below") and sees the whole thing summed up in this absolution. The journalist P. mentions the prophet Isaiah who, together with Moses, Ezechiel and David, sits at the base of the column and declaims: "Bring no more vain offerings, incense is an abomination to me." They are verses from the first chapter, but no one knows the Book of Isaiah and the conversation languishes.

Rome. I open the afternoon newspapers. What a lot of photographs... The fiancé of the victim taken by surprise as he enters the bathroom. The superintendent of the building where the crime occurred smiles and points to the stairway by which the murderer probably went up. Two sisters of the superintendent's wife and one of their cousins, surprised by the photographer as they emerge from a movie theater, pull up their overcoat collars. The victim's hairdresser smiles on the threshold of his shop, next to the superintendent's wife. The fiancé of the victim comes out of the bathroom covering his face with his hands. The barber who cuts the superintendent's hair, with his youngest son, on a motorcycle. The two daughters of the second man point out the house where the friend of the barber was born and suckled. The presumed lover of the victim comes out of the bathroom smiling. The third man goes into it covering his face. The fifth man's superintendent together with his family on the beach at Ostia. The defense attorney for the presumed murderer in a bombardier's uniform points out the place where he was wounded on the Sabotino. The mayor of the village where the victim was born smiles on the front steps of City Hall. The wife of the mayor at the age of ten, in the costume of a little Italian peasant girl. The mayor's barber leaves the bathroom. He runs into the presumed rival of the third man. Both are wearing dark sunglasses and are pulling up the collars of their pajama tops. The inspector in charge of the investigation gets out of his automobile smiling. The superintendent of the building rides up in his own elevator. The friend of the victim in the company of the sister-in-law of the presumed murderer at the time of the first crime. The presumed murderer enters the bathroom: inside he finds the superintendent, the milkman, the tax collector, the mayor, his wife who in the meantime has given birth to triplets, and the young actress Mora Mari, who will be part of the supporting cast in the movie that's being prepared on the life of the victim. A rare photograph of the victim at the age of six months. The presumed eighth man and the inspector in charge of the investigation smile after the interrogation. The superintendent of the building in a picture taken when he was a year old, on a bearskin rug. The actress Mora Mari, in a bathing suit, on the *terrazza* of the building where the crime occurred, plays with the dog of the super- intendent, who probably saw the murderer. Et cetera.

A people that has eight million photographs of itself cannot die.

An evening with friends spent around Emilio Segrè, the phys- icist who, among other things, conducted the first experi- ments at Oak Ridge with Enrico Fermi and who is in Rome to collect the complete writings of his deceased colleague and put them in order. He is a calm and simple man, a good conversationalist, with a wit you no longer find nowadays, it seems to me. He tells about having read that Salvador Dali, "the self-made publicity clown," among the many who beset the daily papers, had declared that he wanted to dedicate himself to the painting of anti-matter. Segrè immediately wrote him a little letter along the following lines (I quote from memory): "Dear sir, your intention to dedicate yourself to the painting of anti-matter is noble and deserves assistance. Having also dedicated my career to this study, I am taking the liberty to send you two photographs of anti-matter, obtained in our laboratories at the University of California in Berkeley. The anti-matter is that little dot marked with an X. Your most devoted..."

I may have overstressed Professor Segrè's modesty in the telling of this anecdote. But I have no misgivings about it, for it will certainly be of some use to the many painters we have in this Country of ours, almost all of them preoccupied with putting a scientific dressing on their researches.

*   *   *

Evening at the Comet, the lovely little theater where they're putting on two works by Ionesco: *Amadeo* and *The Lesson*. "What does Ionesco do?" writes Sandro De Feo in the program notes. "He brings to the fore the mindless automatism, the inorganic routine, the mechanical lunacy in the utterances of fools."

Well said. He should have added, however, that at the theater the real Ionesco is to be enjoyed during the intermissions. What didn't strike me in Paris—because the theater where Ionesco has been playing for three straight years now is so tiny that the small number of spectators (eighty when the place is packed) have to go out into the street during the intermissions and run to nearby cafés so as not to catch cold—here in Rome proclaimed itself to me in all its gravity. I catch the observations of four bored spectators, talking in loud voices, for at the theater no one is ever ashamed of his opinion: "Where's the moral of the story anyway?" "What is he trying to say?" "Did you see how the wife was crying? Poor little thing." "It's the theater of the absurd." "It's futurism making a comeback." "It seems like a lunatic wrote it. I'm not ashamed to say that I didn't understand a thing." "But what's there to understand?" "Signora, your gloves." "Oh thanks, I'm always forgetting them wherever I go." "Shall we have a coffee?" "If I have a cup of coffee now I'll never go to sleep." "Me, I'm just the opposite. If I don't have one, I'll stay awake all night. It's the pressure I'm under." "I can drink coffee whenever I want, but then before I go to bed, one sleeping pill and everything's just fine." "A sleeping pill? Me? Without a second thought, but I don't like to." "Who is this Ionesco anyhow?" "He must be the guy who owns that building in Paris for something about culture." "No, no, that's the Unesco Building." "Well, you certainly have to admit I was close." And so on.

I find it amusing reading the new traffic code, which in certain passages seems like a book of homilies for good little children.

Sometimes the "provision of the law" runs to grandfatherly and loving counsel, and is quite moving. For example, Article 15: "Drivers approaching an intersection must use all possible prudence to avoid having accidents." How true! It would also be a fine act of prudence for drivers to see to it they are wearing warm clothes when the weather's cold. Further on I find these lines, inspired by John Stuart Mill, on the freedom of cyclists (Art. 128): "Cyclists ought to keep their arms and hands free and guide the handle bars with at least one hand." I would have added: and to pedal with at least one foot, just to establish a precedent. On the same page I'm struck by a passage inscribed to the Dioscuri: "Every untamed or dangerous animal must have at least one driver." Naked, as in the paintings of De Chirico? Perhaps it should have been more explicit; but the image is there, distinct. But where the prose of the lawmakers becomes exalted, taking on the style of the more recent Italian classics (I'm thinking of Fucini, I'm thinking of the D'Annunzio of *I pastori*) with an agrestic and desolate feeling that pervades and illuminates the picture, is in Art. 131: "Herds, flocks and all other multitudes of beasts ... may not be left to roam the streets, and at night they must be preceded by a guardian who casts a white light before him, and be followed by another guardian who casts a red light behind him."

You already see the scene: they are going to the Maremma! And I'm not with my shepherds!

I have returned to our lovely Italy after six years, I had been away since March of ... What am I to say to you, dearest friend? Everything here seems to have become simpler with the advent of the radio-television State, which replaces the old "system." You will probably want to know what I mean by the radio-television State. Briefly, I mean this: the State (the one before this) knew it was little loved, that it was tottering, that it was in a precarious way, until it realized that it possessed a force that rendered it absolutely necessary, not exactly as the source of order and well-being, but of entertainment. Today, with the new system, which is developing this force to the full, it is the State that regulates the leisure of the Nation, after having tried in vain to regulate work, upon which it is based.

By leisure I mean pleasures, naturally. Our waking hours, our collective likes and dislikes, but above all our recreative ambitions, the infinite artistic tendencies and the infinite artistic capacity of our Nation—they needed to be given direction, and the State took this task upon itself, with superb results. The faith of the dissolute was languishing, it is renewed today. Our disorder left much to be desired; today chaos is not improbable. Do you follow me? It is through the good offices of the new hedonistic State that today, for example, our production of songs (1 million metric tons in '58) has risen to 6.3. And that the *Official Gazette* (every issue sells like hotcakes) is stamped upon the records made by all the best singers. Thought has already been given to substituting a dance tune for the National Anthem. And I, ought I to be frank? ... even I write songs, as do all the foremost men of letters, down here.

Today—and this is the new thing, the point that I beg you to ponder—it is the State that regulates and distributes popularity, success, fame. There isn't a person here desirous of making a reputation for himself, in whatever field, who can possibly do it without State support. Politicians, industrialists, sportsmen, artists and writers, even philosophers, and let's not even mention actors—they all know that as far as popularity is concerned, the finish line is State Television. Therefore, getting there is what counts! And when they succeed— even if they then say things they would be ashamed to put in writing, or simply to repeat at table, among friends—behold! they feel themselves (and they really are) admired, followed, envied. The people speak of nothing else, when they aren't singing. That is: the time they don't spend in front of television sets, they spend commenting on what they've looked at.

It is "full intellectual employment," the tool of Utopian sociologists, the sorrow of dictators, and we have arrived here
without the slightest effort. How can our hearts not beat faster
before these rosiest of prospects? How can we fail to feel an
upsurge of pride before the spectacle of a Nation which, for
the first time in its history, is united in admiration for its most
illustrious men, mindful that the State can always create new
ones, in accordance with demand?

Everything, dearest friend, is being accomplished by means
of television, down here. Even public education, which used
to leave so much to be desired, has now acquired considerable appeal, so much so that it is almost impossible to tear our
children away from their homework, which is performed with
the aid of a machine based on a simple electronic principle,
and patented under the name Flipper. Places without schools
are being furnished with these machines and the fight against
illiteracy is thus being carried to its very roots. The majority
of illiterates will then be given jobs in television schools, and
even some few in the universities. If you add the number of
illiterates installed in the ministries after the reform of the
bureaucracy and the abolition of Italian (Latin had already
been abolished in '60) you can see that the scores are changing and Italy is now in second place, right behind Sweden.
Check the statistics, if you don't believe me.

Certainly, returning here after a six years' absence, our country gives an impression of serene felicity, of recreative fervor,
it seems like one big bird-cage or, if you prefer, a monkey-
house. Everyone is rabidly having fun, boredom is unknown.
This just goes to show you, my old and incurable pessimist,
how the apocalyptic prophecies of writers like Orwell or Huxley regarding the modern State (which will end up by co-
opting the deepest aspirations of those in its charge) may be
impugned by a grave generic prejudice. Those prophecies
were formulated—and do you remember how much they dis-

turbed us?—without taking account of the egregious characters of various peoples, which rather evolve, each of them,
according to their own natures. Orwell and Huxley, both Englishmen, projected the dourness of the Anglo-Saxon people
into their prophecies, they foresaw a dictatorial workers'
State, regulator of every expression of will, stifler of every
liberty, pyramid-shaped, gloomy, without a single glimmer of
hope. Now take our people: you can see that with us these
prophecies cease to be valid, indeed their authors' reasoning
is stood on its head. For, actually, it isn't the State that will
dominate the underlying population, but the entire Nation
that will express a State after its own image. Our future State,
not being able to combat ideas (which won't any longer exist) nor to repress the collective or individual will (of which
there shall cease to be any) will have to confine itself to
regulating and channelling our Apollonian inclinations toward
song, toward art, toward literature and toward sports, reserv-
ing for itself only the control of Popularity. Don't you agree?
But maybe you'd entrust the job to private enterprise? Our
future is then looking as merry as could be: try to imagine an
enormous and perennial Feast of Piedigrotta, with parades of
allegorical floats, amongst which, naturally, will be the chariot
of the State.

Politically, it seems to me a great step forward. Slowly but
surely, the Constitution is becoming reality. I remember how
those noble articles on health care (owed by the State to its
charges) used to make you smile, or those on the protection
of the countryside, likewise entrusted to the State. Wonderful,
today the countryside is so well protected it can't even be
seen. It's hidden behind the new and more solid billboards of
Popularity; or, in localities of outstanding historical and artistic interest, enlivened by a few refineries or cement factories,
as in the case of Naples, of Paestum, of Gaeta, of the charter-
house near Pavia, and of the Sistine Chapel.

As for health care, it has to be the very best possible, seeing that hospitals are no longer built (the ones that go back to the fifth century have been allowed to fall to the ground) but only sports stadiums and movie houses.

Even the cities are being transformed. The building slump is over. The dwellings that the speculators put up during the years of Reconstruction have almost all fallen to pieces and we therefore have this great furor of Re-Reconstrution. A new, timely law prohibits the use of materials that are of any undue solidity, so that every future building slump may be avoided. Nay, the Futurists' motto: "Every generation will have its own house" has already been rendered ridiculous by the slogan of the building associations: *"Anno nuovo, casa nuova"*—"New Year, new house." The fantasizing of architects who continuously add newer and more new embellishments to their old projects is such that today one buys a new house the same way one buys a new car: because it features one more little balcony, or because there are more brass fittings, more lamps, or because it's painted a different color, or because it seems to have a sleeker line.

In this happy climate, abstract art has become State art; yes, she too has been taken over, poor thing. And yet it's only right, for a State that desires to be totalitarian has nothing to fear from the abstractionists and never will, because with them creating never degenerates into polemics and once they banished Man from their compositions altogether, they also banished passion, affection, enthusiasm, and ideals (except those that are decorative), which are all dangerously susceptible of being interpreted in a political key. The hedonistic State proposes the enjoyment of only the purely arabesque.

I add that art also aids tourism, and vice versa: a law allows the qualification of tourist resort only to those communities that institute some sort of prize or other. For the literati, for painters, for actors, it is a Bengodi, an earthly paradise. Think about it: there are tourist resorts that in addition to having no tourists have neither a public water supply nor a decent school, neither a hotel nor a local library not to speak of a rest-home for the elderly and retired midwives. Well, never mind, these places have all established their own prizes. Once summer comes along there's nothing for our artists to do except make the rounds of these small towns. Whoever arrives late gets a consolation prize. This year, every writer received two and one half prizes. Objects of gold weighing one kilogram are exclusively given to actors (who comprise twenty per cent of the population), provided that they make themselves seen, or that they sing, or that they remain quiet. One certainly cannot believe that they receive prizes for their interpretations! As for artists, they are in the embarassing predicament of having a choice, and this explains why it is so hard, today, to find someone to come and put a handful of plaster on your walls or repaint your doors. Blame it on Art. She has called them all.

The cinema? Oh, it's doing extremely well. These days they're turning out only one kind of film, historical and in Technicolor, which has allowed production "on demand." It works this way: whoever wants to make an historical film, in Technicolor, applies on letterhead stationery to the entertainments agency, providing a few details from the story: the name of the tyrant, the name of the rebel, the degree of kinship between the woman loved by the rebel and the tyrant, the place where the big feast takes place (royal palace, castle, park?), the length of the siege, the setting where the duel between tyrant and rebel takes place. This merely to prevent two or more films from being made on the same historical episode, as has, unfortunately, already occurred. Occasionally instead of rebels you get the Christians, a sect that flourished during the early centuries of the Roman Empire. In this case there is a second application to be submitted, this time to the agency that rules on accidents occurring in the leisure-place, on account of the torture scene, where the Christians get torn apart (by pagans), burned alive, or handed over to wild beasts for supper, not without some risk to the wild beasts. These films have an instructive and moral value, but also, by God! a recreational value, assured by the presence of semi-nude women: slaves, maidservants, poetesses, models, courtesans, queens, female rivals for the throne. Actresses are chosen straight from television and, because they've already made a name for themselves, it is sufficient that they know how to express two or three elementary feelings: boredom, happiness, indifference and, above all else, surprise, which is the salt of their interpretations. (For example: the surprise of the queen when she discovers that the man she is in love with is the rebel.) Novice actresses express more surprise finding themselves in front of the camera lens; but, with time, they all get used to it and, if interviewed, almost always declare they want to dedicate themselves to the theater too, where they want to play Ophelia, Joan of Arc, Antigone: and often they do, thanks to the agency in charge of theater.

In short, dear friend, here one never goes to sleep.

A man gets shot to death on the street. A reporter races to the victim's home, where no one yet knows about the event, and he writes: "The wife answers the door, a woman in her thirties, still attractive . . ."
The same reporter goes to Novi and meets the wife of the late bicycle champion Coppi: "Signora Bruna, enfolded lady-like in her grief, at first sight inspires a reverential respect . . ."

Worth noting here is the difference in the reporter's attitudes before the two women struck by fate in the same way. Signora Bruna, wife of the National Hero, comes across as the statue of grief—"enfolded lady-like" therein—, deserving of an unconditional respect—"at first sight." The wife of the man killed on the street, an uninformed widow, is instead a homey woman, who can even inspire erotic reveries, and in fact the reporter's first impression of her is of "a woman in her thirties, still attractive." Maybe, who can tell, once they get to know each other . . . Whoever is amazed by the huge acting success of Alberto Sordi, who has for years now been playing the same character over and over, should bear in mind that Sordi represents a certain brand of young Italian that is rather vile, indolent, accomodating and conformist. Picture him, for example, in the role of this same reporter: perfect. Sordi well expresses the philosophy of the possible, which in our country is the only philosophy the young are acquainted with, through an animal instinct that makes them audacious with the weak, respectful with the strong, seducers in all other cases. His success then is the fruit of an identification.

I am on my way to Montreux. I have an hour to wait for my connection, and I begin wandering about the station, which looks virtually abandoned. In the waiting room, between the vending machines offering chocolate and cigarettes, there's a barrel organ that runs on perforated steel plates, with little monkeys dressed like clowns, ready to ring their little bells. The repertory is from the last century: an aria from *Boccaccio*, *The Blue Danube*, *La Bella Elena*, a number of military marches, an aria from *Rigoletto*, etc. I put a coin in and choose *The Skaters* by Waldteufel. A railroad man passes through the deserted waiting room and nods to me in greeting. A little later I go out, buy a couple of newspapers, and sit at a table in a café. On a trip, the reading of newspapers always has something detached about it, without obligation, which is in tune with the temporary abandonment of our daily routines and makes us prone to indifference. But I also have the Italian newspapers with me and the comparison between them and the little Swiss papers . . . it's inevitable. Provincial Switzerland's little newspapers have a quality of seriousness that enchants me, the dry bulletin-like tone that goes back to the time when newspapers were meant to be read by men, to be gone through at the café or at the club; and the cafés and clubs kept their newspapers at the disposal of their clientele, clipped within long wooden sticks. The words, the headlines still have significance and weight, there are very few photographs, the defendants in trials are identified by their initials only, a hunter who accidentally kills a swan, mistaking it for a duck, is defined in the headline as "A perfect imbecile!" Italian newspapers, on the other hand, even in their size, have the look of an alarming provincialism. It's visible just in the way they have of giving people names. For us, B.B. means Brigitte Bardot, Ike means the President of the United States, Philip is the Duke of Edinburgh, K. is Khruschev on those rare occasions he isn't called Nikita, Lolla is the screen actress Gina Lollobrigida, Margaret is the Princess Margaret. We give the impression of being connected to the whole wide world by longstanding friendships. What our actresses are up to is never hidden from us: Silvana takes a walk in long pants, Sofia learns French from records, another Silvana is at loose ends: if you don't know these actresses' last names, so much the worse for you. But we are even on a confidential footing with foreign actresses: Ava, Anita, Shirley, we're acquainted with the lives and miracles of each, and today a telephoto (via special service) shows us the perfect image of an American actress as she's leaving a Los Angeles clinic where she has just recovered from some sort of liver trouble. We always want to be present in cases like this. In compensation, our foreign correspondents are forever concerned that in London the English may not know how to have a good time, that in Paris Italian comedies be successful, and that the civilization of pizza and espresso finally penetrate Australia. In the political commentaries the situation is always obscure, the turn of events always dangerous, the clarification always necessary, the agreement always auspicious, the Pontiff's statement always sounds a warning, detente must not mean a lessening of vigilance, and lessons are being drawn from recent history. The daily chronicle succumbs to the same rhetoric: a boundless love for metaphor dictates headlines like this: "EVEN THE SIRENS OF CAPRI IN THE GRIP OF FROST" or: "OPERATION WINTER IN FULL SWING". And all that just to say it's cold outside. A trial that is taking place in Geneva, and which is being reported as an important trial, in the Italian press becomes the TRIAL OF THE CENTURY, the trial that will shake the Swiss bourgeoisie to its very foundations. Let's not even talk about the sports reporting, one no longer finds out who wins or loses, but they inform us that Sampdoria is at its last gasp, that Milan is still alive, that Fiorentina is setting the pace, that Spal isn't fantastic, that the championship could use a little oxygen, and other amenities of that sort. Some time ago in a Roman newspaper I even read: "SCIALBA PROOF OF DIVINE LOVE." The team was beaten by a score of two to nothing.

On the train that is taking me towards the Bernese Oberland I find a little local paper left there by another traveler. It comes out twice a week, in a hamlet of about three thousand inhabitants. It would be worth going to the trouble of copying the whole thing out, for it is a real lesson in journalism. The trial in Geneva is relegated to one column on the third page under the title heading "Billet genevois". The editor begins by excusing himself for having to talk about a trial before the verdict is in, he then summarizes the facts of the case in three lines and concludes that Article 112 of the Penal Code provides life imprisonment for the accused, should he be found guilty. On the front page, the article in the very middle is about "Switzerland and the Emancipation of Black People." Reactionary? Nothing of the sort. The columnist affirms that Switzerland has no racial prejudices. "Fédéraliste, respectant les convictions, la Suisse tend une main fraternelle aux nations de couleur qui accedent à l'indépendance ..."* And further on: "N'ayant jamais eu de vues colonialistes ou d'ambitions territoriales (à part la Valteline, et ce fut un échec), la Suisse est à l'aise, pour traiter avec les pays frais émoulus ..."† And it ends with: "Si les peuples de couleur ne

---

* "Federalist, respectful of beliefs, Switzerland extends a fraternal hand to the colored nations which achieve independence ..."
† "Having never had colonialist designs or territorial ambitions (save in connection with the Valtelina, where they ended in failure) Swit-

se jettent pas immédiatement sur les livres des auteurs suisses, s'ils n'envahissent pas avant quelques temps du moins nos champs de ski, ils seront intéressés par ce que nos industries sauront opportunément leur proposer, ainsi que par nos institutions politiques et culturelles et nos hautes écoles nationales."* A conclusion that mixes faith and irony in doses reminiscent of the good old days.

World politics, in the same paper, are summarized in a one-column *tour d'horizon*. The last page is given over to small local advertisements. For the most part, first class bulls of good milk-producing ancestry are being offered out to stud at rates ranging from fifteen to thirty francs, in accordance with the prizes the bull has won at the cantonal fairs. A certain Paquier invites the citizenry to come and have a look at the plans before he starts building the new fence he intends to put up around his property. No law obliges him to do so, it is simply an act of courtesy on his part. A few words are devoted to the cutting down of three chestnut trees, which has occurred in a square in the Carouge section of Geneva. They were already dead, a danger to pedestrians, a few branches had already fallen off under the weight of the snow. The municipal administration responds to the citizenry's outcry over this "butchery," promising the immediate replacement of the felled trees by some other young trees, probably sycamores. For me, coming from Rome, where about six hundred stout trees have been cut down in a single month to make room for automobiles and more probably because of our administra-

---

zerland is in a comfortable position to deal with the freshly emerged nations . . ."

* "While the colored peoples may not throw themselves at once upon the books of Swiss authors, while it may be at least some time before they invade our skiing slopes, they will be interested in what our industries may in due course propose to them, as well as in our political and cultural institutions and our professional graduate schools."

tors' imbecility, the news has its peculiar import and causes a great sadness to come over me. Dear Switzerland, where they still sell Cavour cigars, "les petits cigares d'un grand homme," Bersagliere cigars and Garibaldi cigars, and where on Sunday, in front of the lake, the town band plays a selection of old and forgotten Italian tunes.

I almost forgot: in the same paper, at the foot of the page, there's a note from the editor-in-chief: "Pensez aux petits oiseaux."

A pistol shot fired at the right moment forestalls all painful discussions. However, the problem is still unresolved: whom to shoot at? At oneself or at one's interlocutor? When in doubt, abstain. But then don't come complaining that all discussions are useless.

Reading is nothing, the difficult thing is to forget what one has read. And these days it's no longer the authors driving us away from their books, but their readers.

An ailing python escapes from the little equestrian circus in which he used to perform in the evening together with other beasts. This happened a month ago in Rome. The python at last makes its way to a garden on the periphery. Normally, it would be able to eat a few chickens, a rabbit, but there's something seriously the matter with its stomach and it isn't hungry: it goes to sleep on top of a wall. Here it's discovered by the horrified crowd; and they decide to kill it, but no one dares. A few policemen respond to an urgent summons. How does one kill a python? Call the fire department? Call the S.P.C.A.? Kill it in a dignified way, like hunters? Afraid of missing it with a rifle shot, they pour a bucket of naphtha over it and toss on a few flaming rags. The python wakes up in time to die amidst the flames. I cannot help being moved whenever I think about this poor snake who after a wandering life as an actor, gets mistaken for a perilous dragon, and is killed in a purificatory rite. In this country it isn't even easy to be a snake.

A certain unemployed man threatens to throw himself off the top of the Colosseum unless they immediately give him a job and let him talk to the Mayor. He gets his wish and they bring him around to City Hall. The brief conversation unfolds like this: "Very well, young man, what exactly can you do?" "Anything, Mr. Mayor." "I understand. What you're saying is that you want a position as a guard. As of this moment you are a temporary guard of the Colosseum, for which you seem to nourish such fondness." The young man thanks him, begins working the same day. One year later, while making his rounds above the tiers of the amphitheater, he loses his footing, falls from twenty meters up, and ... dies? No, he remains suspended in mid-air, waiting for his hiring to become official. Thus they have all the time in the world to save him. All this because I am loath to say anything bad about our bureaucracy.

The professor receives me sitting down at his writing desk, where he pretends to be checking his appointment book. Then he speaks into a dictaphone. He is a sturdy man, happy and lively. His writing desk resembles that of a movie producer: very spacious, covered with a sheet of glass and a display of objects not meant for use: everything is leather-covered except the lampshade, which is covered with silk. "Sit down, Signor Pagliano," the professor says to me kindly, "sit down." Pagliano? But why Pagliano? (It could be that he's just been thinking about that brand of cough syrup.) Already despondent, I sit down, mentally reviewing all the various manglings of my surname: Fagliano, Floviano, Fagiano, Fragano. This doubtless is the way a language evolves, by way of the different interpretations of its vocables, otherwise Caesar Augusta would never have become Saragossa. Very well, the professor stares at me in silence, as if conducting a little exercise in friendly hypnotism; he wants to constrain me to lower my eyes. I have witnessed a scene like this before, but where? Finally, he speaks: he realizes that I am not the common, everyday sort of visitor, he's addressing himself to a person capable of understanding him. He says that we are all, each and every one of us, potentially sick, even he is potentially a sick person. It breaks his heart to think of all the potentially sick people there are in the world who are walking around, laughing and joking, eating and drinking and making love. He, for example, recognizes, he is able to "feel" the sick a mile away; and it is not to be imagined how many people are wandering around wholly unaware of their sickness. I nod, pensive. But where have I heard something like this before? The professor stares at me, sighing.

The telephone interrupts this first scene. On the phone the professor goes on in a clear voice, unconcerned about my presence, he talks about a great scheme for a clinic that his heart is set on establishing in his hometown. There he will try to involve the local doctors so that they won't shrink from helping him, because, he adds, through this project of his he would be head of the entire region. This makes me think back to my own hometown. In it there was once a doctor whom everyone venerated because he spent most of his time caring for poor people; and there was another doctor—by chance he was a cousin of mine—who was only interested in treating the rich. But all that was a long time ago. The good doctor who would spend the night at the bedside of a sick patient, waiting for the crisis to be resolved with the dawn, has lived on in the mythological tales of our grandmothers. The good doctor who used to accept a cup of coffee and who spoke with the sick person about other things than his sickness, to keep his spirits up, has been reduced to a figure of ridicule by antibiotics, by industry, by medical aid centers, by the hurry we are all in, by specialists, by surgeons, and above all by our own desire to be

sick, or our not wanting to feel that we're well, so that we can
flee from the responsibilities of a world that has nothing else
to offer us.

Now the professor addresses himself to me: "I've read your
books, Signor Pagliano, I'm acquainted with what you do, my
compliments. Now then, Pagliano, tell me what's wrong." I
look at him without answering, tempted to laugh. The fact
that he insists upon calling me Pagliano instills in me,
strangely, the certainty that I am indeed someone else and
that I am feeling fine. My only wish now is to go away. Nevertheless, out of timidity, I make an allusion to an ordinary
check-up. "A Complete Physical Check-up," the professor
says, narrowing his eyes, as if tensing before the immensity of
what he's proposing. His behavior changes. From this moment
on I am a lost man, he treats me with the deference he might
bestow upon an object that he must take care not to break
while moving it from one house to another. So there I am, in
another room now, stretched out on a little bed, alone and
half naked. A nurse enters, looks at me and says: "It's raining."
She's a sad and plain little nurse, who flaws the sacredness of
the ceremony, intrudes all her sentimental worries into it. I
spend a quarter of an hour this way. Is this solitude part of the
ceremony too? The patient must be left alone with his appre-
hensions, in anticipation of a ritual of high technology? The
lighting fixture overhead is inlaid with polished aluminum
and casts back my deformed reflection. The little bed is cold,
the rain clatters in the courtyard. Our times are under the sign
of Kafka. Kafka was a sick genius, and he offered his anxieties
to healthy men so that they could take advantage of them; the
same way young Werther instituted "modern" suicide, the
pure refusal of existence, within the range of every pocket-
book. Ah, give me a victorious hero, give me Hercules, who
snatches Alcestis from the clutches of death by main force
alone. Give me the Pickwick Circus!

Nothing. The room is unheated, poorly lit, from above.
Darkness at noon, political guilt, the guilt of being free men.

We are being readied for the entrance of the police officer who would like to make us confess everything, and I think it would be pointless to prolong the torture by adhering strictly to the truth, I would have to admit every hypothesis they suggested to me. "You are not a healthy man, you are a sick traitor." "I am ready to sign the paper." But the police officer is in no hurry. The professor enters with his assistants. They decipher my heartbeats, a long strip of paper that they all scrutinize in silence and with a touch of skepticism. Another assistant comes in to take a little blood from me. To get me to open and close my hand, so as to cause the vein in my arm to swell, he comes out with an oft-repeated joke: "Make *ciao* to the professor." I make "*ciao*," meanwhile thinking that I too am making my little offering on the altar of Mass Persuasion, the only divinity they worship nowadays. I must have a look of provocation about me, because my results are all normal, indicating imaginary health. The professor becomes serious. He observes me at length, he auscultates me and taps me with icy fingertips and hammers. Nothing. He persists. knoc . . . knoc . . . kafc . . . kafca . . Kafka! No, not Kafka, Doctor Knock! *Knock, ou le triomphe de la medicine.* Act III, scene VI: "Ce que je n'aime pas, c'est que la santé prenne des airs de provocation . . ."*

The lazy writer was asleep. The main character in the story he was writing at the moment his dreams took possession of him jumped out of the last chapter and began to rummage through the novels on the bookshelf. "Damn!" he was thinking, "everyone here is having a good time, they're all traveling, talking, getting drunk, they have strange tendencies, they're constantly making love. And me? And me?" The lazy writer woke up and said: "If those are all the things you want to do, do them in the wastepaper basket." And he tore up the pages he had written. And since his character was crying and

---

* "What I dislike is that defiant air health takes on . . ."

wouldn't stop, before going back to sleep he said: "Cry, cry if it makes you feel any better, cry."

We are lacking not only in ideas but also in emotions. Pale fantasies form themselves in our minds, and not a single breath stirs them, swells them, makes them come to life. We're growing accustomed to everything. That which happens is as much as we can repeat, nothing else is of use to us.

"Excuse me, Signore, do you know what time the American satellite passes by?"

"It should already be here, it's eight-thirty."

From the darkness of the garden, a woman's impatient voice: "Mario, has it gone by yet?"

"No, but this gentleman says it should be here right now."

"Maybe it's late. The soup's on the table, are you coming?"

"And what if a shadow got in front of its nose cone?"

"That's possible, but then there's always the one at ten o'clock."

"Buonasera, Signore."

"Buonasera."

Next door to us, in the garden of the *pensione*, the little girls get together every morning. We never see their parents, only at times a few mothers, still young, who come in licking ice-cream cones and shouting: "Simonetta, Patrizia, Barbara!" And a few dogs, of the high-class sort, bored stiff, that emit weak barks, producing a "Bu" (exactly as it's written) at regular intervals, and that have no appeal whatever. The fathers of the girls are far away, at work or on other adventures. We observe the girls: they all have bold eyes, not one of them has reached the age of fifteen but each knows how to make herself the center of attention in a society that is going in quest of its lost instincts. They are the "nymphettes"; I dislike this word, because the associations it brings in its wake have made it detestable; but, just so we understand one another, allow me to use it. Freakishly attired, with tight-fitting shorts, or doll's dresses, make-up cunningly applied, a little radio in their hands, and big purses. For a few days now they haven't known what to do with themselves; the weather has been threatening, the tops of the pines are swaying in the wind, you can't go to the beach, everyone has to stay in the garden. They arrive one by one, yawning, pretending not to know each other, and they sit down, speaking in monosyllables, and even these they pronounce without enthusiasm. (Not a single boy in sight owing to the exams, and the forty-year-olds with their grizzled temples are all in the city.) They don't talk, rather they enunciate their own special syllabary. Beh, bah, bo. "Beh" expresses an inclination to do something, to get up and move; "bah" expresses mistrust in the idea; "bo" indifference. They have no need to say anything else, they are all still sleepy.

Later they decide to play cards. They play six-and-a-half for a hundred lire a point. Someone grows tired of it and takes a piece of knitting out of her purse. It's the signal for the end of the game. The cards are lying on the table and everyone is working on her knitting. They pass the time this way while waiting for lunch, confabulating and laughing, with sudden long silences lacking weight. All told, they give the impression of having skipped over an age and of already being the mothers of themselves, disappointed in a life that has rendered them responsible, remembering sorrowfully their happy adolescence, which opened like a curtain on all their ambitions, and on many legitimate curiosities.

After the passing of Coppi and of Buscaglione, Mario Riva's death, in such a drawn-out and dramatic way, has had an impact on everyone and has been the most productive literary pretext of the year, the inspiration for an infinite number of articles, recollections, biographies, memoirs and testimonials. One could hardly do better. Accustomed as we are to severe and frugal eulogies, usually reserved for men of culture, for scientists and artists, we would have to be astonished by this tidal wave of sentiment were it not for the fact that, in the death and departure of this personality—and, in general, in the death and departure of all those like him—the crowd for an instant perceives its own end, without light, and can't help being dismayed by it.

The death of a Mario Riva casts more doubts upon the immortality of the soul than does the death of an Einstein, of a Benedetto Croce, of a Thomas Mann, who continue to live in their works and in their ideas; indeed, their deaths seem to clarify these other things and to render them eternal. There is something here to be anxious about indeed: with the sudden oblivion that follows upon the demise of the likes of us a few anecdotes may survive, just barely and with time ever more faintly, until they become unintelligible. What then is our fate? We glimpse the end of an ideal of daily consumption, this kind of provisional Piedigrotta that we have managed to cobble together to console ourselves at the edge of the void, and suddenly a bell tolls for everyone and does not feed our excessive hopes, because it announces at the same time the death of our thoughtlessness. And the crowd? The crowd quickly consoles itself, it readily forgets, more readily than it is affected.

"He was one of us," it will say in the end. "We loved him because of this and above all because he wasn't a genius and in reality didn't have one single merit, except for those which we, with assiduous attention, bestowed upon him ourselves; that is, the merits not of his but of *our* popularity."

For, in its mythomania, the Crowd today only worships itself. It wants a Hero, but from him asks for a guarantee of absolute mediocrity. Hercules doesn't have to exert himself, nor does he have to prevail. Take a crowd and give it a toss, when it falls it will be in a circle, in order to worship whoever has landed in the center and who ipso facto represents it. Or it will settle down into a pyramid, acclaiming whomever chance has placed at its top. I know a certain man, the usual honest soul, above suspicion, who has his own idol, a gloomy bicycle-racer. While on a trip connected with his business (which he conducts with such prudence) he happens to be in a restaurant and finds his hero sitting at the next table. He became dizzy from emotion. He confesses: "I was very hungry, but I wasn't able to touch one bite of food."

Now, take this same man, in every way so similar to us, a good father and family man, and every day for two or three years have him come across your picture in the newspaper and in the magazines he buys. You also appear regularly on television. At first he will be contemptuous of you; but in the end, when your person and your existence have been illustrated day after day and become exemplary, he will come to the station to meet you, he will throw himself at your feet, ready to do your bidding. In fact, it is this same man who is going to the airport to welcome the movie star and who will risk being crushed by the crowd just in order to touch the hem of her dress. He is the same man who smiles in the photographs, staring at the lens, struck by a lightning bolt of superhuman happiness, which is the reward of his misery, gladly accepted because only in this way does he feel his existence is justified within the common nothingness. Were he a little more thoroughly acquainted with his movie star or with his hero, perhaps he would become contemptuous of them. It's distance alone that inflames him, because the enthusiasm of his species makes him live in blind adoration of things that are kept at a remove from him, but that are constantly extolled.

On the long dark avenue voices and pistol shots issue from the outdoor theater and spread out in the night air. They are the voices of a waning summer, the voices of an existence that blends with our own, bringing back the memory of other summers. Driver, follow that car. Have another whiskey? If I were in your shoes, Jim, I wouldn't do it. I didn't expect you back so soon. It's ridiculous, I know, but I'm in love. You will die with the rising of the new moon. By the boots of Bacchus, bring in a bottle of Falerian. Don't move, someone is watching us . . .

A few more pistol shots. A swollen moon, promising nothing good, grazes the treetops. From far away come the rhythmed sounds of a jazz orchestra, the languid drum-beats and the sudden trumpets of the equatorial forest. In every jazz orchestra, now that I think of it, there is a musician with a discordant and pensive face, a long chin, sunken cheeks, glasses; a musician who in every way looks like an intrusion into that simulated hurly-burly. Every so often, with a start, he exhibits happiness, but his happiness is always out of tune, has something faintly chilling about it. He attempts to imitate his companions, but is soon distracted. Then he resumes playing diligently and looks at the audience with that face of his of a decadent professor, or else he polishes his eyeglasses.

Piazza del Popolo. A motor coach comes to a stop, forty tourists get out and, without wasting any time, sighting through their view-finders like a party of sappers, they photograph the piazza and climb back into the motor coach, which starts off on its way again. The tourist is a privileged being, who is never hurt by what he sees, by the sight of people above all, the people who go on living in the places that he takes pictures of, who often spend their entire lives penetrating into the mystery of the place. The tourist collects documents that will prove he has travelled, but it would be only too easy to prove to him that he has never moved.

A hobo came up to me and asked me for a loan "because he had to have something to drink." He had a cold. He had caught this cold, he said, from sleeping indoors, in a room, instead of under the bridges. He wanted to entertain us with his paradoxes and kept starting all over again from the top: "If I sleep out in the open I don't catch cold, but I have to keep my strength up with a little wine." And he flung out his arms.

A few days later I encountered a modern beggar. He was young and sly-looking. He was wearing a mechanic's blue overalls, fresh from the laundry, with the air of a person full of health, self-assured. He had me look at a certificate from the prison he had just got out of, which he kept in a cellophane envelope so that it wouldn't get spoiled. And with the gleam in his eyes of a scoundrel, who even seeks the complicity of irony, he said: "Help me re-make my place in society."

The Roman beggar I met this morning is also dressed like a working man, but he recites his lines poorly. He pretends to be lost in the neighborhood, which is new to him. He doesn't know how to get back home, he's in trouble, he'll have to take a bus and two streetcars. He's ashamed to ask a stranger for help, but couldn't I lend him two or three hundred lire until tomorrow. He has a tool kit under his arm. He points to it, says: "You want to see?" Later, I see him again and he's making the same request of another passer-by.

In the end, what we're asking for from a modern beggar is a little performance in dialect. The poor man insists on putting out his hand, calling down divine recognition upon the head of his benefactor; he himself no longer has a future. Whoever wants to get a "loan" these days has to justify it with at least a modicum of imagination.

1963

"This is how I imagine hell," R. was saying to me. "A place where sinners continuously and forever repeat the things that they were particularly fond of on earth and which were the cause of their damnation. Example: the lustful will experience all the horrors and disgusts of eternal copulation, the violent sinnner will repeat his violent acts, incessantly but to no purpose, the glutton will have to devour repugnant mountains of food all by himself, along with his own vomit, the traitor will keep on betraying, forever, even himself, the wrathful . . ."

"Enough," I say, "you're describing life itself."

Conclusion of interview. "Do you believe that television has lowered the cultural level of the public?" "No, I believe that television has lowered the cultural level of the intellectuals." "If you had to define the drama of modern life in a few words—?" "The drama of modern life is this: everyone is looking for peace and solitude. And for the very reason that they're all looking for these two things, they drive them from the very places where they can be found." "And now an indiscreet question: why is it that you write so little?" "My dear sir, I do not have a vocation for narrative. I write, which is something altogether different."

Italians don't love nature because they themselves "are" in nature. This was the starting point of a conversation with L., in a fishermen's trattoria near the mouth of the Arrone. We were lamenting the fact that those same fishermen who frequented the trattoria had transformed the beach into a flattened wasteland, burnt, pulverized, destroying all forty-seven species of plant-life that comprise the Mediterranean maquis and which are interdependent (that is, each one helps the others to live). We remembered together a landscape that was once Arcadian and solemn, just right for a landing by Aeneas, thick with tamarisks, with cardoons, with wild cherry trees, junipers ... shaggy green thickets that protected the young holm oaks from the salt, which in their turn protected the old pines of the forest. The woodlands that stretched down to the shore, with their needles, their purple flowers, their stout outbranchings, and which moulded sand dunes that were every year more imposing and impassable, upon which neither the southwesterlies nor the northwesterlies could make any impression, have now all disappeared. Whenever a car passes by nowadays it raises up a cloud of dust. We asked ourselves then how it could be that the fishermen (who certainly know the sea and the winds) hadn't understood the necessity of saving that vegetable hierarchy established by nature, which defended their houses and tempered their climate. Well, the answer is the one we've already given. The "poor" Italian is impassive before a landscape, that is, he doesn't see it as a harmonious and intangible thing (inspirer of various emotions and keep of memory, if you like) but he dismantles it for its separate utilitarian elements. Whatever is of use to him, he takes, the rest he destroys. He acts, in other words, like a being so thoroughly inserted into nature as not to have the capacity to admire it, but only to make it serve his needs. In certain respects, the poor Italian is a rodent. But the "rich" Italian is perhaps something worse. The "rich man" understands the landscape as an adornment for the things he owns and he even succeeds in dividing it into two categories: representative landscape and serviceable landscape. In order to obtain these two landscapes, which are indispensable to his prestige, the rich man acts the part of a military engineer, he demolishes the sand-dunes that interfere with his view of the sea (which, according to Flaubert, "in him inspires profound thoughts"), he excavates, he fills in, levels, squares, he tears out underbrush and plants trees that don't take root, he erects little walls and fences, embellishes them, he plops his house down next to a palm tree by the shore or thrusts it into the middle of a forest, and there has a tree-trunk to admire that grows up through his living room, from floor to roof; in short, he also modifies the original landscape, which seems un-elegant to him, un-ordered and, above all, un-modern. And wherever he can he spreads a handful of asphalt.

As a conclusion then—and the entire coast of Lazio has become the proof of this drama—whether it's the "poor man" or the "rich man," they both destroy nature: the one because he is a part of it, the other because he wants to make it into his own image and likeness. Can the desolating of certain places continue without becoming unendurable? One is often humiliated by the thought that we are living in a country that is crumbling into ugliness.

The little Swedish girl who saw the flocks of weary quail coming from the sea and alighting in the underbrush to catch their breath knows that an army of hunters is already out looking for them. So she tries to save the lives of those poor migratory birds by rummaging through the bushes with a pole and shouting: "Go away, go away, they're going to kill you!" She demands that her friend get up at night and go with her to warn the quail of the danger that awaits them with the coming of dawn. She doesn't know that the hunters serve to eliminate the weak species indiscriminately. She runs into a hunter and explains to him that he isn't being fair, above all that he isn't being sporting, shooting an animal overcome with exhaustion. The hunter smiles at her, looking at her legs and breasts. Returning home the girl sees a man, a solid, like-able man whom she knows, ferreting between the cabbages in his garden and plucking out two quail. "I'm going to eat them right away," the man says festively. "No, no, no!" cries the distraught girl. The man looks at her uncomprehendingly, makes the timid offer of a gift, thinks better of it, puts the quail into his pouch. Which doesn't at all take away from the fact that the inhabitants of this seaside village are full of virtue, of gentleness, of human kindness, unshakeable in their stubbornness and often the bearers of ancient melancholies.

Brief short story. Giacomo stepped from his car and from his pocket dug out the key to the gate to the courtyard, where the garage was. There he dug another key from his pocket. When he had rolled the shutter down he went back towards the entrance hall: he had to get out another key and fight with the lock, and the glass in the door shook. To get into the elevator door also called for a key, which prevented youngsters from writing dirty words on the wood panelling. Opening the door to his house at present required two keys, this ever since Giacomo had received a visit from burglars. The second lock clicked four times. Giacomo went into his study, opened a drawer in his writing desk with another key, and took out a box. It was of course filled with keys: the residue from other places he had lived, keys to old trunks in the attic, to doors long forgotten, to remote elevators. They all had opened something once upon a time and Giacomo had never dared throw them away from the fear—which keys always inspire in us—that they yet might be of some eventual use or other. Here, exhausted, Giacomo fell to thinking about his future. He formulated two hypotheses. The first of them was full of more keys. Three of these keys were for the villa he wanted to have by the sea; actually, on second thought (gate, front door, service door, garage) there were four—without counting the key to the cellar. Then there was the key to his motorboat (or did it have two keys?) and the key to the cabana. Then he perceived another key ... which would be indispensable . . . the family chapel. However, there was time to think about all that. Right before his eyes, in thin air, there dangled another bunch of keys, genteel ones, tinkling. They were the keys to a *garçonnière* that a friend was willing to cede to him. He hadn't yet made up his mind.

The second hypothesis was keyless. There were no keys to the little hut where he would end his days. In those parts, not only did they not lock doors, but very often they didn't even have doors. Thieves didn't enter houses in those parts because there was nothing to take. Even he, Giacomo, was poor. Just as when he had been a boy, in the pockets of his pants he would have only a soiled handkerchief, a rubber band, and a seashell. Sometimes, to amuse himself, he would go to the the nearby town and loiter about the ruins.

Cheered by this second hypothesis, Giacomo opened the liquor cabinet with a little gilded key and poured himself two fingers of cognac.

Yesterday evening, there I was in a movie-house. During the unpleasant wait before the film started the auditorium was dimly lit. And too: just the opposite of theater-goers, the spectators at a movie-house always give you the impression of being ashamed of something, they scatter themselves among the vacant rows and remain sunk down in their seats without turning or getting up. They seem to be brooding over sinister subjects. Many of them peer up at the ceiling.

Meanwhile, slides were being flashed on the screen, advertising beauty salons, furniture stores, dry cleaner's shops, poultry farms. In the film shorts that followed the following subjects were treated with a petulant seriousness: what to put on your hair to make it shine, why it's necessary to opt for certain pots and pans, why the lady of the house is happy doing the dishes, why pure breath enhances romantic activity. Finally, a young family, which I seemed to be personally acquainted with (or are they all the same?) was sitting at table and eating mayonnaise. Then came other young men and girls pursuing each other on a beach, diving into the waves, protected by a cream for their skin. Other young men, in evening dress, were drinking liqueurs. All these idylls came to an end. The young man was looking at the girl and smiling, the girl responded with a smile of acceptance. Probably they were happy.

When the actual film itself started I felt not only tired but disturbed by the idea of not being in my time, of not loving society, of "not being in touch with the younger generation." Were they all my neighbors, these young people who were enunciating axioms on the screen? Was it possible they didn't have anything else to say? Taking on the same guilty and expectant air the other spectators already had, I ruminated upon the suspicion that mass-man cannot hope to separate his entertainment from the sin that is at its origin and therefore determines it: the dissatisfaction with his own state, the desire to escape it through complacent dreams . . . which advertising makes its allies.

At home, I start to read a novel of erotic experiences and a sorrowfulness takes possession of me, like a toothache. It seems as though the author wanted to allude to something that was the purpose of our existence, but didn't know how to go about it. The messenger has forgotten the message and, dismayed, seeks to evoke its cruder meaning, which has remained stamped upon his memory, but the true message won't come out, it refuses to be composed within a single simple word. I throw the book down and take up a little anthology of Greek poets. The feeling of dismay, of impotence, of imprisonment is now mine, the reader's. A thick pane of glass interposes itself between those representations of love over there and "our" love over here. I can see "their" love, but as an object which no longer belongs to me. I would like to be on the other side of the glass . . . but it would take more than that! The having of the beloved object brought happiness then, just as today it brings a certain pleasure, certain anxieties, a certain boredom? What has love become? For a young man today, an experience: a way of acceding to a certain level of experience. But the collectivity does not counsel him to pursue this experience to its very end, it needs to know that the only true love each person experiences is for it alone. It proposes an agreeable derivative: eroticism, which is agreeable to everybody. For the majority of the young, does love, instead of being the the recognition of one's own existence in another being, become a practice, a technique of systemization through which they are inserted one by one into the collectivity? Something which, through being patiently acquired the way a situation or the esteem of one's superiors is, becomes part of the list that includes the other mechanisms and accouterments of our imprisonment? Thus it comes about that the young recognize "their" love in the books they read and in the films they go to see, where love "is made," where love is not a mystery but a gymnosophy and, like all exercises, can lead to boredom and to loneliness.

At certain times it also leads to innocence. This perhaps is why we lean toward distant forms of art, primitive or barbaric, which are still able to suggest, along with the frankness of erotic representation, ideas of a lost purity, of a recoverable— exactly, a recoverable—innocence in man's relationship to nature and to the mysteries that are closely bound to life. What no longer succeeds in moving us in contemporary representations, moves us in those that precede or deny our civilization. The representation of pleasure in the twelfth century Indian temples carries us back to a lost paradise where love didn't make a mystery of its gestures but forthrightly consecrated them in a ritual in which the man and the woman were the priests: it is a representation without fetters and without caste, and I wouldn't be surprised if it has saved a certain number of tourists' souls.

Then there is the professional artist who sees eroticism as a fault from which he can liberate himself by confessing to it.

Like that sinner of Stendhal's, he experiences the pleasure of the sin twice, committing it and relating it to his confessor in its minutest detail. Immersed in life, the artist asserts he is seeking an explanation of existence: these are two different things. He makes me think of the geologist who, having fallen into quicksand, tries to figure out the composition of the stuff that is engulfing him. For the geologist the conclusion is so foregone and so unescapable that he derives a certain grim satisfaction from it.

The movie producer wants to make a film out of an eighteenth century comedy. The public seems disoriented and needs to be given something solid, stable, well-constructed, without any new waves to it, but . . . naturally . . . in such a way that the end result is a little—even very, in any case, sufficiently—sexy. The director and the actors will take care of the rest, but first it's necessary to come up with a large number of risqué situations, to shift a few scenes from the dining room to the bedroom . . . do we understand one another? A long silence, then F., shaking his head: "It's not possible," he says, "unless you set the whole thing in our own times, I don't think it will work. Sex . . . yes, the *sexy*," and he smiles, "is a commemorative activity that requires a strip-tease of our own clothes, of those that we ourselves wear, not of those our ancestors wore." The producer looks at him with a thoughtful expression on his face. "Yes," adds F., "the costumes of another era act upon the movie-goer like an inhibiting memory, like a brake, a block . . ." The producer bats his eyelashes. "Yes," insists F., "these costumes remind us of our dead, of our grandparents, and we don't like to see our grandparents in scabrous situations. We feel a certain respect for . . ." Another silence. "Okay," F. concludes, rising, "we can telephone somebody, I know who, a psychoanalyst, and ask him for major studies that have been done in this area, have him explain them to us, but I believe that every sexy thing you attempt outside of our own period will have results that are, at best, historical, that is, not instinctive and natural, but cultural."

At that last word, the producer gave a slight shudder and raised his arms sorrowfully. F. took advantage of it to hurry back to the seashore.

1969–1972

The director's Beverly Hills house is up on one of the hills, certainly the best, strewn with villas amidst the greenery. He comes himself to pick me up at the hotel in a black Rolls-Royce. "If you ever come back here again," he says, "you'll be better off getting a car for yourself, not a Rolls-Royce though, something more in line with your work, let's say a black Buick, a convertible. They're real beauties. You can even rent one. If you like European makes, not a Ferrari. Too flashy. Forget about economy cars, unless you're always willing to come up with a joke to explain it. One of my friends used to have a Volkswagen. He had this big key put on the back, the kind for winding things up with, so that people could look at it and think it was spring-operated, like a toy. He did it for laughs, naturally."

We entered the avenue that leads up the hill. "Put your cigarette out. From here on up, there's no smoking along the street. Fires. The fine is five hundred dollars." "Five?" "No, five hundred."

The villa is halfway up the slope, it has a very lively design, edged round and emphasized by the garden. In the distance, beneath a blaze of light, is the ocean, invisible. In the garden are garden statues, copies of the ones you find in Venetian villas: Apollo, Mercury, Venus, and lots of Muses. Already with their own moss. At the base of each statue there's the signature: *Milani sculptor, Vicenza, Italy.* The serene stone that supports the terrace was sent in from Italy too, the red granite on the pathways from Arizona. The director lives alone, he has a cook, a male secretary, and a female secretary. Assured taste in his choice of books, of paintings, of objects. But predictable as well: a taste that is midway between fashion and capital investment. A Braque, a Rouault, a Renoir, a Sutherland, many drawings by Piccaso and Matisse. In the service hallway a Cocteau, somewhat outmoded. In the library, rare first editions and Scamozzi's five volumes on the work of Palladio. In the garden a hummingbird comes and flies around us. I had never seen one before. It simply doesn't seem like the real thing, it flies with the grace and the hesitations of an automaton. The director also owns an enormous and affectionate dog who takes an immediate liking to me and comes to give me his paw every five minutes, to reassure me. He is a dog so very rich, says the director, that in the event of his master's death he will be able to live on his own income. I smile at him, but with strange dogs I never know exactly how to behave, whether to pay attention to them or to pretend to ignore them. One night in Paris I caught myself trying to decide whether or not I should kill a French mosquito. The inquest would have ruled in my favor, under the firm supposition that mosquitoes do not exist in France, being, rather, an insect of Mediterranean origin. This dog then has in every way the air of protecting me, of keeping me from feeling ill at ease. If he could speak he would say kind things to me about Italians, with that exaggeration that hides a certain reserve, usually.

We go back inside, and work is spoken of. The question on the director's mind is that the story I'm telling may not be *romantic*. He asks me about it, waiting for some sort of assurance from me that will set his mind at rest. "Is it romantic?" And he looks at me with an imploring lip. I frown, then ask in my turn: "What does romantic mean, exactly?" He looks about, a bit dismayed, seeking a suggestion from the paintings and from the books, then from the couches and from his shoes. Finally, profoundly surprised, even irritated, impatient: "But romantic ... means ... romantic!"

Work ends there for today.

"Now pay attention," the director says to me. "I'm going to

turn that lamp on by clapping my hands, like a magician." He claps his hands and the light comes on. He claps them again and it goes out. "Try it." An electric eye receives the impulse, it turns on and it turns off. Launched into his technology, the director invites me to lunch and telephones a restaurant to reserve a table. He has a telephonic device with which he can speak without being obliged to hold the receiver in his hand, actually pacing to and fro in the living room. He has three living rooms in all, plus two studies, both in perfect order. He sits down at a table, opens a date-book, chooses a pen from a vase of pens and writes: "Lunch with Flaino." Then he's unsure about it and corrects: "Fliano."

All over the walls of the studio are photographs of actors who have worked in his films. I recognize some of them and the director is amazed at my powers of memory. Finally he points out a photograph of two little girls. "And these two? I bet you don't know who these two are." Okay, I have a choice between the Dolly Sisters, the Materassi Sisters, the Grammatica Sisters, and the Gish Sisters. I am not acquainted with any other sisters. I have to go with the Gish Sisters. The director looks at me with a smile, my answer is absolutely correct! Now we have to leave. In front of the garage he claps his hands, nonchalantly this time, and the door opens up. Once the Rolls-Royce is outside, the door closes implacably. I allow myself to be driven in silence towards Los Angeles, the angels, all the while looking around me with the sinister feeling of being in agreement, of admiring it all.

Not being able to sleep, nocturnal television. One channel shows movies until daybreak. Short detective films, interrupted every so often by a minute of advertising, which improves them. The thing that's special about television is advertising, where one is in a race against time. One minute, two or three thousand dollars (or perhaps a lot more, I don't know much about it), which compels a frenetic diction in order to get as many words and concepts into the spiel as possible. And then: elliptical dolly shots, sudden cuts, lightning quick superimpositions—all things considered, a technique that is silly and irritating in its presumptuous vivacity, but which permits the viewer to believe that, somewhere in the world, there is someone who doesn't mind wasting his talent for his sake.

Advertising improves these films, I was saying, adding breadth to their stories (which are usually inane), spreading them out upon the plane of real industrial and commercial necessity. It gives them something to say, a message founded, if nothing else, upon the sacred concept of the collective well-being. Places and characters in the films: always the same: the private detective, the nightclub, its sinister proprietor, the woman vocalist is Mexican or Italian (alas, on the side of the gangsters), the automobile chase, the shoot-out, love, the crooks caught red-handed, in short nothing would make any sense in these archaic fables without the commercials for cars, for beer, for cigarettes, for restaurants, for motels, all particular parts of the general whole, and pregnant with truth. Generally speaking, these films have unintentionally discovered the true essence of cinema, which is the rendering of reality in ideograms; and also its aim, which is the utilitarian achievement of surprise, between fiction and necessity.

Apropos of a new Las Vegas hotel, a placard upon a taxi announces and promises: "An Orgy of Excitement." That is to say, only hyperbole and over-emphasis will attract the consumer's notice, and only a sexual metaphor guarantees his attention. If the advertising placard of this same hotel were drawn up in simple terms, giving information, number of rooms, quality of service, and so on, "it wouldn't be noticed." Or the consumer would think that that hotel was merely a place to sleep in.

In a restaurant the waitresses wait on the tables topless, that is, bare-breasted. After half an hour, in anticipation of the main course which still hasn't arrived, their nudity becomes a bit irritating; since, once the first pleasant surprise is over, it's good service that again takes on value and we get the feeling that we've been duped, treated like those small children whom the barber at the barbershop plumps in the saddle of a big wooden horse so he can cut their hair. That is, a feeling we've been made ridiculous. Strictly speaking, the patron of a restaurant like this ought to drink milk only, and then beddy-bye.

Travelling is like keeping the faucets turned on and seeing time run away, wasted, liquid, uncontrollable. Struggling with my anxieties over departing, I reach the downtown area where the streets are pretty crowded and laden with the vague menace of faces suspended in mid-air. Then I'm attracted by the sign of a graphologist, which in reality is nothing but a poor electronic computer. You sign your name on a card, put in half a dollar, and wait for the diagnosis, right there on the sidewalk. The machine shakes, rotates, shudders, spits out a dozen cards, each of which contains an exact appraisal of my character; indeed so very exact as to tempt me to try a trick. I make a swift and elaborate signature on a second card, and the responses this time are almost all identical, except for the last one, which says: "Try to be less impulsive."

A visit to the great cemetery they have here is necessary, they tell me, to understand the attitude of the rich in the face of death; which is rather the attitude of a pharaoh, to establish oneself in comfortable surroundings while waiting to be reborn. In the end, however, one doesn't understand why the rich here should have to be reborn: they already have everything. We go then to Forest Lawn, which is an immense and stupendous park, where only small bronze plaques on the sward recall the fact that someone is there underneath. The rest is nature, silence, flowers, venerable trees. In the guest-suites of the deserted church the people just back from a funeral have repaired to the toilets, which are as elegant and

clean as those of a grand hotel. The church library, dedicated
to Longfellow, is empty but ready to welcome us. No one is
there to ask us what we would like. But we become eager to
find out how much a tomb costs. In an office off the vast
hallways we are greeted by a salesman with exquisite manners. He understands immediately that we are a waste of his
time, that we don't want to die or to buy anything; but his
irony, it seems to us, is entirely in wishing to make us believe
that, through the mere fact of our being alive, we are customers nevertheless. If not of that cemetery, then of some other
one. He proposes to us arrangements that run from three to
sixty-four thousand dollars. He leads us into the costliest of
the sample tombs which, on account of its mode of entry,
brings to mind the tombs of the Etruscans. The concrete roof
is guaranteed against atomic conflagration, the plain carpet
extends from wall to wall. The furnishings can be of Egyptian,
Greek, "Empire" or Colonial style, whatever one's choice. The
space is small but elegant: two bronze lamps render it inti-
mate. We don't know what to say other than to repeat: "Lovely, very lovely." The salesman smiles, nodding. Then he
throws his last pitch. Included in the price is the customer's
right to a piped-in musical program, and he may choose between three of them: classical music, easy listening, and pop.
The contract is for five hundred years. He concludes: "It's the
closest thing to eternity you can get."

The medium is the message. If we've understood you correctly, Professor, we needn't bother to open our letters, it's
the postman we ought to read. L'imagination au pouvoir! But
what sort of imagination will be willing to remain there? Culture in crisis. It's always been in one: Shakespeare didn't know
Greek and Homer didn't know English. The crisis of the novel
derives from the comfortable state of its characters, who are
in expectation of nothing but new improvements. The word
truth doesn't mean anything ever since falsehood became useless. Nature is merely a place where we go to be amazed at

how stupid we are. The little girl who tasted an orange for the first time said: "Huh! it tastes like orangeade." And another youngster on summer vacation wrote: "The chickens here walk around raw." A mother asked her little boy: "How are parents born?" And the little boy: "You mean how do they die." Apropos of the next affluent revolution in 1980 one historian will say that when they announce to the president that the people want bread he will respond, annoyed: "But they still haven't finished their brioches!" A computer was writing stories that it collected in a volume. A critic entrusted the review to another computer. The stories didn't come back.

Heliogabalus invited his friends over to an orgy of love. On the carpets and the cushions of a hall in the palace the couples were entwining themselves together, changing partners, one atop the other, overdoing their pleasure in order to please their sovereign, who was eighteen years old. For his part, the sovereign, upon his large throne-bed, surrounded by sodomites and courtesans (he was in reality married to a centurion) kept a rein upon his his own pleasure. And regulated that of the others. Rose-petals rained down from the ceiling, thrown by slave-girls. The rain increased, the petals fell thicker and thicker, then in whole clumps. One of the participants got the feeling it was a trap; knitting his brows, he tried to stand up, and a hundred-pound block of roses smote him to the floor. Amid the screams and the terror, other blocks fell. The lustful below were unable to escape death, whether from being crushed or suffocated. For the sake of his own pleasure Heliogabalus exemplified what the condition of sensual love is: that in the beginning it delights and in the end kills by its very intensity, which increases geometrically, and demands of itself ever new powers and new fantasies without ever being satisfied, until the critical point is reached and it shatters. As a result, therefore, Heliogabalus must be considered a moralist, he had mystical crises, he was faithful to the gods, among whom, in his capacity of emperor, he numbered himself. He was in short a Lenten preacher of sorts, who instead of threatening the punishments of hell demonstrated them.

But he wasn't understood. He met death in a palace revolution. Today, with his ideas, he would be a film director.

After the prodigal son's return, at day's end everyone was weary from all the excitement and the feasting. At table, until late, they went on eating the remains of the fatted calf, with the usual wine which had made for lively talk and which was now inviting them to song. Only the prodigal son was quiet. He was sitting at the right of his father, he was rolling bits of bread into little balls, now and then turning towards his table companions with a smile of humble good will. It was already night when the feast ended. For a little while the premises resounded with the guests' leavetakings, and with singing. The prodigal son found plain and clean linen on the bed, its mattress refurbished, and there he sank into a sleep full of gradually subsiding regrets. At eight the next morning he was still asleep and the house was busy at its chores. The father said they should let him sleep.

No one replied to that. At ten the voice of the prodigal son was heard: he was calling from his room, asking for breakfast and the morning paper. At that a young scullery-maid murmured in a voice that was not so low she could not be overheard: "Let's all laugh." The father went out towards the courtyard.

To further the public's overall well-being men and women are being oriented towards a utilitarian morphology. Already in circulation within the ranks of the young are the models that will be produced in large numbers in the future: nimble, steady men, highly reliable and low on consumption; women of medium stature, easy to maintain and of standard performance. Slight variations in trim. Nature is still producing a few specimens of de luxe men and women meant for the entertainment world and the mass consumption of information, advertising, and illustrated magazines.

I've noticed for a couple of months now that people hereabouts no longer like to look at the moon (*luna*); at least they don't look at it the way they used to. They admonish it for having been up to now the object of useless fantasies and sentimentalisms, a depository of poorly placed tendernesses; in short, a disappointment. Among other things, it used to rhyme with *fortuna* (fortune), *bruna* (brunette), *cuna* (cradle), *nessuna* (nobody).

Your anxiousness to escape, my dear friend, is not prompted by your prison's bare and unhealthy walls, but by the frescoes that decorate the ceilings, by the sixteenth century wrought iron, by the brocades and carpets, by the silverware and furniture, by the plumpness of the cushions, and above all by the faces of the other prisoners, by their artistic and cultural activities, and by their endless good times.

If two actors or singers or two supermarket celebrities leave their respective families, get together and have children, the press says that a loving friendship unites them, that they are sweethearts, et cetera. If you have an affair with some woman or other you are a middle-aged Don Juan, she an adulteress or a scatterbrain, your affair is squalid and reflects the baseness of our customs nowadays, the decline of the family, of moral values, the disorder our emotions are in, the decadence of America and the wicked influence of the cinema. They will tell you that the fault is in the masses, that they cannot live without a mythical projection of their desires, a continual identification. The masses certainly have need of God, of Sunday, but also of a certain number of pharaohs, who are allowed precisely what they, the masses, cannot (and must not) have: conjugal liberty, the easy availability of forever new experiences, incalculable wealth, ubiquity, freedom from all judgment. The masses delegate their lives to these illustrious models, in this way transferring to them part of their wretchedness.

Apropos of a film by Sordi and Manfredi on Africa, which I liked for the correctness of an in-depth observation, namely this: the Italian, in his inherent quality of comic character, is an attempt by nature to de-mythicize itself. Take the North Pole: it's reasonably serious, taken by itself. An Italian at the North Pole immediately adds to it something comical that didn't strike us before. The North Pole is not serious anymore. The vastness of its icy surface is excessive. What's it good for? Why? Isn't there something that can be done to remedy this? thinks the comic Italian character.

The savannah, the jungle, the great open spaces of Africa: two Italians suffice to corrupt them. *"Dottore!" "Ragioniere!"* They won't let go of their titles, they look at the great open spaces, they lose themselves in them, they walk around in them without conviction, dubiously, "You'll never catch me coming to Africa with you again," et cetera. When two Italians chance to run into each other in the outside world, their first reaction is to have a good laugh over it. "Hey, what're you doing here?" "How about you?" In fact it's assumed that if they are away from home it's for motives that are essentially comical: work, boredom, a curiosity full of reservations, women, pleasure, et cetera.

I go to the theater. To see the adaptation of a Flaubert novel, *Bouvard et Pécuchet.* These two characters are the immortal witnesses to stupidity, and with them Flaubert intended to demonstrate that of his own day; availing himself of ideas that were then current, but which today have been refuted or forgotten; testing his characters by having them applying these ideas; organizing an archive of idiocies, compiling a catalogue of chic ideas, that is, ideas currently in style. An immense undertaking that death prevented him from completing. To his friend Louise Colet he wrote that his purpose was to arrive at an extreme form of the comic, one which would not provoke laughter. Not to give a further demonstration of anything, but to write a book that, as Du Camp said, seemed like the work of an idiot. But since then stupidity has made enormous progress. It is a sun that one can no longer gaze at without blinking. Thanks to mass communications, it isn't even the same thing any longer, it feeds on other myths, it sells at an extremely high price, it has turned good sense into something ridiculous, it spreads terror all around itself. The authors of the theatrical adaptation did not perceive, for example, that Bouvard and Pécuchet are the first victims of the myth of free time, stupidity's adopted father.

So, the Flaubertian method would have had to be applied by the adapters, not to yesterday's idiocies, but to those being spread about today as unshakeable truths. And in that case we would have had Bouvard and Pécuchet busy testing the truth of mass culture, of the cultural revolution, of liberated eroticism, of scientific delirium, of the collage as novel, of global confrontation, of the theater of the cruel, of total mechanization, of the space race, of the disalienation promised by the political parties, of art as therapy and therapy as art, etc. What a marvelous series of chapters and scenes! And what a catalogue of unbearably chic ideas! Everybody do his thing.

For today's truth Flaubert would either have rewritten his novel or forbidden the theatrical adapters to use it. For the simple reason that they don't believe in the improvement and incessant variation of stupidity. Which today is no longer so much bourgeois, rationalistic and Voltairean as it was in the time of the pharmacist Homais, as it is oriented towards the future, full of ideas. Today's idiot is full of ideas.

I go to the show. Two parachutists, an Englishman and an American, manage to get inside a German stronghold in the Bavarian Alps during the last war and accomplish prodigious feats of daring. Alone, with spies to contend with, overcoming the most difficult obstacles, in the course of a few hours they kill German soldiers in droves, eliminate the spies, blow up the fort, a cable car, a bridge, they destroy a squadron of airplanes. They kill coldly, with punches, with pistol, with dynamite. For want of anything else, with a hatchet. The depiction of the executions is calculated realistically. Fist strikes chest, bullet punctures forehead, dynamite blows bodies to bits, hatchet cleaves them apart. In the end the Wehrmacht is undone, and we aren't going to be the ones to lament the fact. The spectators exit with a calm, satisfied look on their faces. Those who have cars (almost everyone) leave roaring with happiness, they drive off into the night in a state of heroic inebriation. At home they fall asleep like angels. If it's true that every representation of violence is a safety valve for the latent aggressiveness of the spectator, films of this sort are to be encouraged. As a footnote to them two observations come to mind. The first is that the German soldier these days has replaced the Indian of the westerns, whose death causes no grief, it's only rhetorical, it even has to be repeated over and over again in order to tranquilize the small children in the audience. The second observation brings on a question: where are the Nazis? Excluding the victims, who are deprived of every possibility of escape, riveted as they are to their role of Indians, excluding the parachutists, who are doing their professional duty, without hate and without pomposity, it is clear that the Nazis are the ones who, then as now, get joy and satisfaction from the slaughter, that is, they are the ones who are now looking on: that is, they are the spectators. When certain men of the theater solicit the live participation of the audience in their performances they ought to meditate upon the dangers this may entail.

Because of the number of cases reported we know by now that dying is imprudent. Above all if one dies by the hand of one or more murderers who remain unknown: acting, therefore, not out of passion, but for the sake of simple aggression and rapine. Efforts to hunt down (or at least to identify) the murderers having proven vain, attention shifts to the victim. It is he who is asked to explain the crime. And from his account of what happened things are emerging that can hardly be described as pretty: that he used to smoke, watched television, rarely left the house, lived on an inadequate pension. What's more, his spouse was not of high birth and in her youth had two lovers. As the investigation digs ever deeper the record becomes more and more shadowy: the murdered man and his spouse went on picnics! This is already intolerable, but the picture worsens when one considers that, when they went on those picnics, they would use public transportation, buses, and, still worse, the local railroads. In fact, in the final few years of their lives, they had to sell their little economy car, for reasons that while not clear may nevertheless be surmised—yes, let's come right out and say it: it was because of their urgent need of money. Now, one must ask why people so unprovided for should have an urgent need of money. The hypothesis that it went to pay off an old threat of blackmail is acceptable. Oh, how odious mediocrity becomes!

About the murderers, on the other hand, we still know nothing. On account of those everlasting disagreements among witnesses the identikits offer absolutely ideal faces, not without human warmth, charm and intelligence. The murderers demonstrate it, after all, by eluding capture. Popular sympathy shifts to them. Perhaps it's a question of people who, unable to live without having fun and lacking funds, are therefore compelled, by the nonsensical logic of things, to kill for the sake of a little small change. That it is a question of daredevil types there can be no doubt. They acted unhesitatingly, impulsively, in such a way as not to get caught, to defend themselves, in other words, from censure. Legitimate defense? Why rule it out?

Regarding the victim chilling evidence of squalor continues to come to light: a number of violations, for parking; proof of certain gastric disorders. He was well advanced in years—old,

let's say, and irritable. He even had a quarrel with the milkman, over miserly questions to boot; and the milkman (see
photo) has testified that he was a hunched and taciturn old
man, and dressed without a trace of elegance.

About his friends the less said the better: persons of meager
income, obliged to live modest lives and who now prefer to
keep still, feigning surprise. They say they don't understand
the motives for a crime like this. So the course of justice is not
being aided. They would tell the truth if they were willing to
speak, but they aren't. They would tell us that in this whole
business their friend is the only truly guilty party, by the very
fact of his being dead.

This is a commemorative epoch. The amount of money spent
commemorating things that have happened is enormous. The
same money, had it been spent at the time on these very
things, would have changed the course of history. The mil-
lions thrown away to commemorate Cleopatra of Egypt and
the erotic things she did would have enabled this same Cleopatra to face up to the Roman conquest, and more besides.
The tragedy of Mayerling would not have occurred if the
Archduke Rudolph had had the money that is spent every so
often to explain the mystery. The very creation of the universe, had the good Lord been able to dispose of all the money
spent on biblical films, would, I think, have turned out clearer
and neater.

Now is not a time for harboring great ambitions. If you have
great ambitions drop them by the feet of someone who denies
having them. If a little boy wants the scientific details about
his birth, useless to reveal the truth to him, tell him that you
found him as a bonus under a deep-frozen cabbage: he will
feel included in the promotion of vegetables and he will watch
television with renewed faith. The thing we admire most in
obscure people is their capacity to persist in living in an age
of celebrity. "And do you have an alibi?" the accused de-

manded. "I do, yes," the presiding judge answered. And everybody: "Me too! Me too!" Once in an airliner I happened to have in the seat next to me a young priest who was flying for the first time. He was enthusiastic and chatty. He said to me that in flying man unconsciously realizes his greatest spiritual aspiration, namely, an ascension into heaven. I had him observe that the ascenders are of two sorts, first class or tourist. An art critic once asked the painter Giorgio Morandi if he had ever been abroad. It was his intention to check on the sources of Morandi's inspiration. "Yes," Morandi replied, "but I never spent the night there." Bruno Barilli, leaving a concert at the Adriano di Roma, where, between interminable political applause, we had listened to the *Leningrad Symphony* of Shostakovich, said to me: "Personally, I don't believe in art in public works." And another time, showing me a little cord he had in his pocket: "I'm going to hang myself. You don't mind?" Vincenzo Cardarelli was with Santangelo and me one night when we were stopped by a police patrol, because we were out walking around. They took our names and the policeman who was writing them down asked Cardarelli what his profession was. "Writer," Cardarelli replied. And the policeman, showing us his notebook: "I have pretty fair penmanship myself." They were the days when everyone was singing "Giovinezza."*

The director loves the Theater, but the Theater doesn't love him, she is continually unfaithful to him. The director comes right back, he bustles about, spends all his money, puts her on a "pedestal," but the Theater flies off it, spends her evenings with Stehler, with a variety show troupe, with Carmelo Bene, takes refuge in Trastevere, consorts with Enriquez, flirts with Ronconi, starts afresh with Visconti, is seen with Bosio, with everyone except with him. The director is completely in the dark, no one dares tell him the truth. He continues to sprinkle

* "Giovinezza" (Youth): a fascist song.

the stage with respectable left-wing plays, precise and subsidized, something midway between the party line and the wax museum. He gets angry if the audience yawns. One night he returns home and the Theater isn't there. She has left a note behind: "I want to live my own life, I'm going on the circuit, forgive me and forget me." The director then says: "Evil theatrical companies have corrupted her. She'll be back." He writes dramas of protest, he dreams about exams for the spectators, obligatory theater. He thinks about the revolution that will restore to him his Theater, repentant and docile. He doesn't know, for example, that when Mayakovski killed himself he was thinking about the revolution in the hands of bureaucrats like him.

The restaurant was full of, among other things, handsome young men dressed in clothes from different periods, all of them serious and pensive. They struck you as the illustrations from an anthology of poets, each one was the rare photograph of the Poet as a Young Man. There was a Byron, a Rupert Brooke, several Lamartines, a Silvio Pellico; only a little bit faded, with the melancholy halo of approaching fame about their features. There were also some minor poets and a few bad boy motorcyclists. The girls at the tables, companions or wives of a day or two, appeared more modest in comparison. It's happening here as with the animals, the females have fewer sexual points of reference than the males, fewer colorful feathers, a more modest demeanor. Some have on dresses belonging to their grandmothers, their aunts, somewhat ominous Balkan lace and embroidery. Katherine Mansfield, Virginia Woolf, Ada Negri, various foundresses of theosophical sects. But there were also girls from the cinema in long pants, skin-tight boots, large necklaces, every so often an ostrich plume, fur jackets in rain-soaked tatters, eyes circled with bistre and fixed on some point or other out on the piazza, beyond the heat-fogged window panes, in the direction of the Pincio and the automobiles. The conversation fell off at one point. "One cannot believe in Humphrey Bogart, in Che Guevara, and in Bonnie and Clyde all at the same time," a girl with a priest's hat on her head was saying at the next table. "Well, let's talk about theater then," the younger of her two male companions said, ironically. And she: "Let's. The best actors this year were in Prague." The other young man went on absent-mindedly breaking a breadstick. "Absolutely," he said. Resembling some minor character who is off his timing, the waiter arrived at this point and inquired: "Now then, have we decided on a second course yet?"

He used to go to the cinema every night: thus, in life, he could only remember the events, he forgot about the descriptive passages and couldn't imagine the consequences.

You're mistaking your boredom for moral indignation. You want to smash the china, not because you've decided to throw it away, but only because you are sated now. Freedom horrifies you, now that no one is trying to take it away from you. You yearn for the simple and gregarious life of ants, you need a boss to worship. You have two to choose between: the entomologist and the anteater.

We live in a dramatic age, which uses dramatic words. The word *problem* is the most despairing: it tends to elevate into a problem every question or opinion and, in a certain sense, to communicate to it a suspicion of insolubility. Thus we live surrounded by superfluous problems, which wouldn't pose themselves at all if someone would dare change to another word by defining them correctly. But no one dares. He wouldn't be taken seriously. When Goldoni wished to give a title to one of his comedies about country life, he meditated upon it at length. In his day, *problem* was only used by mathematicians. And since his comedy was about the various problems connected with the country life of his contemporaries, he decided to use the word *mania* (*smania*), in the plural:

The Manias of Country Life (*Le smanie della villeggiatura*).
Mania, according to Tommaseo, is a very lively, impatient
desire. To have a mania for something or to be manic are one
and the same thing. "Someone who gets worked into a rage
over a thing that he wants becomes manic over it. But mania
can more often manifest itself in external acts than in internal
passion." This depicts a few current psychological situations
which claim to be problems.

By calling them manias they would appear to us in a more
correct light. One can speak about a school problem for anyone who goes to school, but manias concerning school are
typical of someone who doesn't want to go to school. I used
to cultivate them. There are the problems of women, but also
the manias of women in the modern world: that is, the mania
of no longer wanting to be women. There are the problems of
political parties and the manias of schools of thought. The
problems of democracy and the manias of demagogy. Traffic
problems are submerged in the collective mania for always
being everywhere at once. Ascending to a higher social level,
other problems, like those of the house, become manias of
prestige. The problem of being somebody deteriorates into
the mania of self-realization at whatever cost, which has become, with Freud, a true epidemic.

There is also the problem of the young, which subdivides
into a number of different manias: that of remaining young
(Peter Pan complex); that of rebelling against parents; the
mania to arrive, right away, at a certain level of power, the
mania for saying no to the System without taking a single step
to stop being a part of it (typical mania in the the sons of
intellectuals, loved, coddled and corrupted by modern comforts); the mania for reducing youth to an anagraphic category (whereby they cut the ground out from under their own
feet, since each passing day sees them become a little less
young). There is finally their ideological mania. More than
two thousand years ago, Ariston, a contemporary of Zeno,
observed that "Young men who leave the schools of philos-

ophy, and who find everything around about them laughable, resemble newly bought dogs who bark, not only at strangers, but also at the people who live in the house."

There are finally the manias of the dissident clergy. Every so often I speak with a young priest so that I can hear about their problems. Well, they want to get married and to go to the theater, two things which I detest ever since matrimony and the theater became problems.

I have searched in vain through the newspapers for news of my birth. Not one single photographic agency paid my father for the privilege of taking the first pictures of me in my mother's arms. Unfortunately, every other person I know is in the same straits as I. My researches in the newspaper archives have brought me to this lovely conclusion: that even the births of Fermi, Carducci, Croce, Pirandello and Garibaldi went unnoticed in the newspapers of their day. I wrote to a vast number of persons, taking their names from a list entitled *Who's Who*, a list so comprehensive that it even included my name, and I received nothing but negative replies concerning the welcome they ought to have received upon being born. One man replied by sending me a newspaper clipping, three lines: blue ribbon. It was all the evidence he could show of society's having grasped the importance of his birth. About him it said that he was in good health, as was the puerpera, who I imagine was his mother. Not much. We get some comfort in knowing for a certainty that something is being done about it. Many new-borns, simply by dint of having been born, today get their weight, the color of their eyes, and their wholesome appearance reported, all of which may be verified by means of the photographs accompanying the article.

The number of particulars is also reassuring, particulars not only having to do with the actual birth itself (hour, day, clinic, gynecologist, nurse) but also with the astral influences that determined it, and above all with the period preceding the birth, beginning with the conception itself, about which nothing is concealed from us. The new system's advantages are obvious. Future historians will no longer have doubts about a fairly large number of persons, nor will they repeat the regrettable polemics concerning Shakespeare, whom many maintain to have been Bacon, the Earl of Essex, Marlowe, and even the Queen of England. As far as the master poet, Homer, is concerned, the absurd contention of seven cities claiming the honor of having been his birthplace will no longer be possible. Behold little Homer II in his cradle, his wet-nurse, his first steps. With time we will reach the point where all new-borns will be guaranteed the attention of the press and of television; which, as of now, by way of experimentation, is limited to the new-borns of workers in the performing arts.

An immense task awaits anyone who should want, today, to put together an archives of idiocies. Bewildered by the choice, I myself defer to other voices, litanies, catalogues of formulas in current favor. In the end, a work on contemporary stupidity becomes stupid, that's the point. One simply can't remain fascinated by it. Nevertheless, it is a task that needs to be done, perhaps by devoting ten minutes a day to it, not more. Today I have been reading Dubuffet, who writes about counterfeit art. Dubuffet is a very big painter, with true talent, whose works are being snapped up, especially in Switzerland, as capital investment. A great merchant himself, he addresses himself to merchants. He manages to disturb them. He says that art has been entrusted to professionals who have reduced it to their own measure, taking it away from society. The art of children and of the insane, free art, is all that is to be recognized as art. About culture: it has become the domain of professors, that is, of students who, once finished with school, ask to "re-enlist" and continue to study and lay the results of their studies down as law. More than that, professors are without passion. For example, it is well known that different cultures clash: the Renaissance fought against the Gothic, art nouveau despised impressionism, et cetera: but the professor explains all these cultures impartially, eager not to displease anyone.

According to Dubuffet, the professor ought to take sides, to inveigh against Renaissance if he likes Gothic, against art nouveau if he is fond of impressionism; and against grown-ups if he loves little children. In short, either choose or keep still. He concludes with the usual anthem: for victory over the bourgeoisie, by way of a beginning you have to destroy its culture, and not acknowledge it. In this, Dubuffet, for his own part, does his best. And he drives home one truth: that talent doesn't exclude a dose of simplicity and bad faith.

He used to be called Freedom. One day he went out on the streets and set to questioning the people he met. The replies he obtained were all along these lines: "Why don't you mind your own business?" "Don't bother your head." "Drop dead." "Leave me alone." "Who's making you do this?" "Is it on doctor's orders?" "You get paid for this?" "You tired of living or what?" "You think living stinks?" "A donkey heads where his master wants." "Don't play the fool." "You're getting yourself worked up over nothing." "Go sleep it off." "Feast day past, the saint's an ass." "Gold doesn't tarnish." "If heaven you'd see, keep busy like a bee."

Freedom said: "These people are very wise, they don't need me." And indeed he began to venture forth less often, and one day he announced he was going away. To the crowd of journalists that descended upon him in order to find out the reasons behind his decision he replied in a rather enigmatic way. He said, smiling: "Freedom must be kept in continuous repair."

I left the house in an unusually happy mood and, just as I do every morning, I went to the bar in the little piazza where the buses turn around. Inside there was already one man who was—or who appeared to be—half-drunk, a cab driver: he had left his carriage (and his brooding horse) by the sidewalk and was now drinking a cup of coffee, from which there arose a strong odor of anisette. He was taking in his surroundings, approving everything, a watery comprehension in his eyes. Leaning forward at the end of the bar so as not to be in anyone's way, he was talking to the owner. The latter, seated at the cash register, without ever glancing at him kept now and then replying, his mind elsewhere: "Good man, you're right, I always said so myself, I like you," exactly the way it's done with amiable drunks who want to make conversation.

"Everything is lovely," I thought, "when we are willing to accept others. In other countries I know of this man would be considered a nuisance and they would toss him out the door, here they accept him." And since the waiter had turned his attention to me, not knowing what to ask for I said the first thing that came into my head, a glass of warm milk. The cab driver winced as if they had popped a lemon into his mouth.

It was going to be one of those tepid and noisy days that seem good for beginning some sort of work or for a spur of the moment visit to the Palatine. There had been a cloudburst during the night and then a vibrant breeze had come to blow the clouds away; and now the neighborhood seemed new. The limpid sun was foreshortening distances, giving a precise order and even a splendor to the modest architecture round about, marking the shadows in deep blue. And so I felt happy on account of the first signs of autumn. Without appearing to be doing so, I was listening to the drunk's conversation, he was talking about the traffic which, these last few days, was quiet, and that pleased him. The bar waiter was heating up my glass of milk with the espresso machine's steam-pipe and he was smiling. In his rapid and sumptuous gestures was the touch of irony young Roman men display towards their work. He was smiling, listening to the cab driver, and finally he interrupted him: "The horse is finished," he said. And he gave me a wink. I was pleased by this confidence which acknowledged my legitimate participation in the life of the bar. He continued: "This isn't the age of the horse anymore, it's the car runs the show now."

The drunk turned slowly towards the waiter and, staring at him because of this sudden attack, said: "You don't understand diddly f——"

"Let's watch our language," said the owner, yawning. And the drunk bent towards me, in so doing wanting to indicate that the owner had interfered. He passed a hand over his face and said without looking at the waiter: "You don't understand that the horse cannot ever be finished. Someday your car will be finished, but the horse . . . not the horse."

"Your horse is nice but he's finished, and in the meantime it'd be a good idea if you put suspenders on him, or he's going to collapse on you at any time." The waiter made a gesture towards the horse parked by the sidewalk, its lowered head touching the pavement, deep in altogether Roman meditation. He added: "Professor, take a look and see whether a horse like that should go around without suspenders on," and he winked at me.

The cab driver chuckled to himself, feeling it beneath his dignity to reply. Now he had another interlocutor. He pointed a finger towards me, delicately, with respect: "You're a professor, no?"

Professor is a title given in bars to dignfied customers about whose calling no one can be certain. Merely out of respect. There being no point in discussing it, I nod my head.

"Well then, you, a professor, you who have studied, you know better than me, an ignorant man, that the horse cannot ever come to an end, cannot ever be finished, because . . ."

He stared at me for a moment, waiting for help. He found it by himself. With that look into which sudden revelation introduces a triumphant gleam of wickedness, he concluded: ". . . because the horse is nature."

I approved: "What you've just said is quite right and quite lovely. What is nature cannot end. That is, let's hope it can't." Then I drank my glass of milk and left, to repeated farewells.

I was pleasantly disturbed in my thoughts. Which were that "At least, the horse will survive us."

Many years ago, in the third or fourth year of his presidential mandate, I was invited to dinner at the Quirinal Palace by Luigi Einaudi. Not invited *ad personam*—the President didn't exactly know me—but as the editor of a political and literary magazine directed by Mario Pannunzio. There were eight of us at table, including the President and his wife. Eights guests is the maximum allowed for a non-official dinner, and so the evening unfolded quite pleasantly, the conversation touched upon various subjects, with a liveliness and unconstraint that were not to the liking of the enormous major domo in eighteenth century livery, who was the only one waiting on us. This major domo, a kind of Hitchcock of vaster proportions but totally devoid of irony, had from the beginning tried to intimidate us by putting the precious tableware down in front of us as if he were afraid we were going to damage it, and darting lightning-bolt looks of distress at us if we failed to single out the correct piece from among the great many there were (some even hidden in the lace of the tablecloth).

Since the President, in his green years, had frequented a Via Della Croce *trattoria*, La Fiaschetteria Beltramme (which some of us still frequent) we also spoke about this, as well as of his companions from the university who used to go there, of the proprietor, of other customers whom he used to catch a glimpse of there: Bruno Barilli, Cardarelli, the painter Bartoli. What for the shifting from one subject to another, for anecdotes which, with the outpourings of laughter they inspired, made him toss about like a wet little bird; what for the reflections that followed the anecdotes, the remarks upon economics and others regarding the future, the dinner was extending beyond its permissible length. The President seemed like a happy grandfather seeing his distant grandchildren again. But here we were come to the fruit.

The major domo brought out an enormous tray, the kind

that the Dutch mannerists and the Neapolitans after them used to paint two centuries ago: everything was there except the sectioned melon. And among all this fruit, some exceedingly big pears. Luigi Einaudi looked a bit taken aback by all that botany, then he sighed: "I," he said, "would take a pear, but they're too big for me. Is there anyone who'd like to split one with me?"

There was a moment of confusion, we all looked instinctively toward the major domo: his face had turned bright red and he may have been on the verge of an apoplectic fit. Never during his long career had he heard such a proposal, not at a dinner served by him, not in these halls. Nevertheless, I took a deep breath and leapt: "I would, Mr. President," said I, raising my hand so as to be seen, like a schoolboy. The President cut the pear, the major domo placed half of it upon a plate and he set it in front of me as if it contained half the head of John the Baptist. A tumult of contempt must have occupied that not very large spirit of his within that vast frame. "Now we'll have to see," I thought, "whether he's going to peel it for me, as if I were a three-year-old."

He didn't do anything, he continued on around the table. But the leap had succeeded and the conversation resumed, livelier than ever; while the major domo, a snob as only certain waiters and watchdogs know how to be snobs, disappeared behind a partition.

Here my memories of President Einaudi come to an end. I never again had occasion to see him, a few years later someone else rose to the presidency, and everybody knows the rest. For Italy it was the beginning of the republic of indivisible pears.

Fregene, Sunday. An automobile stops in the pine forest. Six beggars climb out of it, and spread out in different directions. The parish priest, who here performs the Easter benedictions in the month of August, comes to bless our house and while he's sprinkling walls and floors asks my wife if she's still in-

terested in that piece of land she looked at the year before, et
cetera.

This morning, a long walk on the shore, past a fishermen's
village that's become a modish residential district, beyond the
Arrone, towards Passoscuro. Four or five kilometers of beach.
On the left, a sea that knows when it's guilty and has the look
of a wet dog, and even the smell. On the right, as far as the eye
can see, a sandy waste where no more than ten years ago
there grew strange purple flowers, some prickers atop the
dunes, and cacti that anchored the sand, with all that now
being just a peaceful garbage dump.

The sea washes up tin cans, the refuse from pleasure boats
and oil tankers, cargoes of fruit gone bad. Bundles of grass
arrive from the Arrone, entire bushes, the trunks of rotting
pines, a cat; and the empty canisters that contained the paint
used to embellish the villas. The Roman bathers, who in this
share a trait with the cuckoo, that of fouling their own nest,
leave countless bottles at the end of their stay, the remains of
lunch, opaque plastic toys, flattened beach balls, unpaired
clogs, broken life preservers. And the newspapers.

I note the tranquillity of these bathers, the detachment of
entire families stretched out on the sand taking the sun,
scarcely avoiding the bulkier and more dangerous objects
round about, the boxes of nails, the disemboweled mattresses,
the broken glass.

A lady with a huge paunch exhales the last mouthful of her
cigarette and flings it into the sea, as if into a vast ashtray made
by nature.

No one knows who is supposed to keep this beach clean.
Or the truth may be more modest: no one thinks that a beach
can be kept clean. We know what things are supposed to be
kept clean, even polished: floors, furniture. And the car. All
the rest can be entrusted to chance; and, as regards the sea, to
the big waves of winter storms.

Whenever a bit of wind picks up, the newspapers, today's
and those a month old, rise in ground-skimming flight, like

disturbed sea-gulls; and this is the only sign that remains to bring back to mind the sea of once upon a time, when the sea-gulls used to come, when one could safely take a fistful of sand and let it trickle out *"nel cavo della mano in ozio,"* as the Poet says.

It is well known that more is spent on advertising nowadays than on education. Rome has been invaded by enormous billboards; and from a summary examination of these one could very well deduce that Romans desire principally: to learn the English language, to drink nonalcoholic beverages, and to die. The mortuary agencies are absolutely implacable. Following in order of importance are: the desire to get a suntan, the desire to attend private schools, the desire to be joined together in a bed. This last desire is by nature cinematographic. The next to last is the most mysterious.

One of these "special" schools is close to where I live and I am in a position to observe the behavior of the young people who attend it. They generally arrive in little sports cars or on motorcycles. Forever spellbound by these machines, they examine them and swap them for test runs around the block. After this first inspection, during which heated and ironic discussions often arise, they go to refresh themselves in a bar which prepares, especially for them, enormous slices of pizza, or *schiacciata*, with prosciutto. Every so often someone's glance alights upon the little villa that houses the school. The girls and young men seem happy. On occasion I saw older people enter the little villa, a few professors. The schools are named after our greatest literati of the last century, but also after some scientists. The girls and young men, in couples, kiss—under the by now resigned eye of the bartender, of the wine vendor, of the milkman, of the body and fender men who repair the automobiles here and there all around the little piazza.

One of the professors, whom I met during a stop at the bar, told me (but I hardly dare believe it) that, having asked one of his pupils if she knew *L'Infinito* of Leopardi she promptly replied: "leopardize." The girls and young men are handsome, slender, without hips, yet well fed: the fruit of a social middle class that for twenty years now has suffered neither cold nor hunger, has had no need to accumulate fat on the body and in winter is not acquainted with chilblains. They *want* to "repeat." After graduation, maybe television or the cinema, but with the great technologically advanced houses, or a job with a prestigious firm, a few trips abroad . . . Success, no, they have learned to distrust it, they prefer a nice steady routine. Their humor doesn't exist outside the group and it is practiced in the abstract, against rival soccer teams. When they enter the little villa where the school is, to put themselves in fighting form they give one another shoves and slaps on the head and even kicks.

I have written a book. The thing that a friend of mine reproaches me for, with gentleness and even with sympathy, is that the diction is clear. It's easy to understand everything. "You must not have put a great deal of effort into it," he said with indulgence. I responded that, on the contrary, I had put a great deal of effort into it, that I wrote and rewrote pages over and over again, whereas if I had heeded my natural inclination everything would have remained vague and obscure. "You don't like experiments," the other insisted. "No," I said. "Every Italian, cultured or not, performs an experimental operation at all times, naturally, in *speaking*. It is no mystery that, beside the never abandoned accents of the dialects we were born with, we have a tendency toward jargon, toward anacoluthon, toward turning clauses inside out, to create (according to the flavor we wish to give to the discussion: placid, sententious, indignant, peremptory, and so on) a particular syntax. And that's the thing that adds the salt to our conversations, where often five or six persons are talking all at once and 'understand one another.' We rarely end a sentence, deeming at a certain point that the rest is superfluous. We speak about impressions, always exaggerating in order to make ourselves understood better, always backing off a step so as the better to jump over an obstacle of logic, summoning everything to our aid except syntax.

"The more precise languages such as French (all the French newspapers have grammar and rhetoric columns) don't permit this sort of playing about. Hence that feeling we get of preciseness, which often turns into a feeling of boredom, when listening to a Frenchman speak: everything is where it belongs, inevitably. In French you can't just say "Let's go for a little walk." You have to add where.

"For us the lack of a complement of place is almost sacred, and it points to the profound biological indecision not only of those going for a walk but of a language that needs to create every time in order to render indecision efficacious; and besides, we like it that way. In Italy everyone is forced to learn Italian. It isn't a question of accents, but of vocabulary and syntax. For us, Professor Higgins of *Pygmalion* would have to teach his pupil not to speak precisely, but to fall into vague lapses of memory, to exaggerate through the dreadful use of synonyms, to express herself in a lively manner, that is, in an approximate manner, in order to guarantee her worldly success. Therefore, with us, the true experimental operation is performed in writing 'clearly.' The writer who overdoes punctuation, employs every imaginable tense and mood, metonymy and metaphor, or fishes for long-lost vocables and uses them in some exquisite sense—such writing makes me smile: it is exactly what we do, each and every one of us, when we speak. Like Molière's bourgeois gentilhomme who, when he spoke, recited prose, with us the experimental writer, when he writes, makes conversation."

The naive painters are finished, done with. There is no longer a painter so ingenuous that he is unacquainted with the tricks of the naive trade. But by way of compensation we have naive collectors. Those who buy everything. It is well known that these collectors, for the most part people concerned with investing capital, are not content with the lesser figures, they want the best signatures, the best periods of such and such an artist. And they buy a little of everything, to make up for one painter's decline with the rise of another. In his pamphlet on Belgium, Baudelaire said: "Here, when they talk about prices, they believe they are talking about painting." Today the whole world is a Belgium, and Italy the worst. "What do you think of my Ottone Rosai?" my host asks me with a smug expression. And I don't know what to reply. He doesn't know that Ottone Rosai painted three thousand pictures, of which four thousand are in Rome.

Even Mino Maccari, who is the most prolific of our painters and engravers, gets forged. Even the swiftest forgers ought to get discouraged by his fecundity; instead of that, they imitate him as best they can, without inventing anything, without that degree of quality, of surprise, of felicity that Maccari succeeds in putting into even the most unfocussed of his drawings. Now a certain person comes up to Maccari with a painting he's just acquired, clandestinely. He has a doubt as to its authenticity. So Maccari replies: "Of what importance can it be to you whether the picture was done by me or by somebody else? If you like it, keep it, your admiration is all it takes to render it authentic. If you don't like it and you bought it supposing it was by me, you did something foolish, and it's only fitting if you've had to pay for it."

All that on Maccari incites me to have another look (an umpteenth look) at the ninety-nine extraordinary caricatures by the American David Levine, which Einaudi has published under the title *Identikit*; and which are the most "European" of the post-war period. (Many recall Gulbrasson, and the whole group of artists of *Der Querschnitt*.) We perceive to what low levels, among us, the critical capacity of cartoonists has fallen, even disappeared, that true-to-life concentration of a celebrity's moral and physical features, giving us a secret and definitive explanation of them, not vulgar, epigrammatic. (Maccari does caricatures, but of categories and of social groups, not of persons; he caricatures manners.) Caricature as a critical force, as a re-dimensioning of myths, is still done a little in France (where everyone knows how to do a De Gaulle), in England, in the United States. With us, the hand has passed to the imitator: hence the enormous success of Alighiero Noschese, who mimics the voices and mannerisms of suspect celebrities, but who tends to work within a closed circuit, that is, showing us the same people we see again and again, ad nauseam, on television.

The people in the audience accept him for this reason alone: because he reproduces characters whom they are already familiar with and whom they would never be able to laugh at if they did not see them re-created exactly the way they are. That doesn't take away from the fact that Noschese is a true wizard, even a unique one. Drawn caricature died in Italy with the advent of prosperity, from fear of the powerful, for the politically dominant class lacks a sense of humor. We know that this signals the renunciation of a certain degree of freedom and of culture (it is strange, in fact, that the only caricatures of Montale, of Gramsci and of Italo Svevo are precisely those by David Levine), a renunciation in favor of quiet and boredom.

Will we have a film about the Casati affair? Usually, when anything in the daily news exceeds the humdrum the film is announced immediately. Menichiello had scarcely landed his jet on the Fiumicino runway than a director, a specialist in the news of the day, was already announcing the film about this marine, veteran of Vietnam and defier of the United States' airway system. And now are we to have a film about the millionaire nobleman and his wife, just to quiet a few friends? It's more than likely. But in saying that I am not trying show that the cinema is corrupting society; rather, I wish to maintain the very opposite: society is corrupting the cinema. Cinema doesn't invent anything, it copies. In the best of cases it bears witness; in the ordinary ones it copies. And it will sometimes find itself at a disadvantage because it ought to copy, not vice or depravity, but emptiness. It is born out of an empty whirlwind. That lord and his lady and their supporting cast didn't have even the most pallid idea of what vice is: vice demands intelligence, good will won't suffice. They put to work all the good will they had but succeeded only in coming up with emptiness, and in generating further emptiness. Why I'm writing about this affair is simply because I'm fascinated by the strength of the emptiness that inspires and dominates it. Fascinated by the emptiness of the deeds. These people didn't think, didn't read; they did things. They went fishing and hunting, they went swimming, they took off their clothes, they photographed one another, they admired one another, they utilized one another in bed, they jumped from one party to another, like irreplaceable extras condemned to repeat their scenes over and over again by an implacable director. La Scala opened: there they were. Someone was setting off on a cruise: there they were again. Their friends were naked: action! The spasmodic quest for vice goes bankrupt once it becomes a habit. And out of habit, emptiness was eyeing them suspiciously. And it was yawning. There isn't anything else to say. The actors were images that moved like shadows; and they haven't left us any message, no "intellectual" despair. Useless to be indignant, to lay the blame on the times, on comic books, on pornography, on shady dealings, on consumer society, or on the United States. Satan doesn't enter into it. Useless to blame it on the absence of ideals. It is the old emptiness that would be at fault here, if one could pass judgment on emptiness. Caligula, Nero, the Borgias, Lacenaire, Jack the Ripper were unacquainted with the cinema, with pornography, with comic books: they acted within absolute emptiness.

But chance willed that one evening I should make the acquaintance of someone who played a supporting role in this empty tragedy, the chemist Marangoni, an upright person who gave the police some insights into what had happened, since he knew two of the protagonists and had even offered them some sound good advice. From what he told me I relate one particular: it seems that on the morning of the fatal day, the marquis being out hunting in the Marzotto preserves, or in some other preserves, his wife had called to inquire about his mood; and had learned that during the outing the marquis had brought down 183 (one hundred eighty-three) ducks. As a consequence he was reasonably happy. I no longer remember whatever else Marangoni told me: stories about letters, anxieties, what was on the protagonists' minds, et cetera. I was thinking about those one hundred eighty-three ducks. Perhaps the marquis gave out an exaggerated figure; but not necessarily. I recall having read that at a hunting party (it too held in Italy) in which Prince Philip of Edinburgh was a participant, two thousand pheasants were bagged. So I was thinking of those one hundred eighty-three wild ducks. One single wild duck had been enough for Ibsen to write one of his finest plays, one single dead sea-gull enabled Chekhov to give us his masterpiece. But one hundred eighty-three ducks? How can we justify them? How can the hunter justify them? I know that his wife liked to have their best prey embalmed just as much as he did. Now the Signoracci brothers, who are the most distinguished preparers of corpses in the Roman mortuary establishment, have also had to prepare the two corpses of the marquis and his wife. They were dressed in evening clothes. I have not been able to prevent myself from imagining them stuffed and laid out on a trestle, with the inscription underneath: Italian Marchesi of the XXth Century. My spite is perhaps excessive. But it is because, in the country of St. Francis, the nation's patron saint, in the country, effectively, of a poor friar who spoke to birds and tamed wolves, there are one million three hundred thousand hunters. And it's got to the point where I have to laugh in a few cases: I laugh with all my heart when I read that one hunter riddled another hunter with shotgun pellets. And if I had to give an explanation for this tragedy, I would like to imagine it as in Hitchcock's famous film, as a first rebellion or protest by birds, our wretched fellow creatures; and not as the sign that our society is collapsing under the pressure of its divers sexual activities, which are prompted by fashion or by our decadent manners: they are as old as the world.

Years ago, in one of his lucid writings, Alberto Spaini suggested that Machiavelli's *Prince* should be read in a satiric key. It's possible that the destiny of works of satire, and Swift is a good case in point, is their transformation into literature for children. The only thing that kept *The Prince* from being turned into a Christmas present for boys and girls is the tragic quality of its Machiavellian humor, which doesn't lend itself to illustrations and doesn't open the way to fairy tales; and which then is mistaken for cynicism, a diabolical conception of politics. But the author had his reasons; he was not suggesting that *The Prince* was a how-to-do-it manual on the eventual acquiring and preservation of power, but a story (under the form of a treatise) about what, simply, in his times, princes and dukes, marquesses and popes, republican senates and kings, governors and heads of parties actually did to annihilate their enemies and to maintain their power. The cynicism is not in Machiavelli but in the Italian of those days; who no sooner in command of a state or of a city or merely of an office, than he started weaving plots and alliances to keep himself there. And he would attempt immediately to annihilate his own nearest competitor, favored in this by the absence of any central power: whence the inexhaustible store of hatreds between one city and the next, which endure to this very day.

And so it is not surprising that one day last summer I received a letter, without signature or date or place of origin: its contents I am giving from memory, having unfortunately misplaced it while straightening up my desk drawers. After initially adopting a pro-Machiavelli stance, the letter went on to say that all the histories of Italy that are written today start from the premise that its History is not the history of freedom, which is what the philosopher Pescasseroli maintains, but that its particular aim (and dearest delight) has instead been the Unification of our country. Now it would be interesting—continued my anonymous correspondent—to write about the period that extends from the proclaiming of this unification down to our own times; and to study it no longer as an occupation of Italy by the Goths, by the Gauls, by the Longobards, by the Normans, by the Swabians, by the French, by the Spanish and by the Austrians, and so on; but solely as an occupation by the Italians. To consider the Italians then as a people who have occupied the Peninsula and have been predominant here. Upon these Italians (whom the natives, their reservations by now got over, consider acceptable and even likeable if taken one at a time, but detestable when beheld in political groups of even modest size) the judgments are severe: unification has rendered them arrogant and greedy, contemptuous of their own national monuments, prone to the most unbridled bureaucracy and to a confused interpretation of the laws, attached to their thoroughly abject "individuality," quick to hate their neighbors, and for the most part eternally irresponsible. So that the eventual Prince would not have to crack their skulls in order to govern them, but simply transform their native tendencies into an energetic force that would keep them divided within their union, a paradox that would not be acceptable if we didn't already know that Italians love nothing better than paradoxes and (to cite one) base their domestic politics wholly upon "parallel divergences," leaving foreign policy to be based upon "convergent parallels."

The trick was pulled off once: in the Prince (or leader), who concentrated and exemplified all their defects, and emerged from improvisation and stupidity (two national gifts), the Italians recognized and applauded themselves. They would never be able to free themselves from Italian domination without a war, which raked Italy from end to end. (A war, be it carefully noted, not wanted by the Italians but by their incautious Prince.) Then things changed and now there is a hitch: Italian domination continues, but confusedly. The original tribes have become inextricably shuffled. *Ab ovo,* these tribes, or sects, or clans stood out because of their sharply defined negative character and were of great usefulness to the Prince for his machinations. For example, let's say that one tribe was composed entirely of thieves, a second of builders, a third of wreckers, a fourth of pettifoggers, and so on: complainers, spies, priests, the filthy rich, loansharks, mafiosi, camorristi, historians and philosophers of the regime; and let's not forget the dithyrambists.

At present these tribes, sects, clans do their own dominating, in an ongoing contradiction that nullifies every possible authority and even the most modest harmony. From this foolish dominating all the evils that afflict the natives have come: the "developmental" devastation of the country, the headlong rush towards what are considered the pleasures of life: extermination of wildlife, robbery of the State, intensive construction of horrible habitations known as villas, obliteration of ideas, liberty understood as the imprisonment of one's neighbor, a maniacal fondness for sports played by others, food and drug scandals, deforestation, *son et lumière,* vexatious noisemaking, destructions of green spaces to make room for automobiles—which are the only fetishes now reckoned of any account. The Italian domination in Italy has naturally brought some benefits: the abolition of the frontiers between State and statelets, the construction of an imposing highway network, the rise in income, the rise in bootlegging, the destruction of the schools and the persecution of the Christians. The letter concluded with cordial salutations.

The Nobel Prize for Literature goes to Alexander Solzhenitsyn, he accepts it, braving everyone, we cannot help but admire him for it. And in the same way we can't help but admire Anatoli Kuznetsov, another Russian writer who has been a fugitive for almost a year, having taken refuge in London. At that time this case didn't create much of a stir among Italian writers, at least not among those I am acquainted with.

There are two possible reasons for this failure to participate in his drama. First: Kuznetsov is a very fat little man and wears thick eyeglasses: unphotographable. Second: he has written, they say, mediocre books—no one has read them, but they're mediocre. The statements he gave out to the press have not dispelled the hunch we have that it is a question of a guy who has spat in the dish where others besides himself were eating. To get permission to go to London he said he was writing a book on Lenin and needed to check certain data about the places where Lenin had lived. Moreover, having won the esteem of his leaders, who asked him to inform the literary authorities about what his colleagues were up to, he spread false rumors about some of them. He became a spy. He said that Yevtushenko, Tabakhov, Rajkin and others were collecting money and manuscripts for an underground newspaper. He was re-categorized as a political collaborator and was thus able to get permission to go to London, where he remained.

Doubts arise about a democratic society that grants freedom of movement (the most feared of liberties) in exchange for information about other prisoners. There even arise a few questions: What level of genius or talent does a member of a given society have to attain before his rebellion will be tolerated? Upon whom does the blame fall for the infamous acts that a mediocre writer was forced to perform? Listen: we will never read a book by Kuznetsov, his literature is of no interest to us, but what is of interest is that he be able to write freely about mediocre things, just as we are permitted to do.

The dilemma of Rembrandt and the cat, that is: "Having to save either a Rembrandt or a cat from a fire, which would you choose?" always ends up in favor of the cat, that is, of the life of any being whatsoever rather than a product, however refined, of civilization and art. I decided to verify this noble and sentimental human tendency (to which, however, directors of museums and big art dealers will generally be found hostile) and, it seeming to me that the little cat placed next to a canvas by Rembrandt wins out only because of the privileges its enjoys as symbol, we undertook a personal survey; and, instead of asking one hundred different persons the same question, we chose to question the same person upon one hundred different variants of the dilemma. I'm reporting here a few of the results.

Between a Rembrandt and an incurably sick baby? The baby. Between a Rembrandt and a thief? The thief. Between a Rembrandt and a motorcyclist? The Rembrandt. Between a Rembrandt and an octogenarian? The octogenarian. Between a Rembrandt and a fireman? Let the fireman find a way to save the Rembrandt! Between a Rembrandt and a television broadcaster? Question: Is what we're talking about a real Rembrandt or a fake one? Answer: Let's suppose that what we're talking about is a fake Rembrandt. All right then, the fake Rembrandt. Let's return to the original question: Between a genuine Rembrandt and a hunter? The hunter. I take it you're not altogether sure. Oh yes I am; I'd like to burn the hunter myself, on the side. All right, let's continue: Between a Rembrandt and your wife? The Rembrandt. Why, that's awful! No, my wife would never forgive me if I let a Rembrandt go up in flames, at the prices the Fleming's canvases are fetching nowadays. And to conclude: Between a Rembrandt and yourself? The Rembrandt, provided it's the picture he made of me. But how is that possible if Rembrandt lived centuries ago? That's not a problem I have to concern myself with, it's the painter's problem. Et cetera. As for the rest of the replies, I am saving them. From these I've concluded that the human mind is a mystery; and that every dilemma can be turned into a parlor game.

* * *

Every once in a while I wake up in the dead of night, full of self-reproach, asking myself: "What am I doing for the Novel? Well?" Now, it interests me, this business of the novel as a critical undertaking, what a novel must be, how the narrator must position himself before the facts. This one prefers to put himself in the middle, in the attitude of an Egyptian scribe who watches the facts occur and then sets them down in his register. This other would prefer more mobility in the scribe and to have him wobbling toward the left; and also he would like a choice of facts with socio-political implications. Merely personal facts come out of our noses. And let's not talk about memory. Instead: have a look at history, society, politics, and from the lessons they teach extract a philosophy that will be the driving force behind the novel and be of service to the reader's progress. In the worst of cases talk about sex, or talk sexily. Like those poor drawing room ladies who, at the extremity of desperation, and afraid of being outflanked on their left, appear before the public in shorts.

If I look squarely at what the duty of the novel is I fail to see anything except the thing in itself, the telling of a story; and this is already a critical choice. The politically committed implications are already included in it, although for the time being it isn't able to define them. I remember that English critic who apropos of philosophical novels (socio-piolitical even then) said: "I don't like to find hairs in my soup, I prefer to have the hairs served up on the side."

But the hairs in the soup are always there even if they are invisible to the naked eye. Everything narrated today contains within itself the filigree of our times; every intellectual and artistic operation bears the stamp of the times in which it is accomplished. The philosopher who says: "Philosophy no longer serves any purpose" is philosophizing in just the same way the person who asserts: "God is dead" is theologizing. The hermetic poets of 1940 wrote transparent poetry because hiding behind a mask was then the only way to get recognized. To claim then that a writer should be interested more in everybody's problems than in those of only one person is to ask him to begin at the end. Verga, when he explains his South, first of all performs the work of a writer, that is, he creates for himself a set of fixed standards, a critical system through which he filters the facts. Carlo Emilio Gadda tells about the industrial and bourgeois North, or plebeian and bureaucratic Rome "from first hand experience," by combining society, politics and history into something that "pains him," but without making it appear. The narrator doesn't bat an eyelash at the tortures he undergoes. Were he to let out a cry, he would hand the victory to his torturer. It is his smiling silence (sometimes) that ought to put us in a state of alarm. Everything that lies outside of literature, on the other hand, is propaganda, or homage to fashion. The "committed" novelist must fatally arive at a day of reckoning with a realism which cannot help but be aligned with something. He will have to slip aboard a coach, ride in it, imagining he is a traveller while in reality he is a passenger, a user of the railways of the masses, even if he benefits from notable considerations and reductions. He will have to follow the times, and one day he too will appear before the public wearing shorts, or in the nude, because the masses will eventually ask him for a striptease, the only form of art that arrives at the truth, I suppose.

Dictatorships have this about them that is good: they know how to make themselves loved. I wrote once that the most beloved tyrant is the one who rewards and punishes without reason. It's no longer true, and actually never was true. The most beloved tyrant is the one who punishes for one exclusive reason, the one having to do with his own existence. He who touches the wires of a tyrant, dies. But with the vast amount of information at everyone's disposal and therefore with the multiplicity of emotions that are every day being unleashed in a world ever more on the verge of hysteria, dictatorships have finally discovered magnanimity. These condemn their enemies to death (the world quivers and quakes) and pardon them the next day. Wherewith the world heaves a sigh of relief, wags its tail out of gratitude and pours out more of its love for magnanimous dictatorships.

The hermits once again left the infected megalopolises, which were swarming with philosophers, to return to the desert. They found it full of oil companies. They then went off in the direction of the mountains: there sports resorts and residential villages were under construction. They settled in a dead city, upon the severed columns of temples. They couldn't put up with the crowd of toursists that came to take pictures of them and the reporters who came to interview them. It is because of this that today they prefer to return to the great cities, where they live in the most perfect of solitudes, like lepers. In fact, they're no good for anything.

A letter. "Dear sir, you who write for the newspapers, why don't you propose an educational reform following the principle that school ought to be every individual's reward for a long and active life, and that therefore compulsory schooling should begin for all at the age of retirement? I can already see schools of all sorts filled up with aged and elderly persons desirous to learn: eager, above all, to arrive at the end of life with a certain level of knowledge, after having toyed through their entire childhood, teen-age and adult existence with ideas they were actually unfamiliar with and didn't even know how to express correctly in words. This proposal of mine is based on the necessity of allowing the human instincts to remain free until the age when, having understood the idea of death, he doesn't feel the need for a knowledge that goes beyond his own existence. The average lifespan being established as seventy-five, and the age of retirement set at fifty-five, everyone could easily obtain access to a higher education and even manage to obtain a degree, dying then in the odor of sagacity. The principle would be established that knowledge is an end unto itself, since no one would have time to utilize it for practical purposes. Resolved at the same time, I think, would be the problem of the elderly, at the present time condemned to inactivity and therefore to become a heavy economic burden upon society, as is happening in all the more advanced countries. Moreover, industry would have a new sector to exploit and expand in, and there would be an end to the charge that is brought against the elderly and the aged: their meager contribution to the policy of consumerism: which today's students, on the contrary, in obedience to fashion, promote.

Doesn't it seem to you that our times abound with incredible stories? For example, I and one of my friends, a painter in crisis, went and held up a bank in our neighborhood the other day. Why in our own neighborhood? First of all because we know it well; secondly, a hop, skip and a jump away and you're out in the country and we were thinking that afterwards we'd have lunch in one of those little rustic-type restaurants, where everything is "char-broiled," in as much as, parenthetically, I'm on a no-fat diet. So then, being in a hurry, it was eleven and something, and not wanting to get tied up in the rush-hour traffic, which in Rome is at its worst between the hours of twelve and two, the so-called spaghetti traffic (and they talk about technologically advanced civilization!), we decided to use my car. We could have stolen some car or other off the street, the way everybody else does, so as not to leave clues, but we were afraid that then we'd get there and find the bank closed, because the hours our banks keep are totally ridiculous and they usually close just when I'm getting out of bed; whereas in America they stay open till three. Anyhow, we stopped in front of the bank, double-parked naturally, we went into the bank, which was almost empty, and we asked the teller to give us the money. Unfortunately, we hadn't brought anything with us to put the money into, not even a suitcase or a paper bag, each of us thinking that the other had remembered to bring one. In addition, our weapons gave the teller the impression that we wouldn't be happy with just a modest haul; and so the good man, frightened to death, put more stacks of bills in front of us than we had even anticipated.

Now what to do? My friend left the bank with a first load, to put in the back seat of my car, which I had prudently left with the motor running, while I stayed to guard the rest. I should make it clear that a few steps away from the bank, off to the side a little and right in front of my car, was a policeman on duty. Reassured by his presence, my artist friend immediately re-entered the bank to help me carry away all the rest of those little bundles we had. But talk about the unexpected. Imagine our surprise when, having opened the back door of my car, we found the back seat empty. That is, "they" had left my umbrella, but the money had vanished. Our suspicions fell upon the policeman, and we politely remonstrated with him. The policeman was not a very big guy, but kind of inattentive and melancholic, or maybe nostalgic. I'll bet you he was thinking about his hometown.

Anyhow, at first the man mumbled about not knowing anything, in fact he even said: "I'm not a parking lot attendant, you know." Then, pushed into a corner, he admitted having seen "some guy" (without specifying height, age, attire, et cetera) open the door and go away with "something." He thought that the guy he saw must have been a friend of ours (then he had seen us get out!), an excuse that doesn't hold up under the most benevolent sort of scrutiny. But it didn't end there. While we were having our discussion with the inattentive policeman, another policeman, a traffic cop, one of those traffic cops who are always scribbling out tickets as if impelled by sudden inspiration, was taking a turn around my car, and even though he could see I was the owner, he started to jot down my license plate number in his ticket-book. Wait just a second! In a courteous way I brought it to his attention that my car had been there for scarcely more than a minute, the time it takes to run into and out of the bank, and that furthermore we were just getting ready to leave. In a pronounced dialectal accent, the traffic cop replied that he "didn't know nothing about it" and, without deigning to so much as look at us, he handed us our citation, which would have been no big deal had we not been obliged to fill in all the blanks there and then and accompany him to the post office to send off the fine. This, what's more, came to over three thousand lire, that is, for blocking traffic, while there was plenty of evidence that we were merely improperly parked. Just so as not to ruin my day, I paid. What a jerk! He went away and started to walk around some other car, taking notes the whole time, like a mathematician gone into a sudden ecstasy.

So, to make a long story short, the shifty and evasive behavior of the first policeman and the discourteous and fine-grubbing behavior of the traffic cop put us in a bad mood. In our city scenes of this sort are taking place more and more frequently, and they indicate the point relations between citizens and representatives of the law have reached. That's the reason I'm thinking of clearing out of Italy. Naturally, I took down the name of the policeman and the number of the traffic cop, thinking I might report them to their superiors, but they tell me it wouldn't do any good. What do *you* advise me to do?

My dear boy, what kind of advice can I give you? Unfortunately, you're not in a position to prove your case, having neglected to secure the testimony of witnesses. The chances are that your complaint will not only be filed away forever but will cause those superiors to smile.

Boring cities don't exist; bored people do. Or better: by now all cities have become alike, and whoever has visited them at some previous time, say twenty years ago, finds them all equally "sad." Five years ago it might have been entertaining to spend a night in Greenwich Village or to wander along the King's Road on a Saturday afternoon. Today, any operation of "discovery" whatever is depressing, even in California, which Edgar Morin in his recent *Journal de Californie* sees as "la

tête chercheuse du monde," the avant-garde of future society.
If you have participated in a couple of park-ins, a couple of
rock-ins, visited another couple of "commune" families where
everything is shared in common, children, women, food,
work, and tasted this new freedom, it gets you to the point
where you're anxious to visit Umbria. Everything has been
said, proclaimed, advertised, discovered, used. Marmori is
right, Paris is no longer as enlightened and as hospitable as it
was in the times of Gertrude Stein or more recently in Sartre's; but it is necessary to see to what extent we are still fit to
be enlightened and to be given hospitality. I had not been in
Paris for a year, I go there a month ago, a friend meets me at
the airport and, as much to extend his hand as anything else,
he warns me: "You'll see, Paris is a disappointment." I replied:
"I'm afraid that I'll be a disappointment for Paris."

They say nothing "happens" in Paris anymore. But where is
anything "happening" these days? What's left is to utilize a
great city, if nothing else. The forty theaters, the hippodromes,
the department stores, the great restaurants, the forests and
the rivers of the surrounding area are all still there and ac-
cessible to everyone. No one has touched anything. One even
has the feeling of being rejuvenated: on the Grands Boule-
vards the comedies along the lines of *Boeing-Boeing* have
been running for eight years, at the Huchette performances of
Ionesco have been going on for sixteen years. I limit my
visiting to a few exhibitions and museums, I look for the old
films of Buster Keaton, of the Marx Brothers, of W.C. Fields,
and I still find them. There are cafés where one can read and
write for hours undisturbed. And two dozen places where one
can have an excellent meal without being taken for a tourist.
And extremely well stocked bookstores open till one at night.
And friends ready to welcome you, if, of course, you had the
patience to make yourself one of them "dans le temps," when
(ten, fifteen years ago) the writers, the artists, the journalists,
the theater people filled the cafés and late night bars. Today,
it's true, one has the impression that they are all shut up in the

house, and one understands why: traffic, the general prosperity, the new generations that are invading the sidewalks, the awful "drugstores" that are becoming their meeting places, the sensation of being immersed in the junk of consumerism, the week-ends that fill the city with crowds of provincial tourists. There were years in which one could spend an evening with Tristan Tzara or with Adamov, or with a few young writers, even with Marmori (today impossible to find): they were at home to callers. The scarcely known writer was a "personage," the proprietors of cafés and restaurants coddled him. But the same thing was once possible even in Rome. Today, Rome's few surviving cafés have become snack-bars presided over by the odor of fried food, Via Veneto is a seraglio of warmed over cages for "innocents abroad," traffickers and con-artists, Piazza del Popolo a shop window and a garage. And as far as friends go, some are dead, others are swallowed up by their work.

Once upon a time in Paris there were nocturnal bars that were very cozy and those hundred or so people who counted used to unearth a new one every year, slowly but surely relinquishing the others to the crowds attracted precisely by their having been there. Today you can still find a café worth its salt, Le Café Flore for example, where you're always likely to fish up somebody. Today you also find them filled with homosexuals and people with beards, but so what? True boredom grows in the clubs that are in fashion, like grass in ruins: it is the boredom of illiterates, the boredom which excludes you. If you manage to get in you find fashion photographers in there, disc jockeys, singers, the designers of hats, ex-nudists, girls forever bustling between the toilet and the dance floor, and a few Italian actors. No one talks anymore. "Paris-la-nuit" has become "Paris l'ennui" but it's no different from the world's other cities where every evening must be planned for and programmed, and reservations made, or else you risk not finding a seat.

But for what it offers by way of the everyday, in simplicity, in efficiency, in decency, in tolerance, in large skies and broad open spaces, in beauty and in tranquillity, Paris still strikes all the right chords so far as I'm concerned. You need only ask for the simplicity of her streets, the assurance of interminable rows of brasseries and cafés, of hideaways, of galleries, of specialized bookstores, of old, lively neighborhoods. You still find the writer and the artist who are poor and reasonably happy being so, and who don't talk to you about the end of the world. You still find the authors of books that you still read, good or bad. The echo of television, of the song festivals, of the excitement over sports, over interior decoration and over things to collect, the echo of all of Italy's false vitalism, hasn't made its way here. Here a few humorous or satirical newspapers that aren't indecent continue to come out. If it suits you, you can take long walks without having to climb over automobiles on the sidewalks. Is it no longer a "tentacular" city? Today, certainly, only the province is tentacular, only in the provinces do they stage pink ballets and always keep up with the latest fashion.

Finally, departure and arrival aren't accompanied by that sadness which takes hold of you in Rome for example, in the station overflowing with people who aren't going anywhere, or in the airport that's already old and dirty; where, arriving at night, you find the lights out and the ravenous and abusive taxi-cab drivers waiting for you: thanks to all of which there arises the suspicion that without your knowing it they diverted you to the Near East.

I'm starting to have lapses of vision. This morning I opened the newspaper and read: "Guarded optimism of Colombo regarding thievery (*furto*)." Only after breakfast, returning to the paper again, did I see that it was a question of guarded optimism regarding the future (*futuro*). Too bad, I thought, that optimism regarding thievery didn't get printed. But I didn't smile. In times like these the only way of showing oneself to be a person of wit is to be serious. Seriousness is the only acceptable form of humor.

Then what did I do? Ah, I leafed through a book by Simone De Beauvoir on old age, *La vieillesse*. It's difficult, it's unpleasant, going through it, but I'll read it to the end. The theme is simple: an old man is a social outcast, since he no longer participates in the game of consumption. An old man is a depressing presence, some way must be found to isolate him along with other old men. It's the return of the down and outer, the poor old guy turned into a miser both by the experience of seeing his savings vanish with the wars and by the fear of being without money.

At the age of retirement he starts to die. Society no longer supports him. Absurdly, the old man would be able to "re-enter" modern society if he could find a way of rendering this economically "interesting." The problem is very serious and springs from the emergence of the conjugal family (husband, wife, children) which is steadily replacing the patriarchal family (grandparents, parents, grandchildren). Isolated from the domestic context, without grandchildren and of little interest, the old man is an encumbrance. (It's the defeat of materialism, this.)

For supper I went into a neighborhood *trattoria*, so very squalid, with all its neon lights, that I had never dared enter before. I went in on account of the old waiter who is always sitting off to the side at the first table and who looks at me every time I pass, with an air of saying: "When are you going to make up your mind?" He was visibly pleased. He spoke Roman, the kind spoken by an honest artisan, a gentle Roman dialect, very pure: not the Roman of the movies and of the new breed of canaille. His was a perfect language, right in all its cadences, indulgent in its conclusions. He reminded me of an old departed friend, Santangelo: in fact, they lived in the same *rione*, Ponte. He advised me at length on the fare, he waited on me on the move, circling the table again and again, begging my pardon; and, in the end, the discussion having turned in the direction of contemporary affairs, he asked me: "Guess how old I am." I said sixty-five. He was seventy-seven. I congratulated him. "I went through the whole of World War One, five years, but a lot of good it did me. So here I am here." "Then," I said, "you're a *cavaliere.*" He smiled. "Right, I'm a *cavaliere.*" Meanwhile, a few young automobile mechanics came in, a few bricklayers, the man who works at the bar across the way, always a bit too cheerful. Everyone was joking with the old man, who seemed happy, because of this thing about being a *cavaliere.* They were shouting, "Cavaliere, is that beer on its way or isn't it?" "It's on its way, it's on its way," he answerered. As I was leaving he said: "Shall I see you again?" and not: "Come back" or: "Did you like it?" "Shall I see you again?"—like a *grande dame.*

I went back home and wrote a letter to turn down a particular job I'd been offered. Now it remains to be seen whether I'll send it.

It's been a whole year since I last watched television. On those occasions when I look at it, in somebody else's house, I am seized by a kind of sordid stupefaction bordering on lethargy. They're the same newscasters as ever, plus another one who speaks in English, makes a mistake deliberately, collects himself, produces a few embarassing pauses in order to give an unrehearsed feeling to what he is saying. And actually he's reading. When he's finished with one sheet, he turns it, places it on the table and looks at us. Then someone else appears who gives more news. I have never managed to understand by what criterion they divide the news up among themselves, it being all the same. If the news is about Israel, the map of the Middle East appears behind the shoulders of the newscaster. If on the other hand it's Russian news, the Kremlin appears. This for years now. The language always remains polished, exact, wrought over, it moves forward by means of ideo-

grams. Bureaucratic ideograms, entire sentences which re-
place a single word. The news has to be given calmly,
specifying time, place, the presiding judge, the motives, the
encounters, the anxiety of the whole civilized world, arrivals
and departures. These last all take place in an airport. The
people who appear upon the screen are almost always base-
looking. And it isn't necessary to listen to what the newscasters are saying, it's the tone, the unstoppable flow of ideograms
which constitute the news. But since the way in which they
tell it no longer interests me, I may find myself living in a
world where nothing ever happens anymore. The world of
tomorrow?

A few days ago, from a window, a certain man shot at a motorcyclist with a BB gun. In my own neighborhood, the next
day, another certain man shot at another motorcyclist with
another small calibre air-gun. The first certain man was ar-
rested, they didn't get the second one. I'm acquainted with
this second certain man, he lives right across the way from
me. Like him, I too have had to suffer on account of the
motorcyclists in the neighborhood. The day before yesterday
I ran into him at the bar on the corner and I winked at him,
benevolently. He instantly understood. When I continued on
my way towards Villa Borghese he followed me. In a broad
field, protected on all sides from indiscrete ears, he said to me:
"Thank you." He was alluding to my discretion. Then he
added: "I'm glad I didn't kill him. But I didn't exactly plan it
that way." I replied: "I understand just what you mean." "I'm
afraid," he went on, "that only a few people appreciate my
gesture. But it was necessary." "Yes, necessary," said I, "but
unfortunately not enough. It has to be repeated." "Ah, you're
telling me. That's all I do is think about it."

We sat down on the grass and continued the discussion.
Here, in substance, is what the shooter told me.

"I come from a town in the South. In the South there are
principally two marks of power, of strength and of wealth:

corpulence and noisiness. Corpulence is not within the reach of everyone and therefore it's identified not only with wealth but with beauty itself. 'How lovely and fat you are!' is what is said to people who are well endowed with flesh. Down there I was esteemed because I weigh over eighty kilos. 'Formosa' is what one says about a woman who is beautiful because amply formed. If besides being obese a man is also wealthy, he risks being applauded. He's called 'affluent.' Noisiness, on the other hand, is a manifestation of power that is within the reach of everyone. At the age of development the male advises the female of the virility he has attained by making noise, generally by whistling. To which the female responds by singing: at the public fountain, in the kitchen, everywhere. In the hot hours of the summer you hear nothing else, just whistling and singing.

"Boys no longer like to ride bicycles because they don't make any noise. They can slip a piece of cardboard between the spokes, but that's not much nowadays. So they want motor-scooters and they get them by getting good grades on their examinations. Then they tinker with the exhaust system to produce the desired level of noise. The success enjoyed by sports cars today wouldn't last as long as a blast of cold wind if it weren't for the fact they make more noise than any other sort of car. Now then, it still has to be explained why the fight against noise, which the authorities announce every year at the beginning of summer, never takes place. Here's why: the people who are supposed to be combatting noise are not equipped with auditory organs sensitive enough to perceive disagreeable sounds. In the towns, the local saint's feast-day is celebrated with marching bands that walk around all day long, and with firecrackers, which keep going off all night long. And these same people come from the towns."

Whereupon we parted company, without hopes.

This morning I received a letter that bore no signature. The anonymous writer was lamenting the fact that at the tribute to

Charlie Chaplin, at the Fenice di Venezia, on the evening of the 3rd of September last, many Italian directors and writers were not present. He mentions a few names: De Sica, Antonioni, Rossellini, Zavattini, Ferreri, Rosi, Damiani, Fellini himself, without counting the young directors who today are among the tops in their profession. And he elaborates: "Television, it's true, carried various segments of the ceremony and a couple of lengthy speeches, one that lasted for a half-hour, but I didn't see a single one of these persons on the screen. Yet Charlie Chaplin had come to Venice for a final salute to his Italian colleagues. He is well on in years, the condition of his health is not the best, it was a difficult trip he had to undertake. Can you explain to what cause we owe so many discourteous absences?"

Dear anonymous writer, you weren't watching your TV set very closely. They were all there, except Rossellini who, as you know, teaches cinema in Houston, Texas. Why in Texas exactly? I don't know. But the others were all there. I was present at the ceremony, and I can even tell you what happened. Obviously, the TV cameras didn't catch the scenes that took place on the stage before the curtain went up. And so here they are:

When Chaplin appeared from the wings, supported by the people escorting him, he was immediately welcomed by the applause of those present, some hundred or more actors and directors who had taken part in the international film festival and were there to pick up their trophies. There was a moment of merry confusion, Chaplin was given a seat off center stage, and there he waited for the ceremony to begin. He appeared a little tired and disturbed by such an affectionate welcome. But on the other hand, you have to understand old people, they easily become emotional. Never in his life had he seen so many directors all in one place.

The first to come forward was De Sica. He was smiling, he gave him his greetings and then started to speak, polemically: "Maestro, I have had a number of telephone calls over the last few days from a number of young men competing in this Festival who wanted to keep me from coming to Venice to extend my greetings to you. But could I, a member though I am of the Festival's selection committee, let myself be intimidated this way? Would I not have behaved like a Don Abbondio?"

"Who's Don Abbondio?" Charlie Chaplin asked, full of curiosity.

"Don Abbondio," said De Sica, "was a priest who from fear of a capitalist avoided joining two proletarians in holy matrimony. But it's an old, old story and a long one to boot and I'll spare you having to listen to it. I'll just say that among us Italians Don Abbondio has come to stand for a person who doesn't do his duty from fear of the powerful, from fear of class associations, or simply from fear of being considered *out*, old hat. And so I flew down. Because without your films I very probably wouldn't have made mine." (Applause.) "I wouldn't have made *Shoeshine, Bicycle Thief, Umberto D.,* which I consider my most successful works. And not even *Miracle in Milan*, perhaps the most chaplinesque of them all. Without your teaching ... huh! Let's not go into that!" (Applause.) "From your masterpieces I have striven to extract that lesson in humor, in compassion, in life that have brought me a perhaps unmerited fame." (Voices: "No, no, merited, very merited!") "All of us, dear Maestro," and here De Sica made a circular gesture, "have come out of your famous derby hat, as the nineteenth century Russian authors were said to have come out of Gogol's 'Overcoat.' We came out of your derby hat the same way that doves and rabbits come out of a magician's hat. Thank you, Maestro, thank you!"

Overcome with emotion, De Sica took an enormous handkerchief from his pocket and dried his eyes.

After the applause died down, Antonioni came forward, and said: "I, personally, am completely destitute of humor, and it's not you, Chaplin, whom I prefer, but Buster Keaton, who is more fashionable among intellectuals. Nevertheless, I cannot forget that you made one anti-Nazi film, *The Great Dictator*"—applause—"and one anti-American film, *A King in New York*. In a certain sense I am directly descended from you and this is the reason I am here, and to acknowledge in you a great master of communicability."

More applause. And immediately after, Zavattini took the floor, with that slight hesitatancy of his to which he owes his charm. "Dear—but yes! let's say it—Charlot! Will you permit me—really?—to call you by the name of your most popular character?" (Applause.) "Dear, well then—dear . . . Charlot, do I have to even say it? I'm just the opposite of my friend Antonioni, I have lots of humor." (Applause, laughter.) "Just think that I discovered my vocation as a writer by going to the cinema to see your films. I began in the cinema with a short subject, *I'll Give a Million*, which you wouldn't have disdained in the least. And as for my books? I'm unable to reread any of them without thinking about you. You have taught us to talk about oneself a lot, that the poor are batty, that Totò is good." (Applause.) "You see, we Italians are a great people, we invent little but we know how to make good use of the inventions of others." (Polite laughter.) "Before Charlot appeared on the screen, think about it, our comic actors were Cretinetti and Polidor." (Murmurs: "It's true, it's true!") "Now we have nothing but comic actors, above all comic actors who don't know how to be funny. Immediately, with you, we grasped the essence of the comic—indeed, I underscore the word—by employing your superb weapons of rhythm, of ballet, of *anti-climax* and of *understatement*, foreign words whose meaning I'm not absolutely sure of but which I find beautiful." (Applause.) "Certainly I have been more courageous than you, because I have put a bit of left-wing ideology into my subjects, while you, even with *Modern Times*, remained firmly attached to individual protest. It doesn't matter. I must honestly confess that without you I would be just an ordinary writer or, as I've always desired more than anything else, a tiller of the soil in the Paduan lowlands. And now, permit me a little, the ti-ni-est lit-tle tribute to your person. I want to kiss your hand, just as I would kiss the hand of my own father—there!"

Charlie Chaplin was moved, in fact even upset, for now everyone started rushing up to kiss his hand. "Mah," someone was heard to murmur, "keep it up that way and you'll kill him." It was Fellini, who came forward and said the following:

"My name, Maestro, is Fellini. What can I add to what's already been said? Without you I wouldn't have run away from home at eighteen, I wouldn't have become the cartoonist and comic writer that I became, I wouldn't have 'looked at' life. From you I learned the lesson of freedom and I learned to look at man from every angle, portraying his canine melancholy, his psychic flipflops, his desperation, his great abjection, even his shattered hopes. I cannot see a film of yours again without crying. I've even said so in writing. But crying from utter joy. As an homage to you I made *The Clowns*." (Applause.) "This morning I was in Rome, busy getting ready for my next film; I tossed it all overboard, not the film, I mean the appointments, twenty of them at least, and I came here so that I might also kiss the hand of my master."

Imagine the applause yourself. Chaplin held out his slender, freckly hand to the kisses of the film directors, protesting a little, while two tears rolled down his shiny pink cheeks. And here, to the surprise of most everyone, because they thought he was at the Anti-Festival, Marco Ferreri came forward. A solemn silence fell over the place.

"I," said Ferreri, "didn't want to come. I sneaked in at the last moment. I thought that by neglecting to pay homage to your person I would in a certain sense have disowned my own works. My second film, *El Cochecito*, a film that could have been one of your own Vitagraph comedies, and whose title provided me with a name for my yacht, is yours: I dedicate it to you." (Applause.) "Even *El Pisto* could very well have been done by you. Not to mention *The Queen Bee*, the diminutive reverse side of the golden *Monsieur Verdoux*.

From you I learned a certain positive and intelligent 'wicked-ness.' There is only one point upon which we are divided: you love woman, in your films you make her the sharer and mo-tive force in man's destiny; I, I don't know why, I instead am a misogynist. But aside from that, a critic in the year 2000, if my works ever make it to that distant winner's circle, will not hesitate to cite me, perhaps misspelling my name"—polite laughter—"as one of your most faithful and inspired follow-ers."

Everyone applauded. Ferreri continued: "Furthermore, look how I let my beard grow! Don't I resemble some character out of one of your minor comedies? I realize now that I let it grow unconsciously, but that doesn't detract from the value of my admiration, why no, it increases it." There was a pause punctuated with shouts of bravo! and with laughter. He con-tinued: "I brought with me some fellow participants in the competition. I convinced them that art, when it concerns the destiny of man, has no political boundaries, it aims at a com-mon goal, which is that of truth. And so it is that you, Maestro, have to be honored even by someone who thinks about truth in a totally different way from the organizers of this depre-cated festival. I present to you my companions and colleagues. I am not going to introduce them by name, they're mostly second-rate characters who do their best to tell about things that happen in the newspapers. I call them Sunday magazine section authors. Their purpose is to augment production and confusion. They also make detective films, Carousels, or ad-aptations of novels. In the cinema there is a place even for them, the cinema is a great mamma, and I did say mamma, not manna." (Laughter.)

At this point the master of ceremonies indicated that the moment had arrived to begin. The minister Badini Confal-onieri in his turn advanced toward Chaplin and said: "After the tribute rendered you by the directors, I am adding my own personal homage and I see no point in reading the speech I prepared. Besides, it's tiresome stuff, I drafted it during a session at the Chamber. Let's not waste any further time, let's begin."

Everyone took his place on the stage and the curtain opened. The trophies were handed out to the participants in the twinkling of an eye. After that, Signora Vittoria Leone crossed the pit to go up to Chaplin, who in the meantime had risen to his feet and was dabbing at his eyes. A hurricane of applause burst forth. For a few minutes nothing could be heard but the clapping of hands. At the end, two worldly journalists who were in the pit rose ostentatiously to betake themselves from the hall, and one of them said: "All these honors to that fat old man." A lady heard them, she shouted after them: "Ass—" but the rest was lost in the ovations of the audience.

There you are, dear anonymous writer. That's how things went. If the television cameras failed to pick up the presence of the directors I mentioned there are two possible explanations. First: television equipment has yet to reach the desirable level of perfection. Second: Italian directors have yet to attain a sufficient elegance. In fact, the only justified absence was that of Luchino Visconti, who at least sent a telegram.

Or there may after all be a third explanation: the whole scene just described is only a figment of my imagination and every resemblance to real facts and persons is purely coincidental. How I would have wanted the tribute to Charlie Chaplin to be, and how instead it was not. But, dear anonymous writer, do not take it to heart, what actually transpired was a great deal worse.

Take a potato, enlarge it, peel the skin off: you will have a statue, that is, something that is an end unto itself, which serves no purpose at all, but provokes thought. You will have an example of interior solitude exteriorized, a Leibnitzian monad completely turned into "window." Along with other potatoes place it against a marine background, the sea's beauty will astonish you. Take another potato, enlarge it, crush it, scatter the remains; you will have started a new school: nobody did it before you did.

If, instead, you leave the potatoes the way they are, and refuse even to look at them, you will give everyone a lesson in comportment.

Take a canvas, tear it apart, wash it, set it out to dry in a gallery together with a dog. A critic will explain to you why you did it, and exactly what you did.

Bind your mother up with a chain, strip off all her clothes, wait for the photographers. If your mother cries or protests, call the critic on duty. He will explain to her that you are working for the liberation of women. If someone binds you with a chain and takes off all your clothes, don't be alarmed. You are working for Third World liberation or for your own dignity. Demand, in any case, that the salon where you are exhibited be registered under your name.

If you have farm tools that are no longer good for anything, bathtubs which you want to be rid of (since personal hygiene is of course an antiquated form of godliness), if, finally, you have old trunks, remnants of metallic and motor-driven cranes that are no longer serviceable, don't throw any of it away. Coat everything with anti-rust red paint, the only kind of paint acceptable, and send it all to Venice: everything will be set up in the *campielli* at State expense and with your name attached.

The State has much to ask forgiveness for, its sluggishness, its arteriosclerosis, but in the fine arts it has decided to put itself in the avant-garde. Art is not dead. The truth, more subtle, is that art is being held hostage—by you. It's therefore a propitious moment for you, know how to take advantage of it. The Moon counsels you: decision.

In the newspapers, in the magazines there's disquieting news about Naples. It's a catastrophe. Above all, they advise you against going there by car, you will get lost in traffic jams, perhaps you will never be heard from again. It seems that the city has nothing else to offer but confusion and incommunicability. If this is so, Naples is a frontrunner among cities, ahead of its time. In a few years, maybe even tomorrow, the other major cities of Italy will offer nothing but confusion and incommunicability, but without that grain of genius and of lunacy, of humanity, that warms the heart whenever one thinks about Naples. A verification—what is it called nowadays? On our way to Ischia we decide to have a quick look into Naples, by car, in fact.

On the autostrada, at Caianello, the always surprising South announces itself with the young man who comes to the car door and gently inquires: "Are you interested in a little contraband?" He adds that he isn't talking about cigarettes. Drugs, maybe? No, Swiss watches. He shows us one studded with diamonds that would normally fetch a million. One can make a deal for twenty thousand lire. Even ten. Even less. Instead we ask whether there's a chance of getting through Naples by car. "If you're going to Ischia, then your best bet is to exit at Capua, take the road to Domiziano up to Pozzuoli, and from there the ferry." The young man gazes at us with a pleased look on his face, he's forgotten about his contraband business, he's happy doing this, he carefully points the route out on the map, when we leave he says goodbye with a conspiratorial air. Two days later, thinking back upon it, I will realize that this "contrabandist" is something that still remains of Naples, the courteousness, the pleasure of wasting time, the pleasure of realizing onself on the plane of conversation, a tendency toward everyday curiosity. Seeing that his business proposition wasn't heading anywhere, all that was left for him to do was to smile upon us, to consider me as his equal (perhaps even I am a contrabandist in something) and to be helpful to me. That I at least take away with me a pleasant recollection of him.

One cannot pass through Capua without stopping to visit the Museo Campano. The streets are full of small children getting out of school, many of them have on a neckerchief, not blue or white but tricolored, which makes for a certain air

of festivity, as in the pictures of genuinely naive painters. The
museum is empty. The most recent signatures in the register
are four days old. A guard accompanies us through the twenty-
six rooms, more in order to be helpful than to keep an eye on
us; he is very happy about what the museum contains, above
all about the great rooms dedicated to the *Mater Matuta*, and
about the work the archaeologists are doing in the other
twenty rooms used for storage. Without intending to we entered into the warm and deep belly of Italy, where anything
can happen, even the desire to stay there.

At Pozzuoli we begin to doubt whether we will be able to
reach the port, but it seems that everything was foreseen: at
the city limits, southern disorganization gives way to organi-
zation plus. A boy stationed there on purpose, without asking
us where we are going, makes a sign for us to follow him, and
a minute later we're on the deck of a ferry that will take us to
Ischia. It's supposed to leave immediately, instead it lingers a
while, waiting for more cars, more passengers. The last passengers are two young transvestites. They're welcomed glee-
fully by the crew, there are a few surreptitious whistles, some
applause, deep down a bit of admiration. The two young men
will remain the center of the party for the whole crossing,
which unfolds in a climate of embarquement pour Cythère.
One of the two is amiably impudent, he's immediately in
league with the sailors, he throws himself into general considerations about life and love. The other is more mysteri-
ously adorned. He has on a large and serious wig, he smiles
vaguely, not a word can be got out of him. He has decided that
his charm resides in silence and in the upward turn of his
smile that a few hours before we admired in the antefixes of
the Campanian museum: the remote smile of the Etruscans.
On his sweater he wears the black button that in the South
denotes a recent bereavement.

Then, spreading out before us, in the sea breeze, we see
Naples, the ungraspable, where everything goes badly; or

where everything goes well, according to memories that we have forgotten, have perhaps been contemptuous of, but which in this melancholy sunset, upon this incredible old scow, couple themselves to us as the only ones acceptable.

"I just don't know what to put on," said the Wife.

And the Husband: "Put on your old Chanel, you always look good in that."

But she replied: "It makes me look too ladylike. I'll put my patchwork dress on, or maybe my gypsy girl dress. Or what if I put on long pants and the Indian tunic?"

The Husband said: "I'm going with a turtleneck sweater and sport jacket."

"Why not put on your fisherman's shirt with your foulard?"

"Nobody wears that anymore, it's out of style. Maybe I'll go with my Indian shirt too, and my amulet."

"And then we'll look just like a couple of Indians! No, in that case I think I'd better put on my Moroccan mantle."

From her room came the Daughter's wail: "Mamma!" She was desperate, the crease in her new blue jeans refused to come out. "I tried to iron them, but look, it keeps coming back. I just want to cry."

"Of course it keeps coming back, you have to wash them in bleach first, then iron them dry."

"I haven't time for all that, I'll just put my old pants on."

"You can't go with that rip down the rear. It's too oversexy, too provocative."

"I'll sew it up as best I can. With string."

"No, use light-colored cotton thread. You just can't let yourself be so banal. And what have you done to your pants? Why are they so frayed?"

"Mamma, that's how you wear them. At school we all wear them just like that. Cuffs are totally out nowadays."

"And what are you wearing on top? That T-shirt with the marine sergeant stripes?"

"I'd like to put on that Indian shirt, what do you think?"

"How about that old Brahms T-shirt? It's very becoming to you."

"The Brahms one? But it's laughable. That's stuff from six years ago!"

The Son entered the room where the Father was slipping into his suspenders. "Papa, lend me your motorcycle jacket, will you, mine's indecently new, I don't have time to give it a broken-in look."

"You could slash it with a scissors and dab a little grease on it. But wait a minute! You've got an Indian shirt on too? No, no, no, put on some other dirty shirt, not that one, we don't want to look ridiculous now."

"Mamma washed all my shirts, how can I wear anything good when they wash everything in this damned place!"

Meanwhile in the other room: "Sweetheart," said the lady of the house, "could you lend me your amulet necklace to wear? I'll let you wear my pearl one, or that one with the filigree."

"Sure, just so I can laugh myself silly when your back's turned! No, ask me for anything else except my amulet necklace. You could make one yourself with a shoelace from a hiking boot or something and papa's sports medals. Or I'll lend you that colonel's collar. Or that sergeant's scarf."

"It's a tragedy," the Mother said, "whenever you go out you never know what to put on!"

"Mamma, don't act so hung-up! We have to get rid of this cruddy society. And where else do you expect people to start if they don't start with clothes?"

I belong to the silent minority. I am one of those few who no longer have anything to say and who are simply waiting. For what? For everything to become clear? It's unlikely. Age has brought me the certainty that nothing can possibly be clarified: in this country that I love the simple truth doesn't exist. Countries much smaller and more important than ours have their own unique truth, we have infinite versions of it. The causes? I leave the task of designating the causes to the historians, to the sociologists, to the psychoanalysts, to the round tables; what I am doing is undergoing their effects. And together with me a few others: because almost everyone has a solution to propose: "their" truth, that is, something that won't conflict with their interests. It will even be necessary to invite an art historian to the round table in order to have him say what influence the baroque may have had on our psychology.

In Italy, in fact, the shortest line between two points is an arabesque. We live in a network of arabesques.

Scarcely a month ago I was talking with Mino Maccari. What's he up to? Nothing, he's waiting. For Godot? No, he's waiting for the revolution. Who is supposedly going to enact it, the fascists? "The fascists," I reminded him, "are a negligible majority." Maccari elaborated: "Fascism is divided into two parts: fascism properly speaking, and anti-fascism." Both of them, confusedly but immediately, want the same things: order, work, democracy, the levelling of classes, an authoritarian party, neither of them wants freedom. That is, each wants its own version of freedom, which consists in suppressing that of the other.

Freedom commonly understood, that, for example, of expressing one's own opinions, is something despicable because, for better or for worse, we already have it. We are like those inveterate seducers who despise the woman who yields to their desires. If you succeed in seducing freedom before marrying her, useless to marry her. If on the other hand she demands marriage first, better to let her go to the devil. One can always maintain that freedom is frigid.

"What is our most widely shared ideal today?"

"To be taken for what we are not, for revolutionaries. In reality we are only so many sentimental rebels. This is the country that furnishes the highest quotient of millionaire revolutionaries, to both the right and to the left. The revolution so far as we're concerned is a form of investment, of security for our old age. I am surrounded by 'clear-thinking' friends who have at least two extremists, one on each side, for friends."

"Once upon a time one supported one's son in his studies, today one supports him in his polemical disputes, whatever they may be."

A glance at the day's news is enough. I confess that I do it very much against my will, but one must, or one risks no longer understanding a thing. Every incident comes proposing itself as a tragedy which will never reach its catharsis. Guilty parties do not exist, only the incident itself exists, which grows, develops, runs its course; and, at the end, without a solution, it has no sooner receded into the lap of nothingness than another incident, bigger than the first, looms up on the horizon. The guilty vanish, those presumed guilty remain inside, there's always time to drag them out. You will tell me: they are special cases, cases of temporary "insanity." No, the insane among us are normal and even quite patient (it's enough to see the places in which they are confined): the truly insane are the others, as the philosopher used to say, the ones who have lost everything except their reason. They use it to construct systems of intolerance, of falsehood, of oppression, but above all to impose dogmas. And they all have at least one to impose, constructed upon hasty readings, upon existential rancors, upon their triumphant inferiority, upon their natural vulgarity, upon the theory of the maximum success with the minimum effort. Their aim is to make fearful those who don't think the way they do. Ideological terror is thus kept in a continuous state of repair.

After the furious storm of the other night fair weather has returned, the Italy of Colonel Bernacca, on her feet, scrutinizes the sky and this morning a light sirocco wafts over the waters of the lagoon. I've been here now for a few days for the film festival at the Lido, but in Venice there's also another festival of protest and challenge going on, and it's hoped that next year we will have three or four of them. What is being called the counter-festival has revived, so the newspapers are saying, "the partisan climate" among those attending it: perhaps in a somewhat comic key, according to Marx's well-known law about the repetition of the events of history. Whatever the case, directors and promoters have been seen participating in surprise attacks and other commando actions, as during the war years, in order to get hold of and make away with some film or other, even putting their personal yachts on the line, for among the idealists, towards whom I myself lean, there are people of the most solid reputation, highly considered, as securely well off as can be and aggrieved only by the behavior of the treasury department. In order that the protest be all-inclusive they have asked for and received the support of the metalworkers

The metalworkers must be of fine character: not only are they in an arduous and, at the present time, not very well remunerated trade, they are also running to the aid of those who are well to do; and this is a beautiful thing, because the rich should be aided, we already have too many poor people. A few days ago I was rereading Machiavelli and suddenly I had this modest illumination: it isn't that the Italians are going towards "the left," it's the left that is going towards the Italians, who are as unmovable as Mohammed's mountain. They will make the left in their own image and likeness. That is, extremely elegant.

I went—stealthily—to see a film treatment of one of my stories and I didn't recognize it. And yet, all around me, they were talking about the rights of authors and authors' property. And so amidst all that there I sat, despoiled of my status as author. I later console myself in the lobby of the hotel where I encounter Tretti, a director from Vicenza, the author of two films I very much liked and which have never been released, because they annoy everybody. Tretti sank his personal fortune into these two films and has still not given up hope that the public will eventually get to see them. At this point, who is going to be able to help him? His serene optimism upsets me. He spoke to me at length about a third film he is thinking of proposing ... to whom? Tretti is the typical encumbering author who has not yet understood the game of vested interests and perhaps never will, and therefore I admire and love him. Because he is so un-Italian?

I try again and again to console myself with the retrospective on Mae West going on at the Lido festival, the "official" one, which, in my opinion, has lost its character of footbridge to the stars and autograph-fest to become an exposition of works beautiful and unbeautiful, but in such quantities that it could truly be called democratic, that is, open to every genius however small. There are seven Mae West films, one a day for seven days running, at three in the afternoon. I've seen two of them, I've slept through another two, I've decided to forget about the others. Mae West, I was thinking, ought to say something to my generation. Of her films, "back then," only one ever got to Italy, and I missed it. I was expecting a revelation, one aggravated by my indulgence towards the faraway memories of my youth. I confess that the judgment of Andy Warhol, corroborated by Tommaso Chiaretti, who is writing lovely little things about Mae West these days, can be seducing: "Mae West was a transvestite." I find it a little hasty. Mae West was perhaps worse than a transvestite, that is, she lacked that aspiration towards femininity that moves transvestites to strike graceful poses and to mimic the weaker sex, somewhat overdoing it. Mae West, rather, mimics the "frontier" woman, the ones who followed the gold-rushers out west and opened up the saloons. Probably equipped with an immoderately practical and frank spirit, more in the way of a proprietress than a sinner, her witticisms are all constructed like *mots d'auteur*. And she, always dressed up like a horse in a parade, loaded with real diamonds and white furs, surrounded by fetishistic worshippers and bored second billers, has the appearance today of a Mayan goddess in a steam-engine civilization, with her vampish demeanor, never ceding an inch, incapable of suffering and of truly enjoying, "indomitable," as Messalina used to say of herself. Come on! an apartment house landlady, more a vaudeville star than an actress. I didn't regret my afternoon naps.

Fortunately, to excite our enthusiasm, the "All Chaplin" series was each afternoon offered free of charge—a brilliant idea—to grown-ups and children alike. The at all times lively audience brought me back to certain climates of my childhood, to the feeling of a happiness that perhaps (no, no perhaps) no other author of cinema will ever be able to give us.

And meanwhile the counter-festival, with the arrival of Goddard, of Mastroianni and of Rascel, and probably even of Marilù Tolo, has earned its brave bit of turf, has won the attention of the prudent and of the indecisive. Since it is well known that one trait of the Italians is to hasten to the conqueror's aid, the counter-festival is being populated by authors and directors who have rushed up at the eleventh hour from Rome. It's the realization of the organizers' worst fears. Indeed, this reminds me of an aphorism of Malraux's: "In every intelligent minority there is a majority of imbeciles."

Concerning Satire, Boredom, Faith

The interview that follows was granted to Giulio Villa Santa of Swiss-Italian Radio (Radio della Svizzera Italiana) by Ennio Flaiano two weeks before his death; it was broadcast under the rubric "Opinions on a Theme." We thank Giulio Villa Santa, who is responsible for the title, for his kind authorization to publish what can be considered the writer's last public remarks. [Italian Editor's Note.]

Villa Santa: Flaiano, it seems to me that it has always been your intention to show that nothing today deserves to be taken seriously. Whatever the question, whatever the idea, you dissolve it in a humor, in a satire of which there are not very many precedents in Italian literature.

Flaiano: I confess that you have a point. Satire is not much cultivated in Italy, for reasons that can perhaps be found in Croce's *Aesthetics*, where satire is considered the Cinderella of literature. Here, the cult of art and of poetry reigns in the absolute sense; everyone who writes has *The Divine Comedy, I promessi sposi, I Malavoglia* for models, according to his own intentions and ideology, and no one looks around him to understand, let's not say the ridiculous, but the absurd sides or, in any case, the wild and woolly sides of the life surrounding us. Do that and you put yourself in a position of isolation, but this doesn't bother me. I confess that there are other writers in Italy who practice satire and whom you may be better acquainted with than with me—for example, Carlo Emilio Gadda, the greatest of them all, a man who has attained such a power of style by way of philology, by way of pain, of humanity, of suffering and, let us say, through direct and continuous observation of the reality that surrounds him. Another writer who practices satire in a precise fashion is Piero Chiara. I mean that he writes satirically, knowingly, about us. He knows what we are, what we want and, perhaps, where we are going.

Villa Santa: To what then do you think you owe this difference between yourself and the others, or at least between you and the great majority of them?

Flaiano: Who knows, maybe to the fact that it wasn't my absolute intention to become a writer. My aspirations were a good deal more modest and, I'd say, diverse. When I was young I didn't have clear ideas on the subject; rather, I had a few ideas but they were confused; I'd have liked to become, I don't know, a bookbinder, a carpenter. I was drawn to arts in which I could use my hands and my imagination. Painting, for example, would have been one endless entertainment for me, I even tried my hand at it—with disastrous results—and then, at a certain age in my life, I found myself having to untangle these ambitions of mine and to actualize them, and I was offered a job writing occasional movie reviews. It's clear that next step is a short one: you begin by writing about films, then about theater, then you attempt a story and you do another. And I noticed that I had running through me a thread, a hidden thread, which was of laughing at myself and at others.

Villa Santa: Yet you come from the Abruzzi, an austere country, where they rather tend to melancholy. You've lived in Rome a long time now. What consequence did coming here have upon your inner thread, this hidden thread of laughter?

Flaiano: A catastrophic consequence. I mean to say that it isn't easy living in Rome. It isn't easy because it offers an infinite number of distractions and pleasures, which mine the vital impulse. "Life," Sainte-Beuve once said, "would be bearable if there were no such things as pleasures"; here, in Rome, life, in this sense, is hardly bearable at all, because it doesn't offer anything else but this. As for what Rome has that's good, there's this: it doesn't judge, it forgives, and so anyone working in this city feels a bit like a dog without a collar. At liberty, he doesn't pay dues, because there isn't even a watch dog around, and he discovers that the life going on around him is so very tumultuous, so very fascinating, so very full of humor, so very bizarre that he can't help but consider it from the satirical point of view.

Villa Santa: And to laugh and to smile at everything and everybody is this city's underlying vocation. For if Rome is truly immortal in anything at all, it is immortal in its incredulity, in a skepticism that is impervious to whatever evidence. And to what is this owing, according to you?

Flaiano: I believe it is owing to the feeling one has of the city's eternity, to the feeling that it cannot be possessed physically—or spiritually, let's say. It is owing to this unending mystery that is at once underneath Rome and on its surface. I'm especially referring to Fellini, who is interested in these matters. The various strata that make up this city, whether in time or in space, are such that they lead a man to think of himself as a passenger in transit, and to want to enjoy himself while in this situation, having no other way to get at its truth.

Villa Santa: From the moment you understood satire as a searching for truth, for a truth that is non-literary but rather natural and alive, while entertainment is always an end in itself, have you ever thought about leaving Rome, about moving to another climate altogther?

Flaiano: For fifty years I've been thinking about leaving and moving off to another climate, and every time I leave Rome my greatest sorrow is in coming back here, a sorrow that lasts exactly as long as it takes me to get here, whether by airplane or train. Once I've arrived, my old habits, my friends, the let's say irresponsible heat of this city cause me to postpone my decision to go away.

Villa Santa: That's exactly it: one's friends. One could say that the world always interests us in the form of others, of our fellow creatures, rather than of abstractions and of ideas.

Flaiano: Our fellow creatures—the world's greatest circus, as a Roman would say. Something, that is, that you never manage to get a handle on. One arrives at this conclusion after being in Rome for many years, and watching the—you'll pardon me for using the word—bumptiousness with which the Roman accepts and dominates life. This leads one to consider ideas as having only a relative value, and the climate, this endlessly changing weather, these seasons that never coincide, this way of life lived permanently on a very brightly lit and very noisy stage-front, all of these tend to deaden the meaning of ideas and give them a meaning that's more vague or, if we prefer, give a profounder one to the fleeting moment, which one must seize because even if it isn't beautiful at least it's useable.

Villa Santa: But you don't believe in judging the whole world on the basis of one very particular fellow creature, do you? Is one's Italian or Roman "fellow creature" then so universal?

Flaiano: But, exactly, the protest is precisely in what I write. I am only able to express my point of view about something I am well acquainted with; while I'd take great care about expressing my point of view about a people among whom I was merely an itinerant. And therefore I've understood something, thanks to this conversation, that was not yet clear even to me: that if I'm a satiric writer it's because I live in a society that offers only this one side.

Villa Santa: You see, in my view you have a kind of brother in contemporary literature, and he is the man I consider the greatest writer now living, Saul Bellow. He too is a master of satire, of irony, of bitter humor. But he still believes in certain things, for example, in the seriousness of solitude, of the unknown, and of death. Why is it that in your stories you speak in a satiric voice even about these things?

Flaiaino: I have to start by saying that your fraternal definition moves me and that having myself compared to a writer like Saul Bellow flatters me, even if I can't help smiling a bit. Because Saul Bellow is a great writer; next to him I consider myself a modest one. My modesty extends even to the point of envy, and I have to tell you that indeed one of his books, the one I liked best, *Herzog*—I didn't want to finish it, precisely because I felt that it was one of my books and that if I had had this same idea I would have written it, very poorly, but I would have written it. Certainly Saul Bellow has the advantage over me in that he still believes in the seriousness of solitude, of the unknown, and of death. I believe in solitude, I fear the unknown, and I'm terrified of death. Maybe this explains my retreating to a solution—should we call it one of convenience, one of character?—which is to see things under, not a cheerful aspect, but under one that is steeped in a certain amusement. I am not unacquainted with the problems that loneliness, the unknown and death present; what I try to do is keep them at bay.

Villa Santa: But Bellow takes other things seriously too. For example, in his most recent book, *Mr. Sammler's Planet*, there is also science: that is, the role destiny—perhaps blind, perhaps insane, but grandiose in any case—is beginning to play in the lives of all of us. One gets the impression on the other hand that so far as you're concerned, science is closely related to the wonders of the side show, to papier-mâché, to fraud.

Flaiano: In the long run, the seriousness with which Bellow treats science must eventually arrive at one conclusion, the one I have arrived at by treating science as papier-mâché and as a circus tent phenomenon. We today feel cramped, squeezed; the spiral in which science has placed us, in which we are being squeezed, in which we are being suffocated, is already something pretty much like a circus tent phenomenon: that is, we are not what we were, I won't say ten years ago, but five years ago, because in just these last few years science has imposed on us conditions of life that are unacceptable. It's so true that, today, the protest which goes under the name of ecology is nothing but a protest against *science*. It is said that technology will find the means of eliminating the damages produced by technology; but I don't think so. We have committed the error of believing that one day machines will surpass us through their intelligence. No, machines will surpass by their number, by their quantity, and because man will only be able to keep on making more and more machines.

Villa Santa: At any rate, technology is one thing and science is another. Don't you believe that the latter can help us to understand who we are and where we come from, not to mention where we are going?

Flaiano: Listen, I'll answer you with just one sentence: the professional malady of scientists—what silicosis is to coal miners—is faith. That is, science arrives at a few elementary conclusions, as old as the world, by performing an experiment that, believe me, is painful for mankind. When everything has been discovered, when we have truly decided everything, we will return to the conclusion that it is love that moves the world and the other stars.

Villa Santa: For my part I'd say that it would be no small accomplishment to confirm this through science, through reason. So here, in any case, is something in which to believe, something to be understood even by you—

Flaiano: There is everything to comprehend, more than to understand. And everything to be resolved, each in his own heart and in keeping with his own preferences. I have already chosen mine: they are solitude, writing, and, if you like, ennui, or boredom.

Villa Santa: However ennui is a kind of disease, and thinking about the effect your books produce upon me I must add: a contagious disease. Your books are for me a perilous delight: for a certain while they cause me to live under the suspicion that not only everything in which I believe but my very capacity for enthusiasm as well are worth little more than a chuckle and a yawn. Well, what effect do your books have upon you? Can you truly say about your irony what Saba once said about his poetry: that "a lovely line of verse cures me of every bad thing"?

Flaiano: Saba has expressed what the function of writing, of literature is today: it is a largely therapeutic function. Yes, writing or making poetry can heal; as regards my irony, or my satire if we prefer to call it that, I believe that it liberates me from everything that annoys me; and in this sense it should be considered altogether therapeutic. One thing that perhaps doesn't interest you but that interests me, is that I write something, then I forget what made me write it, what the reason was, that is to say I eliminate it from my existence, and I think about something else. In this sense writing is in effect an organic need for me. I would go a long way toward eliminating the necessity of working from my life—for my tendency is to laziness—if this were not a means of surviving.

Villa Santa: Yet often the method of your satire consists in the definitively destructive formulation of an idea, so to speak: so that henceforth the idea you've attacked can no longer be taken seriously by anyone. For example, a Canadian anthropologist devotes a whole lifetime to studying the influences of the communications and information media upon society, and ends up by synthesizing everything into an aphorism: "the medium is the message," which amounts to saying that television or radio are already messages in their own right, no matter what they tell us. And here's how you settle the matter: "If we've understood you correctly, professor," you say, "it's useless to open our letters, it's the postman we ought to read."

Flaiano: They're low blows, you say, blows not allowed by the rules of the game. But the satiric writer doesn't have to know those rules, that is, he has to rely upon the possibilities that are offered to him, that are outside the game, outside of the rules, he has to strike as he can and with whatever means he has. Satiric writing isn't a sport, that is, it doesn't call for elegance and respect for the rules, it only calls for the strength of an outrage. And at this point all means are fair. If I stand other people's ideas on their head it is because the opportunity is frequently offered to me, often by the very proponents of those ideas. We live in a sea of ideas today and you know very well that today every idiot is full of ideas. I've written this somewhere too: that it is necessary to protect oneself from those who continually formulate new ideas. If I combat these ideas, I cannot combat them with courtesy, but with violence. Therefore allow me to tell you that on this score my conscience is clear—admitting that I have a conscience, or that satiric writers in general have one.

Villa Santa: Well now let's see if we can define a little better what the connection is between your satire and ennui. In short, what is ennui? Leopardi, who was also an expert on the subject, wrote for example that "When man no longer has a feeling for any particular good or evil, he feels, in general, the aboriginal unhappiness of man, and this is the feeling that we call ennui." Do you agree with him?

Flaiano: I agree because one cannot not agree with Leopardi. But I have arrived at another definition of ennui: ennui is truth in its pure state. That is, we arrive at an understanding of truth when we arrive at the heart of ennui. This happens all the time. I once read these words in Kafka's diary, and I was much struck by them: "Such was my boredom this evening that I went to the bathroom three times to wash my hands." Now, if Kafka was bored, I in all modesty ought perhaps to be a lot more bored than he. For his part, Goethe used to say that if monkeys could suffer from boredom perhaps they would become men. Therefore I see in ennui not only one of man's divine sides, that is, the one which brings him closest to the universe's creator—whom I can imagine today as beset by ennui for having made this great masterpiece—I also see in ennui a defense against the wave of activism, of thought, of ideologies, of incitements, of vitalism that this century is hurling at us. Listen, I'm against vitalism, I'm against vitalism because it translates into aestheticism, it translates into mannerism, and it translates, finally, into melancholy. I am not melancholic, I prefer to be bored. A cure for ennui? Well, certainly there is this cure: I believe that it is work. One writer that I admire a very great deal and by whom I have been many times incited to work is Jules Renard, and he once said "Life is short, but ennui lengthens it."

Villa Santa: Don't you think that ennui predisposes us to complicity with whoever releases us from it, whatever the way in which he manages to jolt us out of it, to shatter uniformity? Don't you think that to find yourself still being amused by your neighbor's absurdity (to be amused, here, is simply the opposite of being bored) makes, despite everything, for a certain sympathy with this absurdity?

Flaiano: It's not a matter of sympathy but of observation. Here, I'd like to invoke that Greek philosopher (I believe it was Epictetus, but my memory may be deceiving me) who was a slave and one of whose legs was subjected to the bastinado, isn't that so? It ended with him saying, "Notice that you're breaking it," but without introducing into this sentence anything beyond a statement; neither pain, nor anguish, nor fear of losing the leg. In essence the writer who exploits ennui does nothing more than resort to the same thing: "Notice, if you go on that way you'll break my leg." Everything surrounding us, the pleasure of life, when translated into ennui becomes philosophy—that is, becomes an opportunity to understand it, even becomes an opportunity to reject it. We may put it this way: the work of transformation is what I do, and only in this way can what I write be understood. As to the complicity you referred to before, this complicity does exist, clearly, but it's a strategic complicity, not a political one, a complicity imposed by war, which it is necessary to accept as certain ineluctabilities are accepted, in order to be able to strike better. If isn't a complicity of the heart, only of the mind.

Villa Santa: How about if we move out of the abstract. Let's take an example, and the example is what you wrote on the way Italians travel, that, from the North Pole to the savanna they fail to take anything seriously and continue to be what they are at home. You write, and I quote verbatim: "The savanna, the jungle, the great open spaces of Africa: two Italians suffice to corrupt them. *'Dottore!' 'Ragioniere!'* They won't let go of their titles, they look at the great open spaces, they lose themselves in them, they walk around in them without conviction, dubiously. 'You'll never catch me coming to Africa with you again,' et cetera. When two Italians chance to run into each other in the outside world, their first reaction is to have a good laugh over it. 'Hey, what're you doing here?' 'How about you?' In fact it's assumed that if they are away from home it's for motives that are essentially comical: work, boredom, a curiosity full of reservations, women, pleasure, et cetera." Could you deny that these amused remarks proceed from an underlying fund of sympathy?

Flaiano: Not from a fund of sympathy but from disarmed observation. We know very well that the Italian considers himself, perhaps through his geographic position which has placed him in the middle of the Mediterranean, a sea, a warm lake from which a millenary civilization has sprung—the Italian feels himself something of an only child, that is, he feels that he is inimitable. All the rest of the world is strange, it is absurd that it was ever made, and this is quite true and always causes him to laugh. When an Italian goes to the North Pole he finds that there is too much ice, when he goes to Africa he finds there is too much sand. Couldn't somebody remedy this situation in some way? Couldn't somebody take away a little of this sand? Couldn't somebody get rid of some of this ice? And he finds that the blacks are too black and that the Chinese are too Chinese. This leads him then to consider the rest of the world as though it were temporary and, in substance, a bit ridiculous. Let's think a moment about the Italian who goes abroad, who keeps himself at all times under control, who is careful about what he wears, who's afraid of losing face, who spends all his time keeping a close eye on himself because of this feeling of mistaken superiority. This also prevents him from ever seeing what the country is in which he lives. Have you ever noticed that the writers—let's say "Italian" writers with the word Italian in quotation marks—who have best understood Italy are foreigners, for example Englishmen? The most beautiful Italian novel is *Where Angels Fear to Tread* written by Forster in 1910. Not to mention *Old Calabria* or *South Wind*, both written by Norman Douglas, not to mention *Those Barren Leaves* by Huxley, not to mention Lawrence. They have seen Italy for what it is, an ensemble of historical, psychological contradictions, which come from its mythology and which make a *unicum* of this people, which is ridiculous at certain times because, precisely, of its contaminations. To say that the Italian always feels at home is inexact; he feels himself not at home even in his home; he finds that everything around him is inferior to his own opinion of himself and to what in his opinion his surroundings ought to be. And one cannot help but look at all this with sympathy, because it is the fruit of a state of mind that forms, in short, the ambivalence of the foreigner towards the Italian and towards Italy, that is, this desire to love him and at the same time to detest him. He is an *enfant gâté*, an only child, and as such he should perhaps be scolded, spanked, but in a certain sense also loved.

Villa Santa: In any case, despite the fact that you write, as you did recently, that you are among those who have nothing to say, this evening you've left us understanding that there are things in which you believe—believe, indeed, rather painfully. On the other hand, if it were otherwise there would be no understanding why, in an interview we had together two or three years ago, you said that going off and grabbing hold of the moon, a second world, wouldn't lighten this world's burden of cheats and sons of bitches. Now, invective always presupposes its opposite, it always presupposes terms of comparison, wouldn't you say so?

Flaiano: I'd like to answer you with a line from Cardarelli, a poet whom I knew and very much loved: "I am a cynic who has faith in what he does." If there is any faith in me it is in what I do, that is, in what I believe and in the way I'd like things to be. But these things don't depend upon me. What grieves me is seeing a society that is going downhill, deteriorating—in order to become better, some say; while I think it is in order to lose even that small amount of humanity that remains to it. It is an attitude that is perhaps moralistic, and it may be that in putting it that way I am oversimplifying, but it corresponds exactly to what I think. If there is some belligerence in that sentence of mine you just quoted it is because I believe that society is effectively undermined by people who do not believe; of all the great failings in all the various camps today the greatest is the lack of faith, and I don't mean to identify this with religion or with a church, what I mean to identify it with is faith in man's destiny, a faith which seems to me, today, to be at a very, very low ebb.

Villa Santa: And to what do you ascribe this?

Flaiano: We today are in contact with the whole world through the mass media, principally the press, radio, television. The greatest part of the news that the world has to offer us is bad news, insufficiently alleviated by what groups of men, societies, nations do to keep this faith from perishing altogether. We sense that something is being irremediably squandered through the worship of the golden calf, through the worship of success, through the worship of what we believe we are, that is, sexual animals; whereas we are not sexual animals, we are thinking, reasoning animals. My entire satiric protest in short has this thread mark imbedded in it; and I would like you to see it by holding it up to the light that is coming in through that window.

Villa Santa: I am beginning to get a glimpse of it, and I must say it is a surprising thing to behold. But no one it seems has given much weight to the importance that animals have in your stories, from those crocodiles hunting for washerwomen in your first book to the massacred monkeys in your last. They seem like happy and vindictive carcicatures. What do they represent? Are they a nemesis or the call of a lost paradise?

Flaiano: I love animals. I love animals because they believe in us. They also fear us, and sometimes they place themselves at our service, expressing a fidelity that we ourselves are no longer capable of expressing. For me, the crocodile, in the story you mention, is the devil, the slaughtered monkeys are men. These are two allegories; in reality I love animals for what they are independently of every allegory. I love dogs, cats, I even manage to love chickens, not to mention wild birds, which in Italy are considered targets for rifle practice (and I would like the Italians' patron saint, Saint Francis, to say something more on this subject, to make himself felt in another way). The detesting of animals, the oppression of them, the harming of them, the offending of them is something that has always pained me deeply. I have had some personal contacts, I have even had some sentimental contacts with a few animals. With a cat, about whom I could write an extraordinary story, because she always brought me her kittens to look at: I used to live on a ground floor and every time this cat gave birth she would bring her kittens to me so that I could give them my approval. I've had some equal to equal contacts with dogs, abandoned dogs who in Fregene used to come to me at the end of autumn, especially around this time of year, to get fed, and who would bring me gifts, some shoes, a broken broom, a tin can, because they wanted to repay me in some way for my help. I've had contacts with an injured sea-gull who understood what I was saying to him and wanted to be appreciated by me, not because he was a sea-gull, but because he was a thinking being. I think we have greatly underestimated animals, and, in fact, one of the films of the last few years I like the most (it seems strange that I, a man of the cinema, should mention this film) is *The Birds* by Hitchcock, which foresees birds rebelling against man, a film that not only distressed me but which put me on the side of the birds, because this mankind that considers itself the child of God, divine and brought forth to dominate the earth, is in reality upsetting it, turning it upside down, and does not take into consideration the other guests upon this planet, or takes them into consideration only to make them into fur coats, to eat them as food, to use them in work. It is the most monumental enterprise of enslavement in history.

Villa Santa: I am forced to the conclusion that what upsets you is that thing which animals are by their nature free of: what upsets you is culture in the fullest sense of the world. But you have indicated one way of escape in the story ["Melampus"] where a woman transforms herself into an animal, into a dog, to be exact. Less metaphorically: is this way of escape available to all? And how does one go about transforming oneself into a dog?

Flaiano: This way of escape, as you call it, is available to all and the direction I have suggested is clear: the way can only be love, not canine, cynical love, but absolute, total love. Love that arises of its own accord and goes towards others, love that extends to embrace the whole of our lives, extends to the friends who have abandoned us, who are dead, extends to the persons we have known, extends even to the persons we don't know. This is very difficult to put into practice, isn't it? Because one may fall into a philanthropism that is mannered, artificial, or else at odds with the more philosophical, the more materialistic conceptions of the times, but I don't see any other way of escape. I don't see any other way of escape because all the others suggested by the contingencies, suggested by the tone of our by now degraded lives offer no indications of where to go. The woman you remembered who transforms herself into a dog is a figure of hope, for to save something one must begin by renouncing that which we are, that is, begin by renouncing our "culture," in quotation marks because true culture is something else, it is the one known to illiterates in a certain sense, that is, how to live in the environment, how not to offend it, how to respect others. This is culture; and speaking of love, I don't want you to equivocate.

Love here is understood as something very broad, very vast, very divine: it is the love that includes, above all, the possibility that we someday may no longer be able to exercise it, that we someday will go away and have to leave behind a memory of ourselves that is, if nothing else, at least decent.

Villa Santa: This evening it seems to me, Flaiano, that you have opened yourself up as perhaps you have never done before, that you have revealed an anguish and above all a faith behind your humor. But this gives rise to the suspicion in me that at bottom you are a man from another period if not from another age altogether; is that an unfounded suspicion?

Flaiano: It's a legitimate one. We don't know who we are, we are just so many passengers without baggage, we are born alone and we die alone. Once a woman writer quoted me in a book of hers, and in the English translation the English writer translated my name as Ennius Flaianus, thinking that this Ennio Flaiano was some Latin author. A few months later we met each other in a restaurant in Rome and were introduced and, naturally, she experienced an awkward moment, for she didn't think that this ancient writer was still alive. However, we did agree that certain characteristics of my person, a certain style of life, indicated that she was right. I perhaps was not of this age, am not of this age. Perhaps I belong to another world: I feel myself more in harmony when I read Juvenal, Martial, Catullus. It's probable that I'm an ancient Roman who is still here, forgotten by history, to write about the things that the others wrote about far better than I—namely, let me repeat, Catullus, Martial, Juvenal.

This book was designed by
Austryn Wainhouse, of Marlboro, Vermont.
It was typeset by
American-Stratford Graphic Services, Inc.,
of Brattleboro, Vermont
and printed by McNaughton & Gunn, Inc.,
of Saline, Michigan.